SENSE AND SUCCUBUS

ADRIENNE BLAKE

CITY OWL
PRESS

This book is a work of fiction. Names, characters, places, and incidents either are products of the author's imagination or are used fictitiously. Any resemblance to actual events or locales or persons, living or dead, is entirely coincidental and not intended by the author.

SENSE AND SUCCUBUS
Souls and Shadows, Book 2

CITY OWL PRESS
www.cityowlpress.com

Cover Design by MiblArt. All stock photos licensed appropriately.

Edited by Tee Tate.

For information on subsidiary rights, please contact the publisher at info@cityowlpress.com.

Print Edition ISBN: 978-1-64898-095-4

Digital Edition ISBN: 978-1-64898-094-7

Printed in the United States of America

To Lei-Anne Bailey, for her unwavering support and delightfully irreverent sense of humor. I can't imagine this writing journey without her.

Chapter One

A TURN OF THE CARD

A NINE OF CLUBS. HENRY DASHWOOD TAPPED HIS LAST TWO HUNDRED-dollar chips together and stared at the dealer's eight of diamonds. There had been a run of tens. Surely the streak would continue. Like every croupier Henry had ever known, the harpy's hawk-faced expression was void of anything except challenge. Her golden predator eyes fixed on him. *You know you want to. Get it over with.* Henry could almost feel her contempt.

But a nine. The odds were in his favor. Henry breathed in deeply. He stood at the point of total ruin; once the bet was placed, it would be all down to chance. He felt that familiar rush of endorphins cascading through his body like sex, only better. It wasn't winning he was addicted to —no, it was the *chance* of winning. Like making out, the thrill of the chase excited him almost more than the actual act. This was what he lived for. This was who he was.

Henry placed his last two chips on the table and pointed to the cards. Another nine, spades this time. That was good enough. He swiped his hand, indicating he wanted to stand. Eighteen. The dealer would need nineteen or better to beat him. The harpy slid a card from her shoe and turned it over. A four. She had to pull another card.

Make it a ten, make it a ten. His blood coursed through his veins as he prayed she would bust. This was the moment he lived for. The harpy's hooded eyes betrayed no emotion as she turned the next card. An ace. She pulled from the shoe again. A two. Then a five. *Twenty! A damned twenty!*

With a tiny flutter of her ugly leather wings, the harpy leaned forward and scooped up Henry's chips before he had a chance to react. Oh, sweet Gaia in heaven, he was broke. Flat broke. The sickness of loss hit his stomach in a wave. What was he going to do now? What was he going to tell Mary? How could he look her in the face when he got home?

Where were those sexy succubus waitresses? Now that the money was gone, he could use a free drink, but there wasn't a single one in sight. They all knew he had no money to tip them. Those cookies sure were smart—and quick!

Henry plunged his hands into his pockets and pulled out some loose change and his phone. The money was all he had in the world. Just a few coins. Boy, he could use a drink. As he walked over to the bar, he tapped his phone and stared at his son's number. He *really* didn't want to make this call. John would crucify him when he heard, but Henry was fresh out of favors with his gaming chums, so no other door was left open to him. He bit his lip and called his son.

"Hey Dad, how are ya? Long time no hear!"

His son's cheery voice stabbed at his heart. "I'm over at The Magic Tables." He almost groaned the name.

The phone went silent. Not that John needed to say anything. Henry knew too well what he was thinking. He felt like a total schmuck. He *was* a total schmuck.

"Um, can you meet me for lunch? I need to ask a favor."

There was a brief silence. "How much did you lose this time, Dad?"

"Can we talk about that when you get here?"

Another silence, followed by a sigh. "All right. I was coming into town to meet Fanny anyway. Sit tight and I'll meet you in the restaurant. And Dad?"

Henry groaned on the inside. If there was one woman on this planet he couldn't abide, it was his son's half-goblin wife. "Yes?"

"Don't do anything stupid." The line went dead.

Henry switched off the phone and meandered past the slot machines toward the restaurant. Their jingling music taunted him all the way, reminding him just how much of a loser he was. Every time they rang out a win, he felt a little sicker. It had been some time since they had sung in his favor, and his life showed it. He had some loose change. He pulled it out and looked again. Maybe he could just drop a few dimes or quarters into the slots on his way to the bar? He popped his last three quarters in and pressed play. Three presses later, even what little he had was gone. He stared at the golden little cowboy on the Texas Hold'em machine and wanted to punch him. This just wasn't his day.

A gorgeous succubus stood behind the bar. She had bottle-green hair and curves in all the right places. Her uniform, such as it was, was little more than a black corset, pulled tight around the tiniest waist Henry had ever seen. Her arms were heavily tattooed from her wrists to her shoulders, illustrated with acts of seduction he prayed his young daughters would never see. Her muscular thighs looked hard enough to crack a walnut. The look in her deep-sea green eyes initially said come hither, but after giving him the once-over, her smile faded a little.

"What'll it be, lover?" the succubus said in a throaty voice so deep it made him quiver.

Henry scratched his head, suddenly wishing he could pull out a wad of cash to impress her. By Gaia, there was no way he could humiliate himself with a handful of pennies. John would stand for him, he was sure of it.

"A double Jack," Henry said. "Heavy on the ice."

"Cash or charge, baby?"

"Charge," he said, with more confidence than he was entitled.

The succubus gave him a knowing look, but then turned on her charm. "Coming right up, big boy."

The bar was mostly empty, apart from a smart-dressed man sitting just a few stools away. He had that slick, polished look that screamed professional gambler. He looked like a successful one, too, judging by the shiny signet on his pinkie and the sharp, tailored look to his Italian suit. Henry's hand went to his chin, suddenly wishing he'd shaved a little closer.

"There you go, lover." The sexy succubus dropped a beermat in front of him and deposited his icy drink on top. She leaned forward, treating him to an expanse of cleavage they both knew he couldn't afford. "Rough day, sweetie?"

"Yeah, something like that," Henry said. He downed a little of his whiskey, enjoying the ice-cold liquid as it slid down his gut to warm his belly. Funny how whiskey did that. "The cards didn't favor me today. There's always tomorrow, right?"

The succubus ran a long, polished black fingernail along his forefinger. "I'm sure there are other ways a handsome satyr like you could make some hard cash, if you wanted to. I know a few people."

Henry gently pulled his hand away. Sure, there was a time he'd have been open to all sorts of possibilities. But that was a *long* time ago. "Thanks, hon, but I don't think my wife would like it."

The girl grinned, and though she pulled back slowly, he sensed she wasn't done yet. Henry caught the look she shot to the gambler down the bar. Taking a long sip of his whiskey, he braced himself for trouble.

Sure enough, he heard the scrape of a chair and the man came over to sit beside him. *Here we go,* he thought. He prayed John wouldn't be too long.

"May I join you?"

Henry nodded.

The red-headed gambler had a soft Scottish accent that was surprisingly pleasant on the ears. He had brought his empty glass with him. Reaching across the bar, he grabbed a fresh beermat before sitting down next to Henry.

"I'll take another one of those gimlets," he said, pushing his empty glass across the bar. "And perhaps another for my friend here, since he looks like he could use one. Make it a double."

"Thanks," Henry said. After all, a drink was a drink.

"Name's Wee Angus," the professional man said. He turned in his seat, offering Henry his hand. The man had bright blue, goat-slitted eyes. "But please, just call me Angus. I much prefer it."

Henry groaned on the inside. *Shit. A demon. Just my luck.* Out of politeness, Henry shook the offered hand. Of all the magical creatures, demons were his least favorite. All that double-dealing made his head spin. "Hi. I'm Henry. Henry Dashwood."

"Nice to meet you, Henry," Angus said without missing a beat. He must have seen the groan behind the smile, but he took it in stride.

Occupational hazard, Henry supposed. "What's with the 'Wee'?" The broad-shouldered demon looked anything but.

"Oh, a wee joke," Angus said. The succubus had arrived with their drinks, and the demon took a sip. "Ah, yes! No one can mix these like my darling Lucy."

Lucy grinned from behind the bar. "You old flatterer, you. And you know you're not supposed to use our real names. You'll get me in trouble."

"And you'd enjoy it, my love."

Henry drained his first whiskey glass and started on his second. There was a warm tingle in his belly, and he was already feeling better. Perhaps his luck *was* changing. He glanced at his watch, wondering how long before his son would make an appearance. If the boy had a little cash on him, maybe he could still make something of the day.

"Busy afternoon?" Angus asked casually.

"Maybe," Henry said. "I'm just waiting on my son before I hit the tables again. I just thought I'd have myself a quick breather before he got here, you know?"

"Och, of course," Angus said. "There's nothing quite like recharging your batteries, is there? So, your son, he likes a bit of a flutter at the tables, does he?"

Henry thought about John. There had been a time when his boy would stand beside him, although craps had always been more John's thing. But Fanny had changed everything. The goblin-green hue to his daughter-in-law's skin didn't lie. That girl was a miser through and through, begrudging John even the slightest indulgence. Still, a slippery demon didn't need to know that.

"It's been known," was all Henry shared. "Perhaps not so much now as in the past, but he likes the dice sometimes."

"Just the one boy?" the demon asked.

"Actually, no." Henry sat a little straighter as he thought about the daughters from his second marriage. "I have three young girls as well. And no, before you ask, none of them gamble. They're all far too young and innocent for that."

"Children?"

"No, my Elinor and Marianne are young women now. Little Margaret is still a girl perhaps, but they're sensible, like their mother, Mary. They wouldn't dream of entering a casino."

Angus pursed his lips for a moment. "Satyrs? Like their daddy?"

Henry puffed out his chest with pride. "No, thank Gaia. The girls took after their mother. She's a dryad. They inherited her genes, not a bit of mine. There's not a wicked thought between them, and they have no nasty habits like their dad." He couldn't help but sigh into his whiskey glass as he thought about the one bit of luck he'd had in his life that had never gone bad. His second marriage to Mary.

When Henry put his glass down, Lucy was there again to top it up.

"It's okay," Henry said. "I really shouldn't have another. My son will be here soon."

"Nonsense," Angus said. "And leave me here alone, at this gorgeous girl's mercy? Och, I thought you were my friend, Henry. Go on, just one more can't do you any harm."

Henry was almost off his chair, fully aware Angus was trying to wrong-foot him with some demon thing. But Lucy looked so tantalizingly hot and, well, this was where he'd arranged to meet John. In any case, he had no money to settle that bill. He sat down again.

"All right, just the one. But if my son isn't here soon, I'll have to get going."

"I never had kids myself...."

"Well, you're a demon," Henry said reasonably. "I didn't think you were able to procreate."

"Aye, technically, you may be right. But we love having a damned good go at it just the same."

The two men laughed together, enjoying a moment of bonhomie. For a second, Henry put aside his suspicions.

"Ah, daughters. I think it would be nice to be a father, especially to wee lassies. That special look of adoration, the little bows in their hair, there's nothing quite like it I imagine. Do you have a favorite?"

Henry laughed. "No, they're all very unique. My eldest is the more sensible of the three. Marianne is a bit of a silly-heart, and Margaret has a head full of pirates and hobgoblins. I'm a lucky man to have three such beauties."

"Boyfriends?"

"Ha, no, not yet. The girls are pretty, and I suppose it's only a matter of time. But I'm their dad, so naturally I want to lock their hearts forever. Thank Gaia, they don't seem to be easily tempted."

"Och, is that so?"

Angus turned in his seat to face Henry. For a second, Henry thought the demon's eyes flashed with fire, but when he looked again, he saw the same goat-like slits as before. Perhaps he had been drinking rather quickly. Maybe it was time to slow down.

"Are you all right there, Henry?" the demon asked, his voice rich with concern.

"Yeah, just a little lightheaded. I haven't eaten much today."

"Oh, would you like Lucy to knock you up a little something behind the bar. She makes a kick-ass goat curry, don't you, Lucy my love?"

Lucy beamed. "Best in Ocean City."

"No, no thank you, I'm fine," Henry reassured them. He knew better than to confess any weakness to a demon.

Angus reached into his pocket and pulled out an open deck of cards. He started turning them one at a time, face up on the bar in front of him. Over and over he turned them, in stacks of four. It was a game Henry hadn't seen before, and in spite of his better judgment, he began to follow along.

"Ah, well looky there!" The demon raised his hands in the air in disgust. "Lost again. I can't seem to shake my losing streak."

"I know the feeling," Henry said. "The cards haven't been kind to me for days."

The demon bobbed his head sympathetically and continued to turn the cards. "This streak has followed me all the way from the Magic-Con in Florida. That's one hell of a long time to be plagued by bad luck." He sighed.

Before he knew it, Henry was totally absorbed by the cards, trying to riddle the game out. The demon turned up three aces and a two, but even that seemed to disappoint him, and he thumped the bar in disgust.

"Och, now would you believe it? I've lost again. This is just plain stupid."

"I'm not sure I'm following," Henry said. "Didn't you just pull up three aces?"

"Aye, I did," Angus agreed. "But the point of this game is to get the worst hand possible."

Henry laughed. "I should be good at that game. That's all I seem to get these days."

Angus smiled and took a polite sip from his gimlet. "Fancy a wee bet then? To see who really has the worst luck?"

The demon opened a wallet that looked thick with notes. He slipped a hundred-dollar bill on the bar between them.

Henry knew he should say no. Gambling with a demon was perhaps the stupidest thing to do in both this world and the next, and he knew it. But the fire in his belly began to burn. Nothing in this world, nothing at all, was as alluring to him as the thrill of chance.

But what could he bet with? His wallet was empty, and Gaia knew, there was little if anything in his account at the bank. He looked at his watch. His dad's silver watch was the only thing he had left of value in the whole world. Slowly, he pulled it off.

"Why not?" he said. He placed the watch on top of the hundred-dollar note. "Let's do it."

Angus picked up the watch and examined it. "That's a fine-looking piece. Sterling silver, isn't it?" He returned it to the counter. "Are you sure you'd want to risk losing something so valuable in some stupid bet?"

"Assuming I'd lose," Henry said. He tapped his gut. "I have a feeling my luck's about to change. What do I have to do?"

"Simple really. All you have to do is turn over four cards. Picture cards count as ten. Ace is high, eleven. Whoever has the lowest score wins."

"Fine," Henry said. Still, he wasn't born yesterday. "Um, do you mind if I shuffle?"

Angus set the deck down on the counter. "Sure, be my guest."

Intrigued, Lucy stood in front of them, leaning over the bar. Her feminine delights bunched together and almost oozed out of her corset top.

Henry tore his gaze away, took a deep breath, and shuffled. He dealt out eight cards and put the remaining deck facedown on the bar.

"You first," Henry said.

"Sure." Angus locked his fingers together, then cracked them. "Wish me luck, Lucy love."

"You don't need any help from me," she teased.

Angus raised an eyebrow, but neither agreed nor disagreed. Slowly, he turned over each of the cards. A two, a jack, a nine, and a five. "Hmm. Twenty-six. Kinda blah. I'm sure you can beat that."

Henry hoped he could. He stared at his dad's watch, the adrenaline in his heart racing. This was what he lived for. This was what he did best. One by one, he turned the cards. A three, a four, a king, and a queen. *Twenty-seven!*

"Sorry, Henry."

Henry's stomach tanked as the demon pulled his dad's watch toward him. Gaia, he was an idiot. His losing streak had never gone on this long. And now he had lost his dad's watch. Mary would kick him from here to kingdom come when she found out.

"It's a nice watch," Angus said, staring at its face. "I think it's worth a lot more than my measly hundred dollars."

"Probably so," Henry agreed, feeling sick. "But I have nothing else, so we're done. Thank you for the drink."

"Wait!" Angus said. "Och, I'm sorry. I didn't mean to rub it in. It's just I feel a bit guilty. I'm guessing this watch meant a lot to you?"

"You could say that," Henry admitted. "But a bet's a bet. You won it fair and square."

"Very noble of you. But how about I give you the chance to win it back?"

Henry laughed bitterly. "With what? I'm flat broke."

The demon smiled and placed the watch back on the bar. The idea that he could win it back pulled on Henry's heartstrings. But what did he have to offer? His wallet was empty.

"Och, I'll be kind and make it easy on you," the demon said.

"Yes?"

"Aye. Lucy love, why don't you hand me one of those lovely napkins I know you keep behind the bar? Oh, and a pen while you're at it, love."

Lucy smiled and reached down behind the bar. She came up with both the items requested.

"I'll be happy to take an IOU. I trust you."

"You would?" Henry's eyes filled with hope. He really did want to win that watch back.

"Aye. I like you, Henry. As we say across the pond, you're a good egg. Just blot your X on the napkin, and we'll have another turn of the cards. I'll even let you shuffle again if you like. It's time your luck changed for the better, don't you think?"

That Henry couldn't argue with. He downed the last of his whiskey in a single swallow and stared hard at the watch. It wasn't like this would be the first IOU he'd ever signed.

"How much do you want me to sign for?" Henry asked, taking up the pen.

"Och, I dunno," Angus said thoughtfully. "You know, it doesn't even have to be money. Let me think for a second." He put his forefinger to his lips. "I guess it should be something you value, just to be fair. Something small though, something you can't put in a bank. Something that's not even yours, and that you wouldn't miss if it was lost. How does that sound? Fair enough? I don't want to take you to the cleaners, I just want to have a wee bit of fun. It's not like I'm after your soul or anything."

Hmmm. Henry's hand hovered over the napkin. It didn't sound like much, and heck, if it was something he wouldn't even miss, why not? Maybe his golf clubs? He hadn't played a round in over a year. Mary wouldn't even notice. He licked his lips, enjoying the remnants of whiskey and wishing he could afford another. But another shot wasn't part of the deal. He took a deep breath and signed the napkin.

"Och, this is exciting, isn't it?" Angus said, rubbing his hands together like a hyper child. "You can deal again if you like. You turn over first this time. Maybe it'll change your luck, eh?"

Once again, Henry dealt eight cards.

He turned over a four, a six, a three, and another three. *Sixteen!* His heart began to race. That was a super-low deal. Surely this time he was going to win.

He eyed his dad's watch, imagining slipping it back onto his wrist where it belonged.

"Good one," Angus agreed. "Now let's see if the gods have been kind." The demon turned the first card. A seven. A two. Then a four. Then another two.

Henry's soul bottomed out. *Fifteen!* The damned demon had beaten him again! And by a measly one point!

Henry brought his head down, banging it hard on the bar counter. He didn't care what anyone thought, he deserved the pain. He had bet and lost, and to make matters worse, he wasn't quite sure what he'd gambled.

Sick as a pig, he lifted himself up just as the demon slipped his dad's watch onto his wrist and tucked the IOU inside his jacket pocket.

"What do I owe you?" Henry said, his voice flat.

"Och, what was it I said? Something you value, wasn't it? Something small you can't put in a bank. Aye, something that's not even yours, that you wouldn't miss if it was lost."

"And what's that?" Henry asked.

A flash of fire definitely crossed the demon's goat-slitted eyes this time. He smiled. "Your two eldest daughters' hearts."

Chapter Two

HARM'S WAY

JOHN HATED CASINOS. THAT IS, HE LOVED THEM, BUT HE TOLD HIMSELF he hated them. His wife wanted it that way, and that was how it was going to be.

As he walked through the entrance to The Magic Tables, he spotted his dad sitting at the bar. The old satyr looked rough. His brown hair was unkempt, and he was slumped over a drink, his tail drooping sadly behind him. His drinking buddy, whoever he was, had just signed the tab, and it looked like he was leaving. John slowed his pace, hanging back to avoid saying hello. The less he had to do with these people, the better he liked it.

The man passed him on his way out, and John caught the goat-like slit to his eyes. John's hairs stood on end. *Ugh, demons.* They gave him the willies. The demon smiled as he passed him, almost as if he knew who he was. John thanked Gaia he'd just missed him and went straight to join his dad at the bar.

"Are you ever going to learn?" the young satyr said, his tone more genial than he felt. What he really wanted to do was kick the man from here to eternity. The only thing stopping him was the sexy succubus standing before him. Forgetting his wife for once, he treated her to his full-on satyr smile and started thinking in rhyming couplets. *Boy, this girl's hot. I like her a lot.*

Stop that at once. You're married, you dunce!

"Hello to you too, son," his dad said. "Where's Fanny?" His dad looked over his shoulder. Something about his wry expression suggested he was glad not to see her. As always.

"Held up. I'll see her later."

John settled into the seat beside his dad. The succubus stood before them, her hands on her waist, fully aware of her power.

"What can I get you, lover boy?" she said.

I can think of a thing or two. No doubt, so can you.

"Um, a diet soda, please. Want one, Dad?"

"Sure. With a drop of whiskey in it."

John settled into his chair and tried not to look at the girl's natural endowments. The sight of them was muddling his brain. "Haven't you had enough to drink already?"

"Don't start on me," his dad said. "I've had a shitty day."

John nodded to the succubus, who smiled and turned to pour the drinks. He sighed. There was no need to ask how much his dad had lost. He'd long since given up wishing for moderation.

He pulled out his wallet, then hesitated when he saw the hungry look in his dad's eyes. He pulled out a twenty, which he popped under the tip glass on the bar in front of them. It was stuffed with dollars. He slid the wallet back inside his back pocket, fully aware his dad followed it all the way home. This had gotten beyond a joke.

"How's Mary?" John asked. He could never quite bring himself to call his stepmother Mom, even though he knew his dad wanted him to.

"She's good. She and the girls are, um, you know, just fine."

"Are you still staying at Joe's old place?"

"Yeah, well, just for a while. At least until I can sort myself out. Money's a bit tight at the moment, you know. And the girls love it at Norland Park."

John didn't answer. He supposed he should be grateful his dad had a childless uncle who had bequeathed him a house to stay in. Otherwise, his dad would have put them all on the streets by now. And perhaps would still.

The succubus blew his dad a kiss as she deposited the fresh glass in front of him.

"Thanks, Lucy."

"No problem, lover."

She winked when she did the same with John's Coke. He took a tiny sip.

"Can I get you anything else, big boy?" Lucy ran a rather delicious-looking tongue over her pouty, kissable lips.

With all your curves and obvious charms, I'd love to take you in my arms.

John coughed. "*Ahem!* Pardon me. No, I think I'm good, thanks." He tapped his chest, pretending he'd just swallowed wrong.

Lucy smiled and walked away, and John wondered if she could read his mind. He'd be in *oh-so-much-trouble* if she could.

His dad downed his whiskey in a single chug, then looked despairingly into the bottom of the empty glass. He looked wiped out. His skin was pale and clammy, and there was a slight tremor in his hand. That was new. What on earth had he done?

John knew his dad well enough to know there was more going on here than just one drink too many. Something deeper was eating at his soul. He prayed that whatever it was, it wasn't going to cost him. Fanny would be livid. She'd already told him not to give him any cash. She'd be mad as hell.

"So, it's been a shitty day, has it? Are you going to tell me more or do you plan to leave it at that?"

His dad twirled the ice in the bottom of his glass as he thought. Lucy leaned across to take it from him for a refill, but he shook his head. John thought she sure fit nice inside that corset.

If I were free and you were nice, I'd have that off you in a trice.

Stop it!

"Where's your car?" John tried to look anywhere but at the girl.

"In the lot. I should leave it there, I'm probably over the limit."

"How many have you had?"

"I dunno, I lost track. But they were doubles, so...."

"Okay, let's get out of here. I think I'd rather eat somewhere else. Those slot machines are annoying me. Settle that up for me, will you?" he said to the succubus.

Lucy slipped the twenty out from under the glass, winked again, then turned to cash them out at the register. Henry checked her rear end as she worked it, mapping out the perfect heart shape of her behind.

I'm such a horny little satyr nut, I'd do anything just to grab that butt.

Sick or not, he caught his dad checking her out at the same time. He supposed they had that much in common, and he wondered if older satyrs did the rhyming thing, or if it was something that petered out with age. He'd ask him later once the girl was out of earshot.

Lucy returned with a five and some ones, and John returned the ones to the tip glass. Her perky wings drooped, and she wandered off.

His dad took his time sliding off the chair. Although he'd been called upon to help him on many an occasion, John could never remember him looking quite so wretched as he did now. It tore at his soul. There was 200 bucks or so in his wallet. He would give it all to him as soon as they were out of here. Fanny didn't need to know. It would be their little secret.

"So, what do you fancy for lunch?" John asked as they walked through the chiming casino. "It's a beautiful day outside. We could find someplace on the boardwalk and watch the tourists go by if you like?"

"I've lost my appetite."

"Well, I haven't. I didn't drive all this way not to eat. You can watch me if you don't want anything, but we *are* going to get *something*. I'm in the mood for a big, fat, juicy steak. How about you?"

"Whatever you want, son, is fine by me."

This was getting irksome. His dad might be a hopeless gambler, but he had always had a *joie de vivre,* and this down-in-the-mouth routine was worrying as hell. He desperately wanted to cheer him up, and despite his better judgment, there was only one way he could think of.

He pulled out his wallet and emptied everything except the ten he needed to recover his car. He handed it to his dad. "You're really worrying me, Dad. There. It's all I have on me. If it's not enough, just let me know and I'll see what I can do. Just don't blow it at the tables. You know how my Fanny feels about you gambling."

"I'm not down because of that," his dad confessed. "Not exactly. But I don't want to talk about it." He tucked the wad of cash inside his pocket. "Thank you for this, though. I do need it."

John suddenly felt the call of nature. The one good thing to be said about the casinos was that the bathrooms were in a lot better shape than the ones out on the boardwalk.

"Wait here," he said, suddenly wishing he hadn't handed over the cash quite so precipitously. "I've got to use the bathroom. Don't do anything foolish."

"I won't," his dad said. "I promise."

John hesitated for just a moment, then reasoned there wasn't a lot his dad could do in a minute or two—and that's all he would be, tops.

"Okay. I'll be right back."

His dad nodded and John sped off, looking back over his shoulder one more time before disappearing into the bathroom. It was empty, plush, and most importantly, relatively clean. As quickly as he could, he did what he needed to, washed his hands, and returned to the casino floor.

And of course. His dad was gone.

***

John looked left and right, mad as anything. He'd said he would wait, dammit, so where the hell was he? He'd only been a couple of minutes, so he couldn't have gone far. One by one he looked down the rows of slot machines, but his dad was nowhere to be found.

"Son of a bi—!"

"Hey John, over here!"

John spun on his heels, and there was his dad, pumping a note into a machine in a row just a few feet away. He marched over at once, not believing his eyes.

"What are you doing?"

"You told me to wait for you. I'm waiting."

John was so angry he had to fight to find the words. "I can't believe you're gambling away the money I just gave you after you promised. Dad, you're unreal!"

"Oh hush, son, it's only a few dollars. You were taking forever. It's only a twenty. It's not like I've lost it all."

John looked up to the ceiling where the casino gargoyles were watching all the action in the shadows. He thought he saw the flash of an acute red eye, but it was gone in a second. Those things preferred to stay out of sight and out of mind. He wished he could do the same.

Oblivious to his frustration, his dad kept on hitting that play button like there was no tomorrow. His addiction was infuriating.

"What am I gonna do with you, Dad?" John said, pinching his eyes. He looked at the machine his dad had chosen and sighed. "And darn it, this is progressive slots. You know no one ever wins the jackpot, right?"

"Wait a minute, son. *What the—!*"

Suddenly, the machine started singing louder than any other in the casino. The lights began flickering brighter than police lights at an Epstein slumber party, and the reels began spinning wildly out of control. *Call attendant* flashed urgently on the screen.

"What did you win?" John asked.

"Only the fucking jackpot!" His dad laughed, his eyes dancing with wonder. "Only seven million fucking dollars!"

His dad stared in wonder at the machine, his mouth wide open. As the crowds began to draw, he moved closer to the machine, protecting his claim and looking all around for a floor person to help him.

At last, it began to sink in, and John started to laugh. "Wow, Dad, that's incredible!" he cried, and the two men fell into a hug.

"Excuse me, excuse me," came the voice of someone pushing through the crowd. "Come on den, let me through."

The casino attendant was a three-foot-tall leprechaun, dressed entirely in emerald green. He carried a small footstool, and as soon as he climbed on top of it, he started checking the machine.

"What's he doing?" John asked.

"*He* is making sure da machine isn't malfunctioning," the leprechaun replied. He pointed to a little sign John hadn't noticed before on the top of the machine. It said, *Malfunctions void all wins.*

"And is it malfunctioning?" John asked, hardly daring to breathe.

The leprechaun pressed a few buttons and frowned.

"Nope. 'Tis a good win. Imma gonna need ta see some I.D."

His dad was shaking so bad, he almost dropped his wallet as he pulled it from his pocket. He tried to pull his driver's license out, but he couldn't. Trembling, he handed over his wallet to John.

John pulled the license out and gave it to the leprechaun, who took out a cell phone and began typing into it.

"What are you doing now?" his dad asked, the worried look back on his face.

"Just checking ta see ya not on any exclusion list. 'Tis a gaming license fing, is all."

"And is he?" John asked. For all he knew, his dad could be.

"No, no, not seeing nuffin 'ere. Come with me, we haz some papers ta fill out."

The leprechaun dropped down and, after retrieving his stool, began shuffling through the crowd. His dad ran straight after the little man, though John was afraid to leave the machine, unsure of how things worked. But he followed on at last, and the three of them went to the cashier's window. The leprechaun told them to wait there, while he opened a door and went inside.

"Oh, by Gaia," his dad said, "I've never had such a win my whole life! My heart is racing."

"Mine would be too."

The leprechaun appeared at the window. He still carried his dad's I.D., which he handed back to him under the bulletproof glass along with some papers.

"Fill that out will you. It's for de IRS. Dey gonna want their cut."

His dad looked a little green around the edges himself. "Um, er, son. Could maybe you put this in your name? I er, I might owe a little something to old Uncle Sam." He turned to the leprechaun, who looked like he couldn't care less. "Would that be okay? Can I put this in my son's name?"

"Sure," the leprechaun replied. "As long as his I.D. checks out, sure. Why not?"

"Do you mind, John?"

"I'd be happy to, Dad." John reached into his back pocket and pulled out his wallet again. This was getting better and better. If the money was in his name, he'd have some control over it and his dad wouldn't be able to blow it in a single afternoon at the table. Things were on the up and up. He tried not to show his elation in case his dad noticed and changed his mind abruptly.

While the leprechaun checked his credentials, John started on the paperwork. "I'm so excited for you, Dad. Do you know what you're going to do with all the money? Please, don't lose it all at the tables this time, Dad. Please, promise me you won't do that." John didn't like the way the leprechaun was staring at his father with knowing eyes. He didn't like it one bit.

"I swear, son, I won't. This is Gaia looking down at me from above, I feel it in my bones. I'm going to start again. I will split the money between all of you. Mary and I can get a new house of our own, and everything is going to be just perfect from now on. I swear before Gaia, on my own life, I will never make such a foolish bet aga—"

Suddenly his words ceased and he turned deathly white, his hand desperately clutching his arm. A moment later, he fell to his knees.

"Dad! DAD! Oh Gaia, quick, someone call an ambulance! I think my dad's having a heart attack!"

For the second time that day, they were surrounded by people. John knelt beside his father. He took his dad's hand in his own, a thousand thoughts flashing through his head. With all the power of his being, he prayed to Gaia that his father would be allowed to beat the odds once more today. Only this time, all he had to do was live.

Chapter Three
SHAKER STYLE

FANNY STIRRED THE ONE TEASPOON OF SUGAR INTO HER HOT TEA. IT was her sole indulgence, the one thing her gym instructor would forgive her for. This was her guilty pleasure. *Everyone has to have a little something, don't they?* she thought.

She watched as her husband, John, chewed thoughtfully on his toast, his mind elsewhere as he stared wistfully out the window. Black really wasn't his color. Nor hers. It looked morbid against the green tint of her skin. Not her color at all. She wondered how long she'd have to wear it.

"You know, I've been thinking about the money," she said.

"Oh?" John's focus didn't budge.

"Yes, well, here's the thing. I don't think you should share it with your sisters like you said. Not directly, anyway."

John's brow crinkled, and he took a sip of his own tea. "I'm not sure what you mean?"

"Well, the way I see it, it was your win. Bought with your money, was it not? Your dad didn't have the right to tell you what to do with it. If it weren't for your generosity, he would never have placed that bet in the first place."

"True," John replied. "But he picked the machine. I would never have done what he did."

Fanny sighed and stared at the remnants of her husband's toast. It had been some years since she'd indulged in a little bread, though she still dreamed of it. A moment on the lips and all that.

"Well, I think it was too much of him to expect you to give each of your sisters an equal share in your win. If he meant for you to do that at all. He was sick and probably wasn't in his right mind. You're his firstborn, aren't you? And who did he turn to when he needed help? Not them, that's for sure. It was always you. John do this and John do that."

"True," John agreed. "But I am a lot older than my sisters. They're only just getting jobs now. Well, except Margaret of course."

"Half-sisters," Fanny reminded him. "Not full-blood. That, I suppose, would have been something else. You know, it always bugged me how different he was with them. You, he hardly had the time of day for, except when he needed something of course. Those girls only had to whisper in his ear, and he'd do anything for them. He made it perfectly clear to everyone that he loved his second family more than his first. It used to make me sick to see him rub your nose in it."

John sighed and buttered a second piece of toast. "So, what would you have me do, ignore his last wishes entirely?"

"Ignore them, no. I know you're too good a son and brother for that. But maybe don't give them a full share all at once? Hold the money in trust for them or something. If they need anything, well, then you can step in and help them out at the time. It will make a lot more interest in your hands and will go a lot further. You'd be doing them a big favor if you did that. And remember, it's not like they even know it was your dad's win, right? You never told them. What they've never had, they'll never miss. That's what I think anyway."

John downed the last of his toast, then started buttering another. "To be honest, I'm more preoccupied with the house situation. As you know, their house is technically mine, since Uncle Joe bequeathed it to me. Even if they wanted to stay, they can't afford the taxes on it—not without my help anyway. You know how steep the charges are at the beach. Mary called yesterday and told me they're looking for something smaller now, but she's struggling to find something within budget. Elinor's been looking all over the place, but she's not sure how long she's going to need—there isn't a lot out there at the moment. I think we should let them stay there for a while, at least until things settle down a bit."

Fanny smiled. The house was right on the water and was worth a small fortune in itself. She'd had her eyes on it for years. "Oh, I don't think that's a good idea. The longer you leave them, the more settled in they'll get. You'll never be able to get them out, not while you let them stay there for free. You're far too generous, you really are."

"So what would you have me do? Turn them out on the streets?"

"No, don't be silly," Fanny said. "That would be unkind. No, I was thinking we could go up there, you know, stake our claim. If we're right there in their faces, they'll take the hint soon enough. And in any case, I want to remodel. That kitchen is ancient. I see lovely Shaker cabinets in there, and a nice, big, fat industrial stove. The sooner I can get *mon décorateur* in there, the better!"

"Fanny, really!"

"Oh, come on, John, you want that house as much as I do, you've said so often enough."

"Yes, I know, but so soon?"

"I know, but it's better to get these things over with, don't you agree?"

"At my dad's funeral?"

"Sure, why not? It can't be all doom and gloom, can it? Better to get a head start on these things, I think. No point putting off the inevitable."

Fanny pushed away her tea and put her hand on her belly, ready to play her ace. "And you know, it'll be a lovely place for this little one to live when he comes along. Aww, John, can you imagine? Growing up at the seaside, living the life? I would hate to deprive our new baby of that, wouldn't you?"

"I suppose."

"Good. I'll talk to Mary and the girls after the service. Don't worry, I'll be kind. You know I wouldn't do anything to hurt them."

"I know, my dear," John said. "And you're right of course, as always."

"Excellent." Pleased with herself, Fanny rose from the table and wandered into her office. After unlocking her screen, she pulled up a realty site and started scrolling through similar ocean front homes for sale in the area with the same square footage. The price tags were reassuringly expensive. She smiled and dreamed of kitchens.

Chapter Four

THE FUNERAL

ELINOR DASHWOOD DREW HER YOUNGER SISTER MARGARET TO HER AS their mother stood at their father's grave. She watched solemnly as their mother waved her hand over a closed rosebud, which opened slowly, revealing ebony petals. Her mother kissed the bloom, then dropped it into their father's grave. Margaret's eyes were raw from crying, and as their mother bowed her head to pray, her younger sister turned her head away, clinging to Elinor's skirts as she sobbed uncontrollably. Elinor stroked Margaret's hair, feeling every bit as wretched as her baby sister, though determined to hide it better for appearance's sake.

Their elder brother, John, stepped forward and placed a comforting arm around the grieving widow's shoulder. Gently, he led her away from the grave and back over to her daughters.

"Thank you, John, you're very kind," their mother said.

John bowed his head gracefully, and Elinor smiled softly, grateful for his attentions. Even Marianne smiled her thanks. Elinor passed Margaret a hankie, and she blew her nose, making a noise like a trumpet.

"I'm so glad to see you both at last," Elinor said. "It's a pity it's under these circumstances, but what can you do? How is Fanny doing? Everything going well?"

"Yes, very much so. Couldn't be healthier. We'll be seeing the obstetrician next week, but it's just routine."

Elinor nodded and glanced at her sister-in-law, who was talking to someone on her phone. Elinor had little love for the woman, since it was clear Fanny thought the dryad side of the family was beneath her. But she was always polite for John's sake, if nothing else. "I'm glad to hear it. She looks very well."

"Doesn't she though?" John beamed. "You know, she's hardly gained any weight. But then Fanny's on her treadmill night and day, so we shouldn't be surprised, I suppose. Ah, here she comes." Fanny was striding toward them, putting her phone away.

Elinor took a deep breath and put on her poker face. She managed well enough with the half-goblin, but that didn't mean Fanny didn't get on her last nerve. She prayed today would be one of the good days and that Fanny wouldn't tease them all too much.

She leaned forward to kiss Fanny on the cheek. "You're looking well, Fanny. Pregnancy suits you. Here, I brought you a little something. It's a bromeliad, to keep around the house. It's good for the baby."

Fanny took the little pot and examined it with interest. "Why, thank you, Elinor. What clever things you dryad girls come up with. Of course, when my little Henry is living up at Norland Park, he'll be running around with all that lovely sea air in his lungs. I don't suppose a few plants will make much of a difference, but it's a nice thought."

"You're welcome," Elinor said flatly.

"You know, I find these funerals very bizarre," Fanny mused. "You should bury your dead the goblin way. You know, facedown and with everyone chucking their garbage into his grave to help him rot."

"Ewww, is that really how you do it?" Margaret gasped through her tears.

"Really, Fanny," their mother said, fighting back a fresh round of tears. "Do you expect people to bring all their stinking garbage on a solemn occasion like this? That's just horrible!"

"What? Nooo, don't be silly. It's good for the soil too," Fanny argued. "I would have thought you dryads would be into anything that enriched the earth. I was being kind! No need to get all snooty about it."

Elinor bit her tongue. This was her dad's funeral, dammit. But when was Fanny anything other than tactless? Goblins weren't exactly known for their diplomacy.

"What's that?" Marianne said. Elinor turned, not having seen her sister come over to join them. "You're planning to move in already?" Her sister glanced over to the grave, where her dad's body was barely cold. "Surely there's no rush, is there?"

"I see no reason to delay," Fanny shrugged. "After all, it would be better for my baby if we settled in quickly. Surely you can see the sense in that. It will be hell on earth to try and move with a little one in tow. No, better to do it now. And there's plenty of room. We can all live there happily under one roof until you sort yourselves out. Life goes on after all."

Marianne looked fit to explode, and Mary was wiping her eyes.

"Come on, Fanny," John said, looking around and noting the angry expressions. "This is neither the time nor the place. We can talk about it later, okay?"

Fanny sighed and shook her head but said nothing else.

"It's fine," Elinor calmly replied. "I think we need to get everyone home. We're all just tired and under the weather."

"Well, naturally," John said, puffing up. "This is such a sad day. Come, Mary, let me get you into your car."

John led their mother away, and Elinor held back, watching them go. Despite his unfortunate wife, she knew her brother had a kind heart. He would do what he could for them. Indeed, he was doing very well now, if his new Mercedes E-Class Coupe was anything to go by. She supposed it was nice to have money. John had done well by his marriage. Not that she begrudged him a dime—she just hoped they might all be as lucky in love.

Fanny smiled at her, then followed her husband. Marianne shot Fanny a hateful glance, then gave Elinor a knowing look. Margaret finally let Elinor go and ran after their mother.

Elinor walked quietly to her father's grave and looked down into it. The satyr had been an inveterate gambler; he could be coarse and a little insane at times, risking everything to chance and never taking life quite as seriously as he should. There was a certain cruel irony in his dying in a casino. Then again, that was probably how he would have wanted to go— playing the slots one last time. Her heart was crushed. Oh, how she was going to miss him. She kissed a small nut she had in her pocket and let it fall into the grave. She knew in time it would grow and grow and emerge to become a tree, absorbing Henry into its roots so he would live on, as was the dryad way.

Hear me, Gaia, receive my father unto your loving bosom and care for him. He was a good man and a good dad. Mostly.

Looking back, her brother, John, realized what she had done and nodded his approval.

She sighed. *Damn you, Dad, you blew our savings and left us with nothing, not even the house we grew up in. We're dependent upon the charity of others now.* She glanced at Fanny, climbing into the Merc, and wasn't sure how long that charity would last. *What will become of us?*

But now was not the time to worry. Elinor lowered her head, and with a last blown kiss, said goodbye to her beloved father.

Chapter Five

MR. EDWARD FERRARS, ESQUIRE

ELINOR SAT ON THE SWING AND STARED OUT OVER THE OCEAN. SHE HAD brought a book of poetry with her, but it remained closed on her lap. Her thoughts were lost in the past, thinking of all the times she used to sit here with her dad. Sometimes they would talk for hours; other times they would just be silent and listen to the ocean. Both were nice.

Elinor had planted many trees on the property over the years, like the mockernut hickory, hackberry, and flowering dogwoods that grew around the porch now. As a dryad, nothing warmed her soul more than to talk about their progress. And as a satyr, her dad would wax poetical and make up the most magical stories about them. She was going to miss that a lot.

It still felt strange, him not being here. Maybe she'd never get used to him not being around anymore. But then maybe she wasn't supposed to. It felt like he was with her even now, swinging beside her, watching the world around them.

She could hear Marianne at her piano in the dining room. It was a melancholy tune, played well and with a depth of expression that touched the heart. Marianne had such a gift. And the tune suited everyone's mood today, because Fanny and John were due any moment.

The music stopped, and a moment later Marianne stood in the doorway. Elinor and her sister were very similar in appearance, though

Marianne's hair was a touch lighter, with natural, copper curls tumbling down her black sweater. Elinor's hair also had a touch of red, though a shade or two darker. Their hair changed color with the seasons, with a touch of green in the summer, deep reds and browns in autumn and winter. Dryad girls, in tune with nature.

They both had their mother's green eyes, though Marianne's were wide and bright and Elinor's were calm and intelligent, so she had been told. Marianne was perhaps an inch or two shorter. Beside these differences, they were clearly sisters. Margaret, their youngest sister, took more after their father and was considerably darker in eyes and hair. She had their dad's sense of mischief too. She was going to be a real terror when she grew up.

"Are they here?" Elinor asked, bringing her swing to a stop.

"Just pulled up," Marianne replied. "Should I roll out the red carpet?"

"Try and be nice to her, Marianne. This is her house now, after all."

"I will, but only because you asked me to. But it's not fair. Uncle Joe should have left this house to us, not just to John. We were Pop's kids too. It's 2020 for Gaia's sake, not the 1800s when he was born. Women are actually allowed to own property these days."

"We've talked about this," Elinor said, climbing out of the swing. "Uncle Joe wasn't really our uncle, he was John's mother's brother, so he wasn't truly related to us at all. And under satyr law, properties can't be left to half-blood children, related or otherwise. It has to follow the satyr-line, and since John's mom was also a satyr, he's full-blood."

Marianne snorted her disapproval. "Well, why didn't Joe kick us out before?"

"Well, I suppose he was fond of Dad and let us all stay there. I'm sorry, Marianne, I really am, but it was never meant to be forever. The property is legally John's, and he's free to do whatever he likes with it."

"Yeah, well, it still sucks. Come on. Let's go say hello to phlegm face before she starts counting the china."

"Marianne!"

"Well, I wouldn't put it past her. Would you?"

Elinor didn't answer, but she did follow Marianne back through the house to the main entrance.

Fanny was out on the gravel drive, talking to their mother. John was round the back of the new Merc, pulling a bunch of bags from the trunk.

"The moving van won't be here before tomorrow," Fanny said. "I wanted a night of peace and quiet before all the madness begins. I can't stand all the disruption. I half-thought about John and I going on a cruise and letting them sort it all out while we were away, but I wanted to be sure they put our stuff where I want it to go, and not just anywhere, you know? Oh hello, Elinor, Marianne. Here we are at last! I bet you thought we'd never make it."

Marianne opened her mouth to say something—no doubt some droll witticism—but Elinor nudged her arm, stopping her.

"How was traffic?" Elinor asked.

"Pretty quiet. Oh, I wanted to let you know, we've invited a few friends over for Saturday. John and I have waited a long time for this, and now that we're here, we thought we'd throw a little housewarming party. Just a few intimate friends, you know, nothing too dramatic. We might do something bigger once we're properly settled in."

Fanny looked around, inspecting the house and garden, and Elinor could almost feel her glee. She took a step back and exchanged glances with Marianne, who looked fit to burst. If she didn't speak now, Marianne probably would.

"Um, anyone we know?"

"No, I don't think so," Fanny said. She watched as John labored under the weight of their cases as he headed for the house. They all followed behind him.

"Do you want help with that?" Marianne asked.

"If you wouldn't mind grabbing that smaller one," John said.

Marianne bent down to pick up a small, purple sports bag. She strained to lift it and ended up jerking it off the ground with both hands. Her expression conveyed her surprise at how heavy it was, and she shot John a nasty look.

"Heck, what have you got in here?" Marianne asked.

Fanny glanced over. "Oh, my weights are in that one. Try not to drop them. I plan to work out right up until my due date." She patted her tummy. "Anyway, as I was saying, it's just a few friends. And my brother Edward said he'd probably be able to make it, though he wasn't a hundred percent sure when I asked. I do hope he does. I so desperately want him to see the amazing views. Do you think Margaret would mind giving up her room while he's here? I think her views are the nicest in the house, and I'd love Edward to see Norland at its best."

Without waiting for a reply, Fanny dashed inside the house. Elinor took the heavy bag from Marianne and nodded to the couple of bags left on the gravel. Marianne picked these up and sighed with relief. They followed Fanny and John inside.

Elinor was seething. She wanted to strangle Fanny until her eyeballs popped out and rolled away. It must have showed in her expression, because Marianne glanced at her a few times. "Not. One. Word," she warned. Wisely, Marianne said nothing.

Elinor snapped her laptop shut. "Dammit to heck! None of the properties in this stupid town are suitable. They're either too darned expensive, too urban, too remote, or too apartmenty. You were with me, Marianne, weren't you? I told her we're all dryads, didn't I? I swear to Gaia the stupid woman didn't listen to me at all. Oh, what are we going to do?"

"I can try and get a real job?" Marianne suggested.

"Your online storefront is my lifeline," Elinor countered. "I need your web skills to sell my saplings. We both know I'm rubbish at that sort of thing."

"I know, but maybe something in addition on the side, part-timey. They're hiring at the supermarket. I can stack tins. Or whatever it is they do in a supermarket."

"Yeah, maybe. Once we know exactly where we'll be staying, that might be an idea. Rentals are just so steep."

Their mother sat in a chair by the window. In fact, the whole family often crammed into Mary's room now in their bid to escape Fanny and her *décorateurs*. Especially today. It was the day of Fanny's housewarming party.

"I could try and get a job," Mary said. "There must be something I could do."

Elinor put her arm around her mother and squeezed her gently. The fact was their mother had never worked a day in her life. It was ridiculous she had to think of starting now. But Elinor said nothing. There was every possibility her mother might have to get a job soon, ridiculous or not. If only her tree business was doing better.

There was a knock at the door. They all knew who it was, and no one answered. Regardless, the door opened, and Fanny stuck her head around it.

"Well, here you all are," Fanny said. "I thought you might be—you dryad girls are always squirreled away some place or other, minding your nuts. Come, come on down, all of you. My brother Edward has arrived, and I *so* want you to meet him."

Never quick to respond to Fanny, curiosity got the better of them all. Elinor glanced at Marianne, then both glanced at their mother. Mary shrugged and stood up, so the two sisters rose also, ready to follow. Even Margaret slid out from under the bed. She spent a lot of time hiding under there these days, keeping out of Fanny's way. They'd had a silly argument about Margaret's room, and Elinor still wasn't sure who had won.

"Wipe the dust off you," Mary said. "You're not fit to be seen."

Margaret grinned, proud of her ninja stealth. Elinor helped brush her down and tried not to sneeze as the dust went up her nose.

One by one, everyone followed Fanny downstairs. Elinor could hear John talking to someone in the kitchen. She noticed the second man, who must be Fanny's brother Edward, had a deep, soothing voice, which surprised her since most half-goblins were squeakier than the average human or satyr males. Fanny's shrill voice sometimes made her eye twitch.

"Ah, there you all are," John said jovially. "I was about to send out a search party. Come and meet Edward, Fanny's older brother."

Edward Ferrars was a lot taller than Elinor had imagined he would be, and his style was more casual than his sister's. He wore nice-fitting jeans, a checkered shirt, and a navy sweater with casual brown loafers finishing things off. His mop of hair had a slight goblin-green hue to it, and his slanted eyes were another giveaway, but apart from those two things she would never have guessed at his goblin heritage. His skin lacked the green tint that Fanny's had, and there was nothing calculating or shrewd about his demeanor. She liked him instantly, even before he turned his gentle eyes on her and warmed her heart with his smile.

"You can't be Fanny's brother, you're not green enough," Margaret blurted, like the thirteen-year-old she was.

"Margaret!" Elinor said. "That's just plain rude!"

Instead of looking peeved, as his sister surely would have done, Edward merely grinned. "I know, and it's dreadful. Fanny keeps threatening to disown me, but there's nothing I can do. My ears are a little bit pointy, if it makes you feel any better." He pulled his hair back and tugged at the tips of his ears. To Elinor, they looked more elfin than goblin. Margaret grinned, her expression making it clear he had passed the teenager test.

Edward held out his hand to their mother, then shook everyone's hand in turn. Elinor noticed his shake was agreeably firm and his palms were soft. Her dad had once told her you could tell a lot from a man's handshake. *He'd been right about that*, she thought.

"Nice to meet you," Edward said. "You must be Elinor, which makes you Marianne, and this one has to be Margaret!"

"I am. I'm the youngest."

"And the silliest," Marianne said. "It was very nice to meet you, Edward, but if you'll excuse me, there are some things I need to take care of before tonight."

"Nice to meet you, too," he said.

Marianne grabbed a bottle of water from the fridge and left the kitchen. Elinor watched her go, wondering what was on her sister's mind.

"Did you have far to travel?" Elinor asked. "Fanny never said."

"Oh, well I was staying with some friends in New York. Fanny said I could crash here at Norland for a bit. After that, duty calls and I'll be spending a few weeks with our Mother. Oh!" He turned and smiled at their mother. "Assuming that's okay with you? I wouldn't want to intrude. This is your home, after all."

Mary smiled her approval and nodded. "Actually, this is Fanny's house now. But thank you for thinking of me."

Fanny, who never liked being excluded from any conversation, muscled into the center of the circle and took up her brother's hand in her own. She placed it on her belly. "Do you feel that, Edward? We'll soon have a new little Henry Dashwood running about the place. You're going to be an uncle! Isn't it exciting?"

"I'm pleased to see you looking so well," Edward said, carefully retrieving his hand. "Are you sure you're up to having a party tonight? You look positively fit to pop."

"Oh Edward, you silly, of course. Anyway, there will just be a few of us. My gobby girlfriends will be here naturally, plus my darling sisters-in-law." She indicated Elinor, Marianne, and Margaret with an almost dismissive sweep of her hand. "It'll be so much fun."

"So no other men?" Edward sighed. He stared at John, but his brother-in-law looked away, pretending not to notice. "Oh Fanny."

"Oh, stop complaining, you'll be just fine. I've invited Bethany Morton, you know." Fanny winked as if this were something of significance, but Edward merely rolled his eyes.

"For the love of Gaia, Fanny, I wish you wouldn't do that."

Fanny shared a fake conspiratorial look with Elinor. "Tsk, really, Edward. You know how much Momsie adores her. If it were up to her, she'd have you two married off already. And her family has *so* much money. You'd be set up for life."

"Thank you for deciding my future for me," Edward said flatly. "Anyway, is there someplace I can go and get changed? I've been traveling a few hours and I'm all sweaty."

Elinor laughed at his frankness.

"I'll take you up," Fanny said, already on her way out of the kitchen. "I was going to put you in Margaret's room, but the girl made such a fuss." Everyone stared at Margaret, who, for the present, looked inscrutable. "John, could you come with us? You know I can't carry anything heavy in my condition, and most of Edward's stuff is still in the back of his car."

Margaret grinned, and even their mother didn't try to hide her smirk. *Fifty points to House Dashwood,* Elinor thought.

Edward smiled, noticing the exchange. "Excuse me. I'll see you all later." Elinor hoped he wouldn't tell Fanny. But he seemed genuinely amused by it all, rather than angry. Perhaps he knew better than anyone what his sister was like.

He picked up a small bag Elinor hadn't noticed before from under the table and followed Fanny and John out of the room. They watched in silence as he left, and Elinor found herself wondering why her heart was beating a little faster and why this whole party thing suddenly seemed a lot more appealing.

"Are you all right, my dear?" her mother asked. "You're looking a little flushed."

I was just wondering if goblins are good kissers, Elinor thought but did not dare say the words aloud. But it was an engaging thought. "I'm good, Mom, don't worry. I was just thinking about those rentals."

"Ah yes," Mary nodded solemnly.

But when her mother turned to look away, Elinor allowed herself a saucy grin.

Chapter Six

A MALIGNITY OF GOBLINS

ELINOR'S HEAD WAS SPINNING. WOULD THESE PEOPLE EVER STOP? IT WAS as if her home was being torn apart before her very eyes.

"Ah yes, absolutely," Fanny cried. "All these nasty browns and grays will have to go. I can't abide all these neutral colors."

"Yes indeed," screeched one of Fanny's goblin girlfriends. Elinor had already forgotten most of their names, which was just as well, since not one made any effort to talk to her. Marianne and Margaret had made their escape some time ago, and she expected her mother was already in her room, keeping out of harm's way. "You need more purple and navy on the walls. Drama is the in-thing. What they have here is so lame. But splash a little color on it and it'll be perfect, Fanny."

Elinor wasn't sure if she imagined it, but she thought she caught Edward observing her. If he had been, he quickly looked away. Nevertheless, she felt some very satisfactory tingles running up and down her spine.

"Fanny, you do realize this is a beach home and not some gothic, uptown New York apartment?" Edward said. "I think the color palette suits the place very well, just as it is. It's nice and calming, which is what you want at the beach, surely?"

Fanny snorted. "Really, Edward, what do you know about interior decorating?"

The four goblin girlfriends almost fell off the sofa, laughing at him. Their high-pitched shrills were cutting right through Elinor, and at last, she'd had enough. She rose from the armchair she'd been sitting in and grabbed her sketchpad and a few pencils from the occasional table beside her.

"Excuse me," she said politely. "I feel a bit of a headache coming on. If you don't mind, I'm going outside for a bit."

Fanny barely acknowledged her and waved her off. Edward half-smiled her way, and the others didn't respond at all. Goblins. What annoying little horrors they were.

Elinor stepped out onto the porch. It was a gorgeous night; the sun had yet to set, and the waves were gently lulling the world to sleep. Every now and then she heard a high-pitched cackle from inside, but for the most part it was quiet out on the porch.

A little distance away on the beach, Marianne and Margaret were amusing themselves, tossing a ball between them. From time to time she could hear their laughter, but she was used to hearing them, and their cries hardly bothered her. Unlike the shrill cackling from the goblins who'd invaded her home.

Elinor sat on the porch swing and tucked her heels beneath her, and with the swing rocking ever so gently, she began to sketch. She drew the waves breaking over the familiar rocks on the beach, the curve of the shoreline, and the seagulls in the air, their wings spread wide. She filled out billowing clouds on the horizon, adding shading beneath.

"That's pretty," a voice said from over her shoulder. She hadn't heard Edward approach, and she jumped, ruining her line on her landscape. Edward grimaced. "Oh I'm sorry, I didn't mean to startle you."

Elinor looked down at the pad. The error wasn't much; she could fix it easily enough.

"You're fine," she said. "It's not very good anyway. I wanted to sketch the house so I could take it as a memento, but I should be out there on the beach looking in. I'm getting everything wrong. Have you had enough of the party?"

Edward looked behind him and shook his head. "Um, that would be telling. May I join you?"

"Sure," Elinor said, unfolding her legs and making room for him on the swing. "If you'd like." This was all very unexpected. She glanced back at the house, half-expecting Fanny to come storming outside to see what she was missing.

Edward took his place on the end of the swing and kicked off gently, setting it in motion. "It's very peaceful out here. I imagine it will be hard for you all to leave when the time comes."

Elinor nodded. "Very. We all grew up here. We've never known any other home."

He nodded. "I'm sure us goblins and our brutish ways aren't exactly helping. Hey, do you know what they call a gathering of goblins?"

Elinor shook her head.

"It's a malignity. I don't care for the term myself, but sometimes...." He looked behind him just as another loud cackle broke the silence. "A malignity of goblins. Sometimes it fits perfectly." They both laughed a little.

"If you don't mind me saying," Elinor said, "you're not even a bit like Fanny. I would never have called you brother and sister if I hadn't known you were."

"I take after our mother's side, I suppose. Druids mostly. No magic to show for it sadly, but I dream of starting my own gathering. Not that there's much chance of that. I come from a family of goblin bankers. If Mother has her way, I'll be on the board of directors before I'm thirty. But sadly, that's not what I want."

Surprised, Elinor turned to face him. "I didn't know you had druid blood in you. How wonderful! We love druids. They're just as preoccupied with the natural world as we are, especially trees, which as you know, we revere. Oh, that is such a nice surprise. I hope you can get what you want in the end."

Edward lowered his gaze, momentarily lost in his own thoughts.

Marianne and Margaret had wandered quite some way along the beach, but the light was now fading, and the two girls were slowly making their way back toward the house. They looked so happy Elinor almost forgot their sorrows. Then she remembered their dad and had to fight back a tear.

There was an embroidered throw folded over the back of the swing.

Edward unraveled it and wrapped it around her shoulders. The light touch of his fingers made her tremble; she hoped he didn't notice her foolishness. "It's okay to miss him," he said.

Elinor nodded. "It's getting late. Maybe I should go inside." Even though she said this, part of her wanted to stay on the swing with him. But she didn't trust her feelings. She'd been able to hold back her tears for now, but they could fall at any minute. She didn't want him to see that. She wasn't ready to share her feelings with anyone. Not yet.

"Oh, there you are, Edward." Fanny said. "Really. You've come all this way just to sit out here on the porch like an old fogey? Typical. Come back in. The gobbys need you. We're all having so much fun. And John is feeling positively overwhelmed. He says he needs another man for support and sent me out to find you. Come on."

There was something about the way Fanny was looking at her that irritated Elinor. She knew in her heart Fanny didn't care one fig about where Edward was sitting. All that irked her sister-in-law was that he was sitting out here with *her*.

Edward steadied the swing and stood up. Before he left though, he straightened the throw, making sure of Elinor's comfort. Then with a defiant look at Fanny, he walked back inside.

Fanny was about to turn after him, but then she hesitated, and instead of going inside, she sat beside Elinor on the swing. She stared down the beach to where Marianne and Margaret were currently crouched down, examining something or other in the sand—most likely a crab, if Elinor had to guess.

"He's such a dear, is Edward," Fanny said. "We all expect him to do well. Momsie has her heart set on his running the family business, and we expect he'll make a nice, big, fat pot of money before he's done."

"He's a very nice man," Elinor agreed. "I'm sure he'll excel at whatever he decides to do. Banking, isn't it?"

Fanny snorted. "Yes, well, that's a maybe. But here's the thing. Whatever path he takes, he's going to need a strong woman by his side. We're a proud lot, us goblins, as you know. If he picks the wrong woman, well." Fanny sucked the air in through her lips and shook her head. "Poor Edward if he does, that's all I can say. Momsie will shun him as soon as look at him, and without the family money, Edward will be nothing. It would be the ruin of him. I love my brother dearly, and if I felt he set his heart on the wrong woman—well, I'm sure you understand."

For the moment, Elinor was speechless. She liked Edward more than she'd admit to anyone, but this *warning* from Fanny seemed a tad premature. She had only just met him. "Edward is his own man, I suppose. He'll do whatever he thinks is right."

"Let's hope for his sake, he does not," Fanny said pointedly. "Ah, here are your sisters. Did you have fun splashing about?"

Marianne glanced at Elinor, unsure how to respond. Not that she needed to.

"Well, might as well enjoy it while you can," Fanny said. "Right. I'm going back in to see to my guests. Don't walk any sand into the house. Wash your feet before you come back inside."

Then she turned and left them to it. Elinor's fingers curled into claws. If she thought she could get away with throttling Fanny, she would have.

"Are you all right?" Marianne asked, planting herself on the swing beside her sister as Margaret ran inside. "You look irritated. Has Fanny been at you again?"

"Nothing more than usual," Elinor replied. "But I think we need to move out of here and soon, before I do something I might regret."

"You're not wrong," Marianne agreed. "But what do you think of Edward? He seems a bit of all right, and I reckon he's taken a fancy to you."

"Oh shush," Elinor said, although she was secretly pleased. "What nonsense you talk sometimes."

But Marianne snickered, ignoring her. "Well, he's not my type, but I have to say, you could do a lot worse. And he has a nice butt. For a goblin."

"Marianne!" Elinor laughed and got up from the swing. It was getting a little cooler now. She picked up the embroidered throw, but instead of folding it and putting it back over the rear of the swing where it belonged, she crossed it over her arm, ready to take it inside with her. She had always liked this throw. She had embroidered it herself. But more importantly, she wanted to make sure it wouldn't be left behind. Fanny was going to get the house, but Elinor would be damned if she let her steal all their memories. Both old ones and new ones. She slid open the porch door and went inside. Making darn sure she brought sand into the house.

Chapter Seven

SOME GOOD NEWS, AT LAST

ELINOR WAS JUST BUTTERING A PIECE OF TOAST WHEN HER MOTHER walked in looking pink and flustered. Thinking Fanny had been pressing her buttons, Elinor smiled sympathetically, offered the buttered toast to her mother, then began to butter a second piece. Elinor took a bite and washed the toast down with a sip of tea. "Everything all right, Mom?"

Marianne, who was just pouring a cup for herself, set another cup for their mother and began to pour.

"I'm not sure, I think so," their mother said, nibbling at the corner of her toast. "Thanks, girls."

Intrigued, Elinor sat up straight. "What, then?"

"Do you remember my cousin, John?"

"John Middleton, the one we've never met in our whole lives?" Marianne snorted. "No. What of him? Has he kicked the bucket and left us a wad of cash or something? We should be so lucky."

Their mother peered over the rim of her glasses and shot Marianne a disapproving look. "Um, no, not exactly. He's very much alive and well, if you must know."

"I presume he's written to you then," Elinor said, diverting their mother's attention away from Marianne. "Or called maybe?"

"He sent me a text," their mother said, pulling out her phone. "Out of the blue."

"Oh?"

"He sent his commiserations about Henry, which was nice of course, but then he said he has a little holiday cottage he lets to tourists up in Maine."

"Holiday?" Elinor asked. "He's invited us up to visit? That's nice of him."

"That's what I thought, but no. Apparently, it has three bedrooms, and well, he said if we wanted to we could move in."

Marianne lowered her cup to the table, spilling just a little. "What? Wait...like forever?"

Their mother nodded. "Well, at least for as long as we like."

"Um, Mom, have you ever seen it? I mean, aren't those places seasonal?" Elinor asked. "Before you get too excited, we should at least find out whether we'd want to live there all year."

Her mother slid her phone across the table to Elinor. "There. Take a look. He sent the link he uses to let it out."

Elinor snatched up the phone and hit the link in the text. It opened to pictures of a small cedar-siding cottage sitting on a slightly elevated stretch of land overlooking the bay. The rooms had sturdy, rustic furniture, chosen to be both appealing and practical, and there was a large wood-burning fireplace in the center of the living room. The kitchen was modest but not too tiny, and all floors were walled with solid wood; there wasn't a sheet of drywall in sight.

The outside pictures were just as promising. The property was secluded, nestled within acres and acres of pines. There was a rocky coastline, but the cottage was set back far enough inland to be protected from the worst the ocean could throw at it. Elinor's hopes soared, yet this seemed too good to be true.

"How much is he asking?" Elinor said, passing the phone to Marianne who was itching to take a look. "Is he offering family rates?"

"That's the thing—hardly anything," their mother said. "And we can move up there whenever we want and stay as long as we like."

"It's very small," Marianne observed. "And only three bedrooms?"

"Yes, I know," their mother said. "That's the only downside."

"Well, the rooms look a pretty decent size. You and I can share," Elinor suggested. "Or maybe convert that tiny dining room into another bedroom for Margaret. I'm sure we could make it work."

Elinor turned to look out the window. Edward was just returning from a morning walk along the beach. She thought about what Fanny had said. Screw Fanny. What business was it of hers anyway? If they liked each other, that would be that. Shunning. Ha. Stupid goblins and their ridiculous ways! What would any of them care about that? And leaving Norland wasn't exactly the end of the world. If Edward liked her, as she hoped he did, he could come up for a visit. Or text her, call her, send up smoke signals— whichever he preferred. She checked whether the cottage had internet. It totally did.

"I think you should text Cousin John back and accept before he changes his mind," Elinor said. "We're not likely to get a better offer than that."

"I wonder what he's like," Marianne mused. "I wish we'd met him at least. He could be a monster for all we know."

"If he is, he's a very kind monster," their mother reasoned. "I don't remember him being at all bad, but you have to remember, we haven't seen each other since we were kids. He's a satyr, like your father was. So how bad could he be?"

"Well, anyone who wants to help us gets my vote," Elinor said. "No one else is."

"I thought your brother would help us out more, but he didn't even offer us his town house in New Jersey. He could at least have let us stay there for a bit."

"What, and have Fanny lose the chance to make a little rental income on the side?" Marianne scoffed. "Ha. You know we couldn't pay her what she'd want for it, and there's no way in hell she'd let us stay there for less than it's worth."

"Yes, but John is my stepson and your half-brother. He could have put his foot down."

Neither of the sisters was going to dignify that with a response. They both knew who ruled the roost in that nest.

"Well, I shall text him back. You all need to start thinking about what you want to take. You saw how big the size of those rooms are, so don't get crazy. And Elinor?"

"Yes, Mom?"

"I want you to think about what seedlings we should take. It's much colder up there, but I think we should take a little something from our home soil. And a gift, just for him. Think of something—it's the least we can do. Marianne, you can help Margaret go through her things. There won't be enough room for all of her toys."

Elinor nodded. It felt good having a plan. Fanny was going to be delighted, of course, but who cared? They had to think about themselves now. And this was an exciting turn of events, better than they could ever have wished for.

Elinor picked up their breakfast things and returned them to the kitchen. Edward was there, helping himself to a mug of coffee from the pot. He smiled when she joined him and turned around to lean casually against the counter.

"You look happy," he noticed.

"I am, we just had some good news. Mom's cousin has offered us a place to live up in Maine."

"Oh, right. When do you think you'll be going?"

Elinor rinsed the cups in the sink and loaded them in the dishwasher. He didn't exactly sound overjoyed. But then she could guess what he was thinking. She was sorry to be leaving him, too.

"We don't have a set date yet, but pretty soon. It's time we got out from under your sister's feet. This is her home now, not ours." Just saying the words out loud caused her throat to tighten. She had never felt so miserable, and Edward looked at a loss for what to say or do. She could feel his desire to comfort her. So why didn't he? He liked her well enough. Her dryad senses went on super-tingle whenever he got within a few yards of her.

Elinor popped an organic dishwasher tab into the machine and turned it on. Edward frowned and scratched his chin, as if he was churning over something in his mind.

"Yes?" Elinor prompted. He looked a little gobliny when he did that. She managed a faint smile.

"We haven't known each other very long," he began slowly, "but I feel like...." He paused.

Edward turned a slight shade of green, and she wondered if he was always like this when he was perplexed. Funny, those goblin genes.

"I feel like you and I could be good—friends," he got out. He stared at her pointedly, anxious, she supposed, for her to be following along.

"Yes, I think we are."

"And friends should always be open with one another."

Elinor nodded, but what was he saying? She'd talked to him, what, twice now? And exchanged a dozen words. She didn't want to be untrusting, but like it or not he was a goblin. Could he really be so different from the rest of his species? And his own sister? Perhaps he was. Perhaps she ought to give him a chance. What did she have to lose? Plenty, if Fanny found out! She pushed this thought aside and said, "Go on."

"So, I think I should tell you a little something of my past."

Elinor smiled. At twenty-four, she could hardly imagine he had much of one. "Oh? Is it naughty? Full of lewd and wicked things?"

Edward chuckled at that. "Perhaps, in a way. When I was at college...."

He was cut off when the front door slammed and there was a commotion in the hall. Elinor heard her mother tell Fanny the gist of what had happened. Fanny squealed with delight, then a moment later she burst into the kitchen, her arms full of Gucci bags that she dumped on the table. She looked positively delighted.

"Oh sweet Gaia above, I've just heard the news. Isn't it marvelous? Ooh, your very own quaint little cottage. How lucky you dryad girls are, always falling on your feet. I only wish John and I had half as much luck. Have you heard, Edward? It's the best news we've had in a long time. And Norland Park will be all mine at last. This kitchen is next. I want a big, fat marble island right here."

Edward gave Elinor a sympathetic look, but Elinor just stared down at the tile, wishing she hadn't loaded all the mugs in the dishwasher, so she'd have had something to throw at Fanny. Luckily, she did not. Instead, she took a deep breath and composed herself.

"Yes," she said. "We're not sure when exactly. But as for me, I hope it will be soon. Your hospitality has been something else, I assure you."

Fanny waved her hand in front of her face, as if she'd been paid the greatest of compliments. "Pfft, never mind all that. It was the least we could do in the circumstances."

"The very least," Edward said under his breath.

Elinor bit her lip and held in a snort. "If you don't mind, I'll be taking a few of the saplings with me from the orchard. We'd like to start a new garden when we get up north."

"Oh, take them all," Fanny said. "I was thinking of digging them up anyway and putting up a pagoda or something. Maybe a pool, I dunno. But I won't miss a few silly old trees, so please, help yourself."

Oh sweet Gaia! "There are spirits in those trees. Please don't do that. You'll bring bad luck to this house and regret it forever." Well, maybe the latter wasn't quite true, but Fanny didn't know that.

Fanny shrugged. "Whatever. Edward, help me with these things, darling." She indicated the bags. "I bought way too much, but there was a sale, and you never know when you're going to need more tops. They're all a bit small right now, but they'll be perfect when I lose the baby weight. Come, come!"

With that, Fanny swanned out of the kitchen, dismissive of Elinor and leaving Edward to collect her things and run after her. He dutifully picked up her bags and gave Elinor a sad, lopsided smile. There was no changing his sister, and they both knew it. "We'll talk again later."

As soon as they left, Elinor strolled to the sink and gazed at the trees. Her heart was breaking. She wished she could save them all. She resolved to take as many saplings as she could, giving them a chance to live on in their new home. Fanny be damned. She wished they could leave this place tomorrow. Elinor had had enough. If she never saw her sister-in-law again, it would be too soon.

The sun slipped gently over the horizon, casting a soft, yellow glow across the sands and bathing the windows at Norland in golden light. It was a little chilly out on the beach, but Elinor didn't mind. She loved the dawn. As the other occupants of the house slept, the world around her came alive. She pondered in silence the cry of the gulls overhead as they combed the beach for easy prey such as eggs or fish trapped in shallow pools. She smiled at the skittering of the ghost crabs as they shuffled around their secret hideaways, preparing to sleep away the day. All these creatures were her companions, and she would miss them dearly.

Still, it was not the beach that called to her this morning. She turned and made her way to the orchard. It was time to say goodbye to her dearest and lifelong friends. The melancholy notes of birdsong echoed the feelings in her heart. Her departure was known to all, and their sorrow filled her soul. Once there, she strolled quietly to the center of the orchard and knelt among the trees. The pain of parting became intense, like a lead weight on her shoulders. It didn't help that by leaving them to the care of her cold-hearted goblin sister-in-law, who had little affinity with nature, she was abandoning them to an uncertain future. In her heart, Elinor knew none of this was her fault, yet the guilt came anyway. She held out her hands palms up in penitence and prayed for her friends' forgiveness.

Two branches of an elder tree lowered and circled her open hands with their tips. At their touch, the collective soul of the orchard stirred within her. Their heartbreak was equal to her own, but there was something more —a dignity and majesty that had always been there, but she sensed it now more than ever. The trees knew that the future was never certain, but they looked ahead with a proud calmness. Indeed, their one concern was not for their own future, but for Elinor and her family. Rather than lament the changes to come, they infused her with the strength to face her own challenges. The generosity of their spirit fortified her, but it also overwhelmed her. She had come to support her old friends, but instead she had received a blessing from them. Elinor could hold back no longer, and in the privacy of her orchard, the tears came. The branches gently wound around her body, supporting her and rocking her gently. She felt their love, and through her sorrow, she was comforted.

Chapter Eight

BARTON COTTAGE

JOHN MIDDLETON WAS SOMETHING OF AN ODDITY. AS SOON AS ELINOR drove their battered Forester onto his drive, the old satyr came bouncing over, his furry legs and cloven feet very visible under his red tartan shorts. He had a long set of tongs in his gloved hands, and smoke was pouring from the vent on his barbecue grill behind him.

He was surrounded by a swarm of young satyrs, all similarly attired and screaming in their excitement.

After the long, five-hour drive, this was quite a reception. Elinor put the car in park and braced herself as she opened the driver door.

Almost immediately, the two tallest and most excited satyr boys started pulling at her top, almost dragging her from the car. "Come and play! Come and play!"

Her mother and sisters, observing the assault, remained in the car.

"Come, come now, boys, that's enough!" The jolly satyr looked as likely to join in their antics as put a stop to it. He turned the two of them back toward his house, a large cedar lodge that reminded Elinor of the small cottage they were to occupy, but on a much grander scale. "See everyone back inside now, will you, while I take care of our new arrivals. Off you go!"

The two boys grinned mischievously but did as they were told.

"Well now!" the elder satyr said, looking from Elinor to the others in the car. "I'm guessing you must be Elinor, am I right?"

Elinor nodded. Now that the boys were out of the way, her mother, Marianne, and Margaret climbed cautiously from the car.

"I'm your cousin John—well, your great-cousin, I suppose. How was the journey? Did you find the place all right? I'm sorry about the boys. They're not used to visitors, you see, but they're good kids—just high spirits. Ah! Mary! It's so wonderful to see you again after all these years. My, but you've blossomed into a most beautiful creature, and your daughters...well, what can I say but wow."

When he paused for breath, Mary stepped forward and embraced him warmly. Marianne stepped forward and shook his hand, and Margaret stayed back, apparently a little overwhelmed by everything, not to mention tired after so long in the car.

"Well, here you are, and I'm preparing a little something in your honor." He looked back to where the grill was billowing smoke. "I'll just have you run quickly down to the cottage. You ladies can settle yourselves in, then come back in an hour for some dinner."

"Really, John," Mary said. "You shouldn't have gone to all this trouble."

"Trouble? Pah, this was no trouble at all. The missus and I are delighted, I tell you, delighted to have company after all this time. And such pretty girls too! That cottage has been sitting empty far too long. It'll be nice to see it come to life again. Now, off you trot. I'll get the boys to help you with your cases, then like I said, have a quick wash and come back up. There's plenty of food, and no need to dress up." He opened his arms, giving them all a good look at his hairy chest and tartan shorts. "We don't stand on ceremony here. Just make yourselves comfortable and come back, quick as you like. See you in a bit. BOYS!"

The two elder boys came sprinting back out of the large house in response to John's bellowing. Elinor glanced at her sisters, who were both looking overwhelmed by all the noise. She could totally relate.

"Go with them and help them with their luggage. Thanks, boys. Oh." He reached into his pocket and handed their mother a set of keys. "I almost forgot. You're going to need these. The boys will show you where everything is. I'd come myself, but I don't trust these rascals to flip my chops. You'll figure it all out, I'm sure. Have fun!"

The satyr boys ran along the path, and Elinor and the others climbed back into the Forester and followed slowly behind. The cottage wasn't very far away. All they had to do was pass a small clump of trees, and there it was. Just as lovely as it had appeared in the pictures, except a thousand times more real and appealing. Just ahead, the ocean opened up before them.

"Oh my, it's beautiful!" Marianne exclaimed. She was the first to get out of the car, and she wandered over to the ocean, taking everything in from the top of the rocks. There was a pine island right in front of them, with a few houses that could only be reached by sea.

Elinor was just as enamored as everyone else, but she was anxious to see the inside of the cottage. They were all tired, and she wanted to be sure they could be comfortable there.

"Mom, can I have the keys?" Elinor asked, seeing her mother and Margaret were as spellbound by the view as Marianne clearly was.

"Er, sure. I'll be right in behind you, just a moment."

Elinor took the offered keys and traipsed along the pretty cobblestone path leading to the front door. All around the cottage were blooming perennials, like red columbine, blue cardinal, and yellow jewelweed. They were running a little wild, but that was just how Elinor liked them.

A weather-beaten sign over the front door read *Barton Cottage*. She turned the key in the lock and went inside.

The place looked just as it did in the pictures, only now she could smell the cedar in the walls and the smoke from a log fire that still lingered in the air. While the two boys dragged their luggage inside, Elinor wandered from room to room, inspecting the accommodation and running her hands over the furnishings as she tried to connect with their new home. It was sparse but comfortable, and her fears began to ease. With a little work on their part, and if they could find jobs, there was no reason the family couldn't be happy here.

Her mother found her in the bathroom, just as she was checking the state of the shower behind the curtain.

"Just the one bathroom?" her mother asked.

"I think so."

"Hmm. That'll be interesting, given how long Marianne takes in the tub. Are you sure we can make this work?"

Elinor shrugged. It wasn't like she could do anything about the number of bathrooms. "It's really nice, Mom. I think we totally can. Come and see the dining room. I think we were right about making it over into a bedroom for Margaret, and that tiny table can go in the corner over there." She pointed to a spot behind the sofa. "That should give us enough space, and the table will be more useful there, right next to the kitchen. What do you think?"

Her mother still looked dubious but nodded. Marianne and Margaret came inside.

"Wow, this place is gorgeous. Have you seen the trees? Margaret and I went to touch them. The souls inside were dormant, but we should be able to wake them up and bring them to life."

"I already did," Margaret said, excited. They all looked at her.

"Good," Elinor said. "We can introduce ourselves and ask their blessing for our planting in the morning. Talking of...." She paused as the young boys dropped a large case unceremoniously on the floor. "Would one of you get the plants off the back seat? Carefully."

"I'll get them." Marianne shook her head as the two satyrs ran around her and went outside.

"Anything else, cousins?" one of the two boys said.

Elinor wasn't able to tell them apart yet. "No thank you, that was very nice of you, we appreciate...." But they were already gone, running back up the path to their home, lured by the promise of sausages, no doubt.

"Why don't we go upstairs to the bedrooms?" their mother said. "Let's sort that out and then we can eat. I don't know about you, but I'm starving."

"Good idea." Elinor followed their mother upstairs. The three main bedrooms were a nice size. Their mother settled on the main one, with large windows and a sweeping view of the ocean. The older woman stood, staring out at the view. It wasn't hard to guess what she was feeling. Elinor missed him too. "Dad would have loved this place. He would have loved to see Cousin John's family too. All those hairy legs and hooves. He would have been right at home."

Her mother sniffled, and Elinor put her arm around her shoulders, drew her close, and kissed her head. "I know. I miss him too. We all do."

Once the sniffling abated, Elinor left her mother to her own thoughts.

There were two other good-sized bedrooms on this level. She chose for herself the slightly larger room with a view of the trees—elder sister dibs. The ocean was there, if she craned her neck to see it, but she could certainly hear it. The other room was a little smaller but overlooked the rugged rocks and directly out to sea. She left this one for Marianne, since she knew her sister would like it more.

Elinor bounced on her quilted, pine-framed bed and found it surprisingly comfy. She pulled out her phone to check for a signal and was delighted and relieved to see two bars. She opened her messages. Nothing. Before they left Norland Park, she told Edward she'd let him know when they arrived safely. It would have been nice if he'd jumped the gun and wished her a safe journey or something before they'd got here. But no, he had not. Oh well. She began to type.

Got here okay. 5-hour drive. Cottage is gorgeous. Trees! Ocean! Soft bed! Talk soon, if you're lucky.

She grinned and tapped send.

She turned her screen off. It occurred to her that there were four women and only one bathroom. There was no time to lose. She pushed herself up off the bed, and feeling a little jaded, she headed downstairs in search of her toilet bag.

Chapter Nine

CHRIS BRANDON

HER SISTERS OFTEN TEASED MARIANNE ABOUT BEING THE LAST OUT OF the bathroom and the slowest to get ready. But her hair was fuller and curlier than theirs and required a lot more care and attention. No one appreciated the hard work she had to put into looking perfect.

She looked out over her new bedroom window, over the rocks and to the island beyond. She loved, loved, loved this cottage. She had loved Norland, too, though her fond memories had been somewhat sullied after Fanny's arrival.

But this place was awesome! It appealed to her sense of romance. She smiled at the little built-in bookcase by the window, already imagining her novels stacked along it. The only thing this place lacked was a piano. They'd had a nice one at Norland, but Elinor had reasoned they'd have no place to put it here. Elinor could be as annoying as hell sometimes. Her sister was too sensible for her own good. Sometimes you just needed to have some fun!

"Are you ready yet?" Elinor's voice boomed from her room. Sound certainly carried in this place. Dammit, she should have brought the piano, Elinor or not. Although from a practical viewpoint, trying to find room for it in the back of the Forester could have posed a problem. But they could have sent it on later. Really!

"I'm just coming." Marianne pulled her hair into a navy scrunchie and checked her chin for spots. Thank Gaia, her skin was clear.

There was a long mirror hanging over the back of her bedroom door. She looked good, dressed in blue jeans and a blue, button-up cardigan worn over a crisp, white blouse. Behind her, her suitcases were flung open, and clothes were strewn all over her bed. No doubt, Elinor's would already be neatly put away on wardrobe hangers and in drawers by now. Marianne's could wait. She had some serious exploring to do.

She traipsed down the stairs, enjoying the unusual clunk of the wood, and ran past everyone waiting for her, anxious once more to be outside. She raised her hands in the air, drinking in the sun.

"Oh Elinor, isn't this glorious? Have you ever felt such a day? The spirits in the trees here must be very happy. Now we're here, I don't think I shall ever want to leave."

"I'm hungry," Margaret said, joining her. "Can we go get some food?"

"I'll race you! See you up there, you two!" Marianne stole a quick glance back at Elinor and their mother, who were chatting away as they left the house, then sprinted up the path beside Margaret. The smell of smoke and grilled meats assaulted her senses, reminding Marianne she was pretty famished herself.

"Well now, there you are," John said, while adding another chop to a child's plate. It was piled so high Marianne expected it to topple over. Yet somehow the kid kept it balanced.

She didn't think she'd ever seen so much food as was changing hands here. And it looked so good. John clearly knew what he was about at the grill.

"What will you have?" John asked. "I have sausages, pork, steaks, burgers, and such, and the wife over there has potato salad, buns, and all the fixings. There's drinks in the cooler. Help yourself to whatever you want. There's plenty to go round."

"Um, can I have a burger, please?" Margaret asked.

John beamed at her politeness. "Absolutely, and how about you Marianne? What'll it be?"

"I'll take the same."

Elinor and their mother joined them, and Marianne wandered over to the next table with Margaret to get a bun.

A heavily pregnant nymph was stirring the potato salad.

"Hello," Marianne said. "I'm Marianne Dashwood, and this is my younger sister, Margaret."

"Oh, h-hello," said the nymph shyly. "I'm, I'm Gemini. I'm John's wife." Her smile was sweet, but she sounded a little tongue-tied.

"Oh, thank you for lending us your boys to help us. How many children do you have?"

"Eight. All boys." She sighed and patted her tummy. "Another on the way. I would have liked a girl. Maybe next time."

"Wow, eight boys!" Marianne couldn't help but blurt. "They must be a handful."

"Yes, well, John's very um, er, would you like a bun?" She pointed to a plate of buns just in front of her, as well as the fixings along the side.

"Yes, please."

Marianne and Margaret loaded their plates. Then Margaret wandered back to their mother and Elinor, who were busy talking to Cousin John, leaving Marianne and Gemini alone. They stood for a moment in awkward silence.

"I, um, I really like the cottage," Marianne said. "And the view is spectacular."

"I'm glad you like it."

"I do. I imagine there are some amazing walks around here, and I intend to start exploring them immediately. Can you recommend any in particular?"

"I'm sorry, I'm not much of a walker."

Marianne chomped on her burger, wondering what to say next. She supposed Gemini wasn't used to much adult company, not with so many boys to run after, but she wanted so much to like her. After all, she and her husband had shown them more kindness than anyone on the planet. She was determined to persevere.

"I think the only thing I will miss is my piano back home. It was too bulky to bring with us, though it's probably a good thing. The cottage is beautiful, but I don't think I could have squeezed it in there. Not unless we kicked Margaret out of the house or something." Marianne laughed and noticed Gemini's eyes light up.

"We have a piano," Gemini said. "A very nice one too. I used to play it all the time but rarely get the chance now. Please, I would love you to come into the house whenever you like and play on it. Really, it would make me so happy if you did. Would you play something for us now? I mean, after you've eaten of course."

Gemini was suddenly so animated, Marianne could hardly refuse. Not that she wanted to. She loved showing off her playing whenever she could. She snarfed down her burger in double time.

"Well, I'm ready now, if you like?" she said through a mouthful of burger. "If you have time to show me where it is?"

Gemini looked over the array of side dishes, and reassured that everything was as it should be, she led Marianne up to the main house.

Elinor was watching her curiously.

"They have a piano!" Marianne called out. "I won't be long."

There weren't quite so many flowers around the perimeter, but it was an impressively large house with some very austere-looking maples that Marianne was determined to investigate later. Inside there was a big reception area, leading to a large open-plan living room with panoramic views of the sea. Wow, this was even nicer than Norland Park and their cottage put together.

The piano was over by one of the walls—whether neglected or just out of the way, Marianne couldn't tell. She took a seat on the stool and opened the keyboard cover. It was a very old piano; the keys were made from sugar pine and were slightly yellowed with age. She tested it and found it still nicely tuned. She read the maker's name and realized it was a classic, worth a mint.

"Wow, this is a Van Strandler. You don't see many of these around. And you never get to play it?"

"No, but she should." It was a strange, deep, almost manly voice that answered. Marianne turned to see a much older nymph had joined them. She was carrying a small satyr in her arms. He looked to be about one year old and was wriggling excitedly.

"Marianne, this is my mother, Mrs. Jennings. Mom, this is Marianne. The others are outside waiting to meet you, but Marianne wanted to play on our piano for us."

"Somebody should," Mrs. Jennings said. "Feel free to call me Betsy. Mrs. Jennings makes me sound like such an old fuddy-duddy." Betsy was a large woman with long, slender hands that didn't quite go with her rest of her. She wore a loud purple and pink dress and had an air of frankness that was the polar opposite of her shy and anxious daughter.

"Nice to meet you, Betsy," Marianne answered. She sat a little awkwardly, unsure of whether it would be polite to play now or not.

"Oh please, go ahead," Betsy said. "This place could use a little music, if only to cover up the sound of all these screeching boys."

It wasn't the best invitation to play Marianne had ever had, but she gratefully took it. Turning in her seat, she laid her fingers on the keys and closed her eyes. An echo of the spirit in the pine thrilled through her fingers, connecting with her soul. Marianne took a deep breath and began to play.

She was soon lost in a world that was all her own. There had been no music to read from, so she played a song she had written. Her fingers easily found their rhythm, and before long, she closed her eyes and entirely lost herself.

When she was done, Gemini and Betsy gasped in appreciation. But that wasn't all. Someone behind her was clapping, and she turned, wondering who it might be.

"Christopher! There you are," Betsy cried. "I was beginning to think you had changed your mind. Come and meet our lovely new friend, Marianne Dashwood. Her mother and sisters are just outside—did you see them as you came in? I've yet to meet them myself. I've been too busy listening to Marianne play. Have you ever heard such music? I thought it was really lovely."

Since Marianne remained seated, Chris merely nodded his hello. He was an older man—Marianne judged perhaps a little younger than her dad. But then she considered everyone over twenty to be old. He wasn't bad-looking at all, but he had a pale complexion and was rather serious in appearance. The cut of his goatee made her think mage or warlock, perhaps. It was hard to tell with those guys.

"Remarkable," Chris said.

"Remarkable?" Marianne asked, unsure of whether this was a good or bad thing.

"I don't think I've heard that tune before," he said.

"No, well, I wrote it. I like writing my own songs."

"Interesting."

Marianne thought interesting was just as vague as remarkable, but since she only just met him, she didn't want to ask him again what he meant. If he meant amazingly talented and gifted, couldn't he just say so?

At that moment, John, Elinor, Margaret, and her mother came into the house.

"Ah, Chris, you're hiding in here, I see," John exclaimed. "No doubt drawn in by that lovely music. Everyone, let me introduce you to my good friend, Chris Brandon. He lives just up the road in that ridiculously big house on the hill. You probably passed it when you arrived, Mary. Chris, this is my cousin, Mary Dashwood. It looks like you've met her lovely daughter, Marianne, and these two lovelies are Elinor and Margaret."

"Nice to meet you," Mary said.

"Hello," Elinor said.

Suddenly shy, Margaret hid behind their mother, but Chris just smiled warmly.

"I see you've sniffed out their piano," Mary said, chiding Marianne but smiling. "She'll be happy, since we had to leave ours at home, and she loves to play."

"Ah, well, in that case, why don't we run this one down to the cottage?" John suggested. "Gemini never has time to play it anymore. All it does is sit here and gather dust. It would be good if someone got to play it. You wouldn't mind, would you, dear?"

"Well, um...." Gemini looked doubtful. Marianne suspected she might not have time to play, but she'd still miss it. She noticed Betsy was frowning too.

"Oh no, I couldn't possibly do that."

"There's no need for that," Chris said. "I have my mum's old piano doing nothing in my house. I only ever use my grand. I'll have it sent down tomorrow. It's a fine instrument, and it wouldn't be missed."

Marianne looked hopefully to her mother.

"But there's so little room...."

Chris smiled. "I don't think that will be a problem. My mother's piano is a miniature upright, very compact. In fact, it's only this size." He drew a sparkling outline of the piano in the air with his finger. *Huh,* Marianne thought. *He is a wizard!*

Their mother's voice faltered just a little. "Well, if you think it will fit?" With a click of his fingers, the outline disappeared.

"Um, we wouldn't want you to go to any trouble...."

Chris dismissed her concern with a wave of his hand. "Look at it this way—you'd be doing me a big favor. I've been meaning to get rid of it for some time. At least now I know it'll be in the hands of someone who'll appreciate it. Just figure out where you want it to go, and I'll have someone bring it over in the truck. I'll see if I can rustle up some music to go with it as well. There, that's settled then."

"Sir, your kindness overwhelms me," Mary said. "But are you sure?"

"It's no problem at all, I assure you. I'm happy to do it."

Marianne looked at Elinor, expecting her to object. But her sister just smiled and said, "Thank you, Mr. Brandon, you are excessively thoughtful."

"Please, call me Chris."

"Well now," Betsy said. "Looks like you already have an admirer, Marianne. Now we just *must* find someone for your sister. What do you say?"

"Elinor already has someone," Margaret blurted, finding her voice and looking all coy. "His last name begins with an F, and he's very good-looking."

"Margaret!" Elinor and Mary cried at once.

"Oooh," Betsy said. "Do you hear that, Gemini? A mystery! We love a good mystery, we do. We'll have to riddle this one out."

"No, please," Elinor objected. "My younger sister doesn't know what she's talking about." Elinor nudged Margaret to be silent, but Margaret looked all the more mischievous.

"It's true. I saw them making ooey-gooey eyes at each other. He didn't kiss her, but I could tell he wanted to."

"Margaret, enough," Elinor said, flushing pink. "You're talking nonsense."

Marianne couldn't believe Margaret was doing this to Elinor in front of strangers. "John, I think I'll have another one of your lovely burgers, if that's okay?" Marianne said, rising from the piano. "Margaret, I thought you said you were hungry? Come with me."

Before Margaret could object, Marianne grabbed her hand and marched her outside. Not that her sister would have objected. Nothing came between Margaret and her food. She had a healthy teenage appetite, after all.

As she left, Marianne looked back over her shoulder. Chris was watching her. He smiled at her, and she felt an odd tingle of uncertainty but dismissed it. He was going to give her a wonderful present, and he clearly liked music, which was a good thing. But he was old. Surely he didn't think she would be interested in a man of his age. No, he was just being neighborly, welcoming the family to Camden. She smiled faintly in return, just to be polite, then turned around again and put all thoughts of him out of her mind. A piano! She was going to have her very own piano!

Chapter Ten

JOHN WILLOUGHBY

THE PIANO HAD BEEN WITH THEM FOR A WEEK NOW. AS LUCK WOULD have it, it had squeezed perfectly into their window recess—well, that's what Marianne had told herself. Chris had waved his hand a few times, gold and purple sparkles had filled the air, and somehow the piano had slid right into the spot.

Once installed, Chris handed her some sheets of music to practice. Marianne took one glance at the score and raised her hand to her chest.

"Are you sure?" she asked. "This looks very complicated. I'm not sure I...." She shook her head, unable to express her self-doubt.

"You underestimate yourself," Chris said. "Please try. This was my mother's favorite. It's been a long time since I've heard it played."

Marianne stared down at the sheets again. It really was quite daunting. But Chris, her mother, and Elinor were all smiling at her—and, well, he had been ever so kind.

She sat at the keyboard and spread her fingers on the keys. She felt the familiar and delightful tingle as she connected to the wood. She knew they would help and guide her, even on a score as unfamiliar as this.

Her performance wasn't perfect, but she persevered, and Chris was still smiling when she looked up from the pages. Mary clasped her hands in delight, and even Elinor had closed her eyes as she listened.

"I, er, I stumbled here and there on the difficult bits, but it's a nice piece. I like it." Marianne closed the score and put the fallboard down.

"You played it well," Chris said. "Excellent, really, considering you've never played it before. You're a wonderful pianist."

Marianne blushed. "I shall practice every day and see if I can do better, since it was your mother's favorite. Oh, and Mom?"

Her mother had been filling the coffee machine with water. "Yes?"

"Do you think Gemini would mind if I go over to the house later? I thought we could play together. I know Betsy would like to hear her play more, and it would be nice to have a musical friend."

"Well, why not indeed? I think that's a fine idea." Her mother beamed.

Chris was also smiling. "I think she would welcome the distraction," he said. "And she liked you a lot. I could tell."

"Do you really think so?" Marianne asked. "Then I'll go in a bit. Elinor's not much into music, and Mom never has the time."

"Well, if you're ready soon, I'll walk you over," Chris said.

Elinor shot Marianne a knowing look, and Marianne blushed. *This is awkward,* she thought. Would it be rude to say no, especially after he'd been so kind and generous to her?

"Um, sure. I'll just grab my coat."

Her coat was hanging on the back of a kitchen table chair. Elinor was sitting at the table, browsing through her laptop. When she was sure Chris wasn't listening, Marianne whispered in her ear, "Come with me, *please.*"

Elinor shook her head and just grinned.

After that, Chris had shown up every day on the pretext of delivering some new music sheets to her. Surely he could have given them all to her on that first day, but noooo! He'd found it necessary to come. Every. Single. Day.

She had just finished breakfast when Margaret called from the window. "He's coming again, Marianne. He *fancies* you."

"Don't be silly," Marianne said, irritated. She wandered over to the window and sure enough, there was Chris Brandon walking down the path, armed with more music sheets. *Is he ever going to leave me alone?* "Anyway, he's probably not here for me. He's probably come to see Mom for something."

"I don't think so," Margaret teased. "He stares at you *all* the time."

"You know, it's a lovely day. I think I'll go for a walk. And you're coming with me."

"What? No. It's horrible out there. I'm sure it's going to rain."

Marianne didn't care what Margaret thought. She'd teased her and Elinor one too many times, and the little twerp could use a lesson.

"Come on," Marianne said, peering out the window and figuring they didn't have much time before Chris got to the front door. "I want to go and tend to the trees, and I need your help. Let's go."

Margaret looked none too thrilled, but she grabbed a raincoat and followed Marianne out the back door.

Marianne peered around the side of the house, keeping Margaret close behind her as they waited for Chris to knock on the door. As soon as they heard the door opening, Marianne made a run for it.

"Where are we going?" Margaret cried behind her.

"Keep your voice down. I told you, we're going to see to the trees. Come on, keep up!"

Marianne ran off at a pace, feeling a little guilty knowing she was leaving her mother and Elinor to make excuses for her. But really, seven days in a row was too much. She was beginning to think the man was obsessed. With what, she didn't know. If and when she was ready to look for a boyfriend, she would make a formal announcement to all.

She reached the trees much sooner than Margaret, who was dragging her feet and looking miserably up at the sky. "It's gonna rain, I know it," Margaret whined.

"What if it does? Come on, the trees will protect us."

Marianne ran to a set of trees near the drop to the ocean. She began to laugh and spin, her hands raised up to the trees. "I love this state," she cried. "Did you know ninety percent of Maine is forested? We are going to be soooo happy here!"

As she said this, she closed her eyes and summoned the spirit of a maple to reach out to her. The maple inclined a branch down to her, sweeping Marianne up into its arms and pulling her safely to its trunk. Then as the rain began, she reached out to another and another, allowing herself to be passed from tree to tree, laughing in her joy while Margaret watched in a half-sulk on the ground. Beneath her, the ground was getting wetter. Margaret stood with her back against a tree, taking maximum shelter from it. Her arms were folded, and she had a scowl on her face.

"Come and dance with me, Margaret," Marianne said, reaching down to her sister. "It's easy, don't be afraid. The trees just want to play with us, see? Wheeeee!"

Marianne reached out, ready to embrace the next limb that was to carry her, but she lost her grip on the slippery bark, and before she knew it, she was falling, the rough limbs of the clumsy maple cutting her skin as she fell. When she hit the ground, she rolled perilously close to the edge of a granite cliff and bashed her ankle against a rock. A sharp pain shot up her leg like a lightning bolt, and she cried out loud.

Margaret screamed in terror. "Marianne! Marianne!" She ran close to the edge but stopped.

"Stay back," Marianne shouted, fearing for her sister's safety. Heights were not Margaret's thing. Come to think of it, they weren't Marianne's either, not this high up anyway. Below her, waves crashed upon exposed rocks. Marianne swallowed hard. "I'm okay, but I've hurt my ankle. Run home, get help. I'm not sure I can walk on my own."

Margaret turned away and began running, but suddenly stopped in her tracks and screamed again. A tall, raven-haired stranger flew down from the sky, his great, leathered wings spread wide, as he descended to the ground, blocking Margaret's path.

The rain-soaked man rose from his crouched position, drawing himself up to his full height, with his leathery wings folded behind his back so their clawed tips peeked above his broad shoulders. He ran around Margaret, careful to avoid making contact, and hurried to where Marianne lay. He was at once terrifying and beautiful, with dark, oval eyes and a firm, chiseled chin. He was slim, Marianne observed, yet also muscular. Her gaze followed his leather pants—*oh my Gaia*—to his silken shirt that appeared impervious to the rain. He had a handsome face, with little horn nubs protruding from his smooth forehead. His aura was coated in black. She knew of only one species that had such an appearance. She shrank back in fear. He could only be an incubus.

Yet the winged man didn't look dangerous. He leaned over her now, his face a picture of concern.

"Please, please don't be afraid," he said. "Only I was flying overhead, and I saw what happened. Would you mind if I took a look at that ankle of yours? It looks swollen."

Speechless, Marianne could only nod.

The stranger pressed along her ankle, and Marianne yelped when he tried to turn it.

"Are you okay?" Margaret asked. "Should I go fetch Mom?"

The winged man turned around to where Margaret was hopping from foot to foot, hovering and unsure of what she should do. "How far is your home?" he asked.

"Not far," Marianne said, answering for her. "If you help me up, I could try to walk."

The stranger looked doubtful. "Here, let me help you. Let's see how you do." He held out his arm but she was half afraid to accept him.

Her heart racing, Marianne tried getting up from the ground, but it was no use. Her bad ankle couldn't support her weight, and she slid back down to the wet ground. *Gosh, he's so good-looking,* she thought. *I bet I look like a drowned rat. What must he think of me?*

"Have you ever flown before?" the winged man said.

Marianne shook her head.

"Wrap your arms around my shoulders."

He was so close, Marianne could smell him. Her acute dryad sense of smell caught the scent of honeysuckle and cut grass mixed with rain—all of her favorite things. But still, he was a stranger and possibly an incubus, so she hesitated.

"Don't be afraid. I promise I won't fly more than a few feet off the ground, but it'll be the easiest way to get you home. Your sister can show me the way. Come on."

Before she even realized he'd done it, the winged man scooped her up in his arms and they were hovering a few feet off the ground. His powerful wings beat so strongly that wind rushed through the trees as if driven by a storm, agitating the branches so they danced around her. If her ankle still hurt, she barely felt it. With her arms wrapped around his shoulders, Marianne was inches from his face. Her heart pounded in her chest; she'd never seen anyone quite so handsome, who smelled quite so good, and who could actually fly.

"This way!" Margaret cried from the ground.

Slowly, the winged man followed Margaret's lead, his eyes hardly ever leaving Marianne's. A thousand impulses she had never felt before soared through her body, and she felt locked in time, in a world where there was only the stranger and herself.

Love. Was this love? Was this how it felt? An arrow of some kind had pierced her heart. When emotions were kindled this quickly, it had to be love, surely?

She stared into his deep, dark, fathomless eyes, which hinted of poetry and otherworldly delights. She gripped a little tighter, faking fear of falling, and the stranger only smiled and held her tighter still. The hardness of his muscles made her breath catch in her throat.

All too soon, he brought her back down to earth; the two drifted gently down. He slowed long enough for Margaret to run before them and open the door.

"Mom! Elinor! *Mom!*" Margaret cried.

Her mother and sister dashed to the door, then hurriedly stepped aside when they saw Marianne being carried to them by a flying man.

"What the—!" Mary gasped.

The winged man breezed past them, flying into the cottage and not stopping until he was able to put Marianne down gently on the sofa.

"What happened?" Elinor asked, the first to find her voice.

"She fell from a tree!" Margaret cried. "She hurt her ankle!"

Elinor stepped forward at once. "Margaret, please, go grab some towels from the bathroom."

Margaret ran off, and Elinor sat calmly on the end of the sofa and looked at Marianne's ankle.

"Can we get your shoe off before the swelling gets worse?" Elinor asked.

"Yes, um, sure," Marianne said. Elinor was fussing about something, but Marianne only half-heard the words. It was as if she was having to think through a fog.

"Do you think we should call the doctor?" their mother asked.

The winged man, who now had his feet planted firmly back on the ground, stood a polite distance away over by the fire. "Um, that might be a good idea," he said. "I saw her fall. She was quite high up, and though I think it's just a sprain, it might be wise to have a doctor look at her."

Mary nodded and reached for her phone.

"You, um, seem to be well looked after, so if you don't mind, I'd better get going," he said.

Marianne nodded dreamily. "Yes, er, thanks. Oh wait, please. Can you tell me your name? I don't think you mentioned your name."

"Oh." He grinned, and Marianne noticed two adorable dimples on his cheeks. "My name is Willoughby. John Willoughby of Allenham. I'm glad I was around to help. I'll come and check on you all tomorrow, if I may?"

"Certainly," their mother said, to Marianne's surprise.

And with that, he left. Marianne fell back into the sofa, her lips forming his name and repeating them over and over. *John Willoughby of Allenham, John Willoughby of Allenham.*

Their mother began speaking to their cousin on the phone. "Hello, John? It's Mary. Yes...well no, actually. Marianne fell and hurt her ankle. Do you happen to know a good doctor's number? You do? Yes, do you think he would mind? Yes, if you could, as quickly as possible. Thanks. Goodbye."

"Did you see his eyes?" Marianne asked, as Elinor popped a cushion under her ankle to elevate it.

"Yes, I did notice," Elinor said, her voice oddly husky, as if she had a sore throat.

"Or his wings?" their mother added suggestively.

Even Margaret, now that the shock of the accident was behind her, was making her favorite ooey-gooey face. "He was *nice*. Really nice."

The only one not to add to the chorus of admiration was Elinor. Her sister frowned and wandered over to the window and looked out beyond it. She opened the window to let air in and took a few deep breaths, like she was trying to clear her lungs. Marianne couldn't see what Elinor was looking at, but right now she didn't care. Marianne had met John Willoughby of Allenham, and everything was all right in her world. She took hold of the end of the bath towel, and with her head still in the clouds with Willoughby, she slowly dried her rain-sodden hair.

Elinor turned around. Frowning, she said, "You know he was an incubus, don't you?"

Chapter Eleven

FLOWERS FOR THE PATIENT

THE DOCTOR HAD PRONOUNCED A BAD SPRAIN, AND THOUGH HE prescribed something for the swelling, all Marianne could do was rest up and keep her foot elevated for as long as possible.

The morning sun streamed through the windows. There wasn't even a hint of yesterday's rain. Marianne stared at her toes, thinking happy thoughts. John Willoughby had said he would come today, and she'd arranged her hair as prettily as possible and had put on a little makeup. As soon as she was settled, their mother had set off to take Margaret to school and run a few errands. The older sisters had the house to themselves.

As Marianne ran her strawberry e.l.f. lip gloss over her lips, Elinor cleaned all around her, moving quickly, her duster hitting a little harder than usual. Something had ticked her sister off—but what?

"You're going to break something if you're not careful," Marianne said, shifting her bad foot as the duster came perilously close to it. "What's gotten into you?"

"Me?" Elinor said. "Oh, nothing. Other than getting tired of babysitting your lovesick boyfriends."

"What?" Marianne shifted uncomfortably on the sofa as Elinor moved to dust the table behind her. "I don't know what you mean."

"Oh, yes you do. Chris. Do you have any idea how long he waited for you yesterday? Mom and I had to sit with him for half an hour before he finally gave up and left. Gaia, it was embarrassing!"

"Did he say anything?"

"About you not being here? No. But he knew you were avoiding him, I could tell. Talk about awkward. Mom hardly knew where to look. Look, it's none of my business, but if you don't like him, you should say so. Don't lead the man on."

Marianne's cheeks flushed. "I am not *leading him on!*" she protested. "I don't ask him to keep coming—he just shows up uninvited."

"Well, it's obvious he likes you, so you really ought to say something. It's not fair to me and Mom to have to do your dirty work."

"I didn't ask you to."

"No, but you left us to make your excuses. Or did you think we'd just leave him standing at the door? You're not a baby anymore, Marianne. You should know better."

Marianne's back was beginning to ache, so she lifted herself up a little and sat straight.

"I'm not stringing him along. But it's hard to be mean to someone after they've been so generous. I don't know what to say to him. What if he gets mad at me and takes the piano away? Not that I mean...it's just...oh heck, Elinor. He's old enough to be my father. What am I supposed to do? I didn't ask for this."

Elinor parked at the end of the sofa and pulled Marianne's blanket over her exposed toes. "Maybe not. Just be kind to him, okay. He's a nice man. And he's not that old."

"You go out with him then."

Elinor didn't respond, but instead stared wistfully out the window. Marianne knew who she was thinking of now. And it wasn't Chris Brandon. "Have you heard anything?"

Elinor shook her head.

"He said he would come though, right?" Marianne asked.

"Not in so many words."

Marianne was confused. It had been pretty obvious to her and everyone else that Edward had a thing for Elinor. "I'm sure he'll come soon—you'll see. Have you checked your email? Or your phone? The signal around here is weak as anything. Maybe it's just a delay."

Elinor shook her head. "He never promised me anything. And Maine is a long way. He might never come."

"Well, there's always Chris Brandon," Marianne laughed.

Elinor laughed with her. "Um, no. But thank you." She rose from the sofa and peered through the window. "Talking of men friends."

Marianne caught her breath. Willoughby had said he'd come, and now he was here. Her heart began to race, and she could feel her color rising. "Oh?" she said, trying to keep the excitement out of her voice, knowing Elinor would tease her mercilessly. "Is it John Willoughby?"

"No," Elinor said. "It's Chris."

Marianne's joy vanished as quickly as it came. "Oh."

"It's early yet," Elinor said. "I'm sure your incubus friend will be along a bit later."

"Please don't call him that."

"Call him what?"

"*Incubus friend.* Like it's something nasty."

Elinor raised her eyebrows and moved to open the door before Chris got there. "All right, I won't. But please be careful. Those men are never to be trusted."

"Oh, come on, Elinor. I don't believe a word of it."

"Don't believe what? That incubi seduce women as they sleep? Do you think I'm making this up? Don't you remember Mom giving us *The Talk*?"

"Well, maybe one or two of them are knaves, but they can't be all bad. John was a perfect gentleman. You saw him! Don't paint them all with the same brush."

Elinor opened the door. "Ah, Chris. How are you? What a lovely surprise. Have you come to see Marianne?" As she said this, Elinor cast a mischievous glance back over her shoulder, which Marianne returned with daggers.

"Er, yes," Chris said as Elinor stepped aside, inviting him to enter. "I heard what happened on the grapevine and came to offer my condolences." Despite his choice of words, Chris was smiling warmly.

He nodded as he passed Elinor but made straight for Marianne. "How's the patient?"

"Feeling much better, thank you," Marianne replied.

There was a brief silence, then Chris said, "Oh, I almost forgot." With a wave of his hand, Chris conjured a beautiful bouquet of purple violets. They were strung together in the form of a heart-shaped note, made with an entwined treble and bass clef. "These are for you."

"Um, thank you," Marianne said, in awe of the intricacy of the spell but a little embarrassed by the not-so-subliminal message. "Er, Elinor, can you put these somewhere for me? There's no room on the little table."

"Oh, right," Elinor said. "Chris, can I get you something? Coffee?"

As Chris turned to answer, Marianne glared at her sister. Elinor pretended not to notice.

"Coffee would be lovely, thanks."

Elinor was just about to make some when there was an unfamiliar knock at the door. "Excuse me, please, I must see who this is. Who has come knocking upon our door at this hour of the morning, unexpectedly?"

Marianne could tell from her tone that she was enjoying this.

"Oh hello, John, isn't it? How lovely to see you again. Do come in, won't you?"

"Please, Willoughby. Everyone calls me Willoughby."

"Okay, if you like."

Willoughby stood in the doorway dressed in casual jeans and a navy shirt, his wings neatly tucked behind him. In the harsh morning light, he looked so young and handsome, perhaps even more so than when he'd rescued Marianne in the pouring rain the day before. She had to check she was still breathing, and once she trusted the air going in and out of her lungs, she managed to say, "Hello."

"You're looking very well this morning," Willoughby said, his dark eyes flashing playful mischief at her.

Marianne smiled, remembering being carried in his arms and the sensation of flying.

"Thank you," she said. "I'm feeling a lot better, thank you."

"Ahem!" Elinor coughed, reminding her they were not alone in the room. "Willoughby, I was about to make Chris some coffee. Would you like some?"

"Oh, sure," he replied. He took one look at Chris and his easy smile faded. "Black, please."

"Er, Chris, have you met Willoughby? He's the man who rescued me from the cliff last night."

For the first time, Marianne realized that Chris was no longer smiling. Indeed, he was almost scowling. Did the man honestly think he owned her?

"We've met," Chris said.

"Indeed, we have," Willoughby said. The two men stood awkwardly staring at each other. Marianne wondered what it meant, but Elinor had already turned away and was making coffee, so she couldn't read her thoughts.

"Well, um, clearly Marianne is well, or at least will be soon," Chris said. "I won't overwhelm you with too much company, so for now I'll be off. I might pop back again later, if I may. I'll talk to you then."

Marianne hardly heard him. She was mesmerized by Willoughby's face, and it was only Elinor's sharp reminder that snapped her out of it.

"Marianne!" Elinor said, holding two steaming mugs of coffee in front of her.

"It's okay," Chris said. "Thank you, but I won't be staying after all. I'll see you later, Elinor. Marianne."

"Thank you for the lovely flowers," Marianne said, remembering her manners. "They're very beautiful."

Chris paused, but merely nodded and let himself out.

The second he was gone, Willoughby dashed to Marianne's side and planted himself on a small chair right next to her. Elinor handed him his coffee but shot Marianne the dirtiest of looks. Marianne ignored her but accepted the coffee her sister carefully placed into her hands.

"You know Chris, then?" Elinor asked.

"We both live in this neighborhood," Willoughby answered. "It would be difficult for me not to know so famous a warlock."

"You don't like him?" Elinor asked.

"*Don't like* would be a bit strong. He's just...we're from different generations, that's all." Willoughby smiled at Marianne, who smiled back, completely understanding him.

Elinor shrugged and retreated to the kitchen.

"You look very different today," Willoughby said. "If I'd have known how pretty you are, I'd have hung around longer yesterday."

Marianne grinned. She loved a good flirt as much as the next person.

And she could never turn down such a compliment. "I could say the same about you. You look different in the sunlight. Have you shaved?"

He laughed and pinched the point of his chin with his fingers. "Perhaps, perhaps. Maybe I wanted to make a good first impression."

"But you've done that already," Marianne laughed. "When you saved me."

"Oh, I hardly did that," Willoughby laughed. "I suspect you'd have found a way home somehow." He put his hand into his pocket and pulled out a handkerchief. He handed it to Marianne.

"What's this?" she asked.

"Open it," he said.

Marianne unfolded the clean linen handkerchief and found a single pressed cornflower inside. "What's this?" She frowned, unsure of its meaning.

"I plucked it from the ground where we first met," he said. "I hope you like it."

Marianne gasped at his answer. *How thoughtful!* "It's beautiful," she said. "May I keep it?"

"I pressed it just for you, so yes."

Marianne laid it gently on her lap and stared at it. It was such an old-fashioned yet charming gesture. "Cornflowers are my favorite flower," she said.

"Are they?" Willoughby asked, raising an eyebrow.

Marianne giggled. "Well, they are now."

They both laughed together.

"So, where you do live?" Marianne asked.

"Oh, I have a small place in Allenham village. I come here for the summer, you know."

"You have more than one home?" Marianne asked.

"Oh yeah. I have another place down in New Jersey. It's a smallish estate with land, but it has a nice view of the sea. Maybe one day we could go visit or something?"

"Really?" Marianne gasped. "That's where we came from. We had a place in Ocean City! We only just moved up here."

"No kidding, what a coincidence," Willoughby said, a twinkle in his eye. "We might have been neighbors and never knew it. How funny is that?"

"Do you live with anyone?" Marianne asked. "Like, um, family?"

Willoughby smiled. "Not anymore. I left my parents' house some time ago. I live by myself now."

Marianne wanted to ask if he had a girlfriend, but she figured he would probably tell her if he had. She really hoped he didn't. Oh, those eyes of his. She could lose herself in them forever. She suddenly realized she was staring, and she blushed as it occurred to her that he was staring back.

She took a sip from the coffee that was rapidly cooling in her hand. Breaking eye contact left her a little dizzy, but she assumed that was from all the sitting down.

"Are you okay?" Willoughby asked. "Do you want me to get your sister for you?"

"Um, no, I'm okay. There's no need."

"All the same." Willoughby stood up and planted his mug on the table behind her. "I should get going."

Marianne looked up, suddenly annoyed with her own injured foot. "You really don't have to."

"Sadly, I do. There are a few things I need to do, but I wanted to make sure you were okay. Perhaps, if you don't mind, I'll come by later. Do you have your phone?"

"No, no I don't." Marianne mentally kicked herself for leaving her phone upstairs by her bed.

"Never mind. Give me your number, and I'll text you later."

Marianne didn't hesitate. "555-234-7130."

Willoughby closed his eyes for a second, then opened them again, smiled, and said, "Never mind, got it." He bent down and kissed Marianne softly on the cheek. The scent of honeysuckle and cut grass filled her nostrils, and she breathed deeply, wanting to imprint his scent on her soul.

Elinor chose that moment to return from wherever she'd been hiding. Marianne wondered if she'd seen him kiss her. "Are you off then?" Elinor asked.

"Yes, I'm just leaving," he said. "Thank you for the coffee." He recovered his mug and handed it to Elinor.

Then with a final smile for Marianne, Willoughby turned and headed for the door. She watched, entranced, and stared wistfully after him, even after he spread his wings and flew out of sight.

Elinor also watched him go, but Marianne noticed she wasn't smiling. She'd had enough of Elinor's disapproval for one day, so without a word she put her coffee cup down on the table, settled into the sofa, closed her eyes, and dreamed of flying.

"Well, unless I miss my guess, you won't be receiving any more daily visits from Mr. Brandon."

Marianne groaned inwardly. If only that were true, but she wasn't so sure. She hugged her cornflower to her chest and thought of incubi abs.

Chapter Twelve

AN UNEXPECTED VISITOR

ELINOR STOOD AT THE KITCHEN SINK, HER ARMS ELBOW-DEEP IN SUDS AS she watched Marianne and Willoughby sprawled out on a blanket over toward the sea. It was a pretty day for it; the sun was high in the sky, and Willoughby was reading something to Marianne while she gazed up at the drifting clouds. Elinor continued to wash the breakfast dishes, clattering them into the drying rack as her irritation grew.

Marianne's sprain had healed quickly, and before too long she and Willoughby had been running around Camden, living it up, having more fun than Elinor thought was good for them. Their family was new in town, but tongues were already wagging. They were dryads, not common nymphs. They were supposed to live their lives beyond reproach. Until they were called on for bonding. Her sister would lose her power if she wasn't careful.

And yet, a little part of her ached to act just as Marianne did. The two lovers smashed the world around them; they were oblivious, self-absorbed, living in a special universe just for themselves. *Oh Edward.* He had sent her one text since she'd arrived, but it hardly lit her world on fire. Just a hello, how are you sort of thing. He could have been writing to anybody, and her heart had died a little when she'd finished reading his short note. Even so, she had read it a thousand times, looking for meaning that in the end just wasn't there.

Hello, hope you are settling in okay, busy, busy, talk soon.

That had been over a week ago. Not one more word since.

Willoughby put down his book and pushed a lock of Marianne's hair behind her ear. It was such an innocent but intimate act that Elinor couldn't help but feel a twang of jealousy. She yearned to feel just a little of what her sister was feeling. She had fallen in love first, hadn't she? It should be her out there on the lawn being loved on, not Marianne. By Edward, of course, not Willoughby.

It appeared Chris was all but forgotten now. They hadn't heard a word from him since the day he'd visited Marianne and Willoughby had showed up. Elinor found it hard not to feel sorry for him. His only crime was liking Marianne, and she'd heard the two of them ridicule him for it.

It was a pity her own heart was engaged elsewhere, or she might have made a play for him. But as to that, Chris had shown no inclination in her direction, and if she were honest with herself, he wasn't really her type at all. Oh well. All's fair in love and war, so they say. Except it wasn't fair, not even a little bit.

There was a knock at the door behind her. Her mother and Margaret had left a little while ago, and her mother had a key, so Elinor wondered if this was Chris making a reappearance out of the blue. Or maybe Gemini had come to call on Marianne. It wasn't as if they got a ton of visitors at the cottage. After setting the cup she'd been washing on the drainer and drying her hands on a tea towel, Elinor crossed the small living room and opened the door.

A part of Elinor's brain knew her mouth was open and that she still carried a tea towel in her hands, but it wasn't the active part. That had completely shut down.

It was Edward. "Hullo. Can I come in?"

"Er, yes, sorry, of course." She turned aside, inviting him into the house while her brain frantically rebooted.

"I'm sorry," Edward said. "I should have called, but I was in the area and thought you wouldn't mind if I just popped in."

"I, um, no, I mean, yes, that's perfectly fine. Wow. It's so good to see you, Edward. Oh my gosh, how have you been? I was beginning to think you'd forgotten us." *That you'd forgotten me,* she thought.

"No, nothing like that. But I have been rather busy with studying and such. Anyway, I had to come to Maine, and I didn't want to leave without paying my respects, so...here I am!"

They stood awkwardly. The longer the silence continued, the more difficult it felt to break it.

"You could offer me a cup of coffee, or ask me to sit down," Edward said, grinning. "Unless, of course, I've come at a bad time and you'd rather I left?" He made a show of looking into the living room. "I'm not interrupting a tryst with a man friend, am I?"

"Er, no, no, I'm sorry. Please, come and sit down. You've just taken me by surprise, that's all."

Elinor closed the door and wandered over to the coffee pot, which she filled with water. She was going through the motions fine—water, filter, coffee—and yet she worked on automatic, her brain in an entirely different place and her heart a total mess. *Why was breathing, never mind talking, so difficult?*

Edward sat down at the kitchen table, watching her as she worked. It was so surreal, like he had never left them, like there hadn't been this wall of silence between them.

"Milk?"

"Yes, please. No sugar."

She pulled a gallon of milk from the fridge, amazed that her hand didn't tremble as she poured a little into two mugs. She sat opposite him while she waited for the coffee to brew. He was smiling polite as could be, and unlike her, he seemed perfectly composed. Perhaps she had been mistaken in his regard for her? If that were so, thank Gaia she'd had enough self-control not to make a complete fool of herself.

"How have you been?" Elinor asked as the coffee pot began to chug along behind her.

"Good. Keeping busy." The smile left Edward's face, replaced by a more somber, faraway look.

"Is something wrong?" Elinor asked.

Edward shook his head. "Other than the fact that I can be an idiot at times?"

Elinor laughed. "Can't we all."

The front door burst open, and Marianne came in. "Oh sweet Gaia, I thought that was your car. How are you doing, Edward? It's so great to see you."

"I'm good," Edward said, his smile returning.

Elinor rose to fetch the coffee pot, inwardly cursing Marianne's bad timing. As she poured, she looked back to the door. "Where's Willoughby?"

Marianne slid onto a chair beside Edward, her grin still fixed in place. "He had to scoot. He said he'd text me later. Oh, can I have one of those?"

Elinor slid her mug over to Marianne, then set about fixing a third cup for herself.

"How long are you here for? Elinor never said a thing about you coming." Marianne shot Elinor a reproachful look. "Are you staying with us? This place is a lot smaller than Norland, but I'm sure we can make room. Margaret and I can share or something."

"Elinor never told you because I didn't know myself before today. And unfortunately, I am only in town for one night. I thought I might book a room in town, it's no bother."

"Nonsense. Marianne's right. You must stay here with us. There's no need to book a hotel." Edward opened his mouth to protest, but Elinor was adamant. "Really, if you've only got one night, why waste it in a stuffy, old hotel room? We would be honored to have you stay with us. I know Mom would be, too, so don't worry about that." The very thought of losing a single minute of his company filled her with angst. He had to say yes, he simply had to.

"Well, if you're sure."

"We are," Marianne said, beaming. "Now that's settled, do we have any cookies to go with this coffee? I'm positively famished."

Elinor pulled a packet of Oreos from a cupboard and dropped the open packet in front of her sister. "You know we do, lazy bones. Is there something wrong with your legs?"

Marianne grinned and helped herself. She waved the packet at Edward, but he smiled and shook his head no.

"So is there anything in particular you want to do?" Elinor asked.

"There are some lovely walks around the house, and the town is nearby. There are some good bars and restaurants we could take you to, or we could hire a boat. It's not horribly expensive, and the boats are a lot of fun."

"Um, I'm afraid you'll have to excuse me," Marianne said through a half-eaten Oreo. "I promised Willoughby I'd meet him later. Elinor will have to take care of you by herself."

Elinor didn't need to look at her sister's face to see the mischief dancing in her eyes.

"So who is this Willoughby?" Edward asked. "New boyfriend?"

"Sort of," Marianne said. "I don't know as I'd go that far just yet, but he has potential."

"Yeah, right. Who are you kidding?" Elinor laughed. If she really thought that, Marianne was delusional.

Marianne grinned cheekily. "Well, I'm going to leave you two alone to plot some mischief while I go and grab a few things out of my room. Then I might take a soak in the tub while you're out. If you're not here when I come down, I'll see you later, Edward."

Marianne grabbed her coffee mug, rinsed it out, and left it in the sink.

"I'll be upstairs if anyone needs me."

Elinor waited as Marianne went upstairs. As soon as she heard a door shut, she stood up.

"Well then, what shall we do? Do you want to go into town? It's a lovely day. We could walk once you've finished your coffee."

"Or we could sit here for a while," Edward said. "I haven't seen you in forever, and it would be nice to just catch up."

Elinor smiled. "Lovely thought, though Mom and Margaret will be back soon. You'd be lucky to get a word in edgewise."

Edward laughed. "Well, in that case! Walking would be nice. I could use the air. Mind if I use the bathroom before we go?"

"Not at all. Just down there, door at the end of the hallway."

Edward downed the last of his coffee, and after he disappeared, Elinor sat and thought. He was being very cordial and civil, but there was something in his eyes that suggested so much more. Was it desire maybe? She yearned for him to give her some sign, some clue that he returned her affections. Plenty of girls were taking the initiative these days. Maybe she should just grab him and throw him up against a tree or something? And yet, what if she was wrong? Was she willing to take that kind of a risk with his friendship?

When Edward returned, Elinor couldn't help noticing how well his jeans hugged his body and how broad his chest was. She looked away quickly. He smelled so good. She wasn't in the habit of sniffing men, but for him she would make an exception. She would have laughed out loud at herself if Edward hadn't been there; he would have thought her a lunatic. Instead, she grabbed her vintage rope bag, slung it over her shoulder, and gestured toward the door.

"Well, it's a beautiful day," she said. "After you."

He preceded her outside. As Elinor closed the door behind her, she turned her face up to the sun, enjoying its radiance. She only had one day with him. She was determined to make the most of it. Not confident enough to hold his hand, she linked her arm through his, and together they wandered down the little path.

"Wait until you see the maple trees, they're really something!" she gushed, no longer able to keep her excitement in.

Fanny would have frowned at such a pointless thought, but her brother threw his head back and laughed. Elinor loved the sound. "Let's go see these maple trees of yours then," he said.

They were like old friends. The more they talked, the more Elinor found it impossible to believe Edward was any relation of Fanny's. Whereas she was all selfishness, guile, and bitterness, Edward was all consideration, openness, and compassion. He was sometimes quiet and would walk along silently, studying the world around them, but if any demons tormented him, he never shared it.

"It's a pity we only have you for one day," Elinor remarked as they neared the town, having said hello to the trees and continued along the cliff path, which gently descended toward Camden. "Maine is such a long way to come for so little time."

"Actually, I've been up here for two weeks already," Edward explained. "This is my last day, and I really have to get back." He paused just as soon as the words left his mouth, no doubt realizing how insensitive this must sound.

Elinor stopped dead in her tracks. *Two weeks? And not one mention of it? Not one email? Not one text?* She coughed, and instead of punching him like she wanted to, she composed her thoughts and asked, "Oh? What were you up to? Anything fun?"

He shook his head. "No, if only. One of my professors lives in Bar Harbor. Believe me, if I could've gotten out of it, I would have. But I'd been putting him off forever, and it couldn't wait any longer. I had hoped to get away sooner but...well, things didn't turn out as I had hoped."

Elinor wanted to ask him more, to find out exactly what he did up there—he had mentioned that he'd been studying—but something about his tone was clipped, and a shadow crossed his face when he spoke of it. He clearly found the subject unpleasant, and since they only had a few hours, she thought it wise not to push him.

They entered the town via a cobblestoned side alley that opened into what was the main street, full of little shops and eateries. Elinor looked around for her mother and Margaret but didn't see them. "And I suppose your business at home is just as pressing? You couldn't postpone for a few more days?"

Edward shook his head. "No, not really. I have a deadline on this paper, and Fanny has some event I have to attend on pain of death."

Pity. "Well, the Drouthy Bear is a nice pub. They have good ale, and if you're hungry they serve Scottish food. Do you like that?" She hoped he would. The pub had low lighting and exposed brick, and she fancied being close to him in a cozy, intimate setting.

Edward nodded. "Sure, in a bit. I'm not terribly hungry right now. Are you?"

Elinor shook her head, hiding her disappointment. "Not especially."

They were standing right outside the door of the pub. Elinor was just about to continue down the street when Edward gently pulled her back. He was staring at something just across the road.

"What?" Elinor asked.

"Is that a psychic shop over there?"

Elinor directed her gaze to where he was pointing. Across the street was a small shop painted entirely black. There was a lilac, neon palm in the window flickering slightly. There was no sign other than the palm, but Elinor had heard of the shop by reputation.

"Yes, that's Lady Eliza's place." Elinor lowered her voice and spoke almost reverently. "I've heard she's very good."

There was a twinkle of mischief in Edward's eyes. "Shall we be wicked and check her out?"

Elinor hesitated, suddenly a little afraid. "Is that wise? What if she tells you something you don't want to hear? They say she's only human, but I don't know—I heard her predictions are scarily accurate. Like when old Mrs. Jennings took Gemini in to find out if she was having a boy or a girl, and she told them they'd have to pop out a lot more babies before a girl ever showed up. So Mrs. Jennings said, anyway."

"You surprise me," Edward said. "I would have thought as a dryad you'd be more open to this sort of thing. Divination is hardly new."

"It's not an issue of belief," Elinor argued. "More one of preference. I would rather not know and just take life as it comes to me."

"I'm part druid. Divination is in my blood. Unfortunately, though, the one fortune I can't divine is my own. Come on, let's go see if Lady Eliza is the real deal or just some old hack with a fake crystal ball."

Elinor shrugged. It might not be her cup of tea, but Edward clearly wanted to and well, he was her guest, after all.

"Sure, why not?" Elinor said. "As long as you don't expect her to do mine. I'm just not into it."

"Fair enough. Don't worry, it'll be fun. When psychics realize I'm part druid and know what I'm talking about, they usually poop their pants anyway."

Elinor laughed, and together they carefully crossed the busy street and went inside the shop. A tiny bell tinkled. All noise from the world outside eerily ceased as the door closed behind them.

Edward was still grinning, but the hairs on Elinor's arms were tingling. These psychic places gave her the willies—this shop especially. It wasn't the decor, since most of these psychic shop parlors were alike; like most of them, the place was elaborately decked out in soft velvet drapes and willowy sheer fabrics, and the near silence was designed to kindle the senses and put the customer on alert. From somewhere inside came the watery tingle of wood chimes and the distinct trickle of running water from a fountain. Elinor's ears pricked up as she listened out for the proprietress, but she heard nothing.

"Anybody home?" Edward called.

There was no answer. "Maybe they're out to lunch and forgot to close the door," Elinor suggested.

"Possibly," Edward said. "Let's take a look."

He pressed ahead, lifting a great curtain that led into a chamber, which for now, boasted a small round table and empty seats.

"See, no one's home," Elinor said, thinking of the pub across the street and how nice it would be to have a glass of wine there. And possibly some Scottish steak and sausage pie with soggy pastry, mmm.

"Looks like you're right," Edward said, his disappointment apparent.

Just as they turned to leave, a deep, feminine voice called out. "Oh hello, I didn't hear anyone come in."

Edward shot Elinor an amused glance, and they both turned around. Lady Eliza, if indeed this was she, was dressed all in black and stirring something hot in a teacup. Apart from her black blouse over black jeans, she wore no jewelry, and her face was devoid of makeup. Her Viking blonde, shoulder-length hair curled gently on her shoulders. Elinor had expected someone in her fifties or older, but the psychic looked no more than thirty—she certainly looked good no matter her age. Annoyingly. Edward couldn't keep his eyes off her. She took a seat at the table and beckoned Edward to sit down.

"How did you know I wanted the reading?" Edward asked.

"Fifty-fifty odds," Lady Eliza said. "That, and your girlfriend looks like she's wetting her panties to get out of here."

Elinor didn't know whether to blush or leave at once. *Not much of a psychic if she doesn't know I'm not his girlfriend!* she thought. Edward gallantly pulled out a chair for her to sit down, but Lady Eliza shook her head. "You might not want to do that."

This time it was Edward's turn to look surprised. "Do what?"

Lady Eliza stared directly at Elinor. "I know you don't want to be here, and that's perfectly okay—I get that a lot. But even though your part-druid friend would have you stay to ridicule me, I think I am doing him a kindness now by asking you to step outside. Just for a few minutes. If I'm wrong, he can call you back in and I'll finish his session for free. Otherwise, my standard fee is a hundred dollars an hour."

"A hundred dollars!" Elinor gasped.

Lady Eliza waved her hand dismissively. "Your friend can afford it. In any case, what I have to say to your friend won't take more than a few minutes."

She took a sip of her drink and looked up at the two expectantly. "Of course, you're welcome to stay if you want."

Elinor hesitated, but for just a moment. There was something in the tenseness of Edward's shoulders that gave her pause. She laid her palm gently on his shoulder. "Edward, what would you like me to do?"

Edward looked from Elinor to Lady Eliza and back again. "Um, if you're okay with it, I think perhaps I'd better hear this alone."

Elinor nodded. There was an eerie sensation in the room, a sort of power she was anxious to get away from. She was glad he'd asked her to leave. "Very well," she said. "I'll just pop next door into the gift shop. Come and find me when you're done."

Edward nodded, and Elinor left. She loved the world of magic, but the darker arts she didn't fully understand and had no desire to learn more about them. It had been immediately clear that Lady Eliza was no hack, which was all the more reason for her to get out of there. Still, time was running out, and she and Edward had so little time as it was. She wished to Gaia she had never brought him into town so that he'd never have seen this stupid shop. She should have shown him her bedroom instead and kept him locked in there all day, stopping only to feed and water him. Or maybe not.

The gift shop was full of tourists. Elinor idly browsed the counters full of cheap jewelry, moonstones, and Camden souvenirs, but she couldn't focus on any of them. She pretended to look at some books, but her mind was a complete wash. She had so desperately wanted out of that psychic shop, but now that she was out of there, she wished she were back in it. What on earth was Edward telling her? And another little voice niggled even more. That Lady Eliza woman was awfully pretty. What had Elinor been thinking, leaving Edward in there alone with that mind-twister?

Minutes seemed like hours as she pretended to shop. The assistant behind the counter kept glancing her way.

"Can I help you find something?" the woman asked at last.

She probably knew Elinor wasn't a tourist. Her whole family walked into town often enough; there was every chance the assistant had seen them out and about.

"No, just browsing." Elinor felt like an intruder. *Oh Edward, come on!*

Elinor was just looking at some stuffed toy lobsters when Edward called to her from behind. She turned around, relieved instantly at the sound of his voice. He pushed gently past an older couple fussing over whether to buy a salt and pepper mill set with *Camden* written down each side.

"How did it go?" Elinor asked, her voice upbeat in contrast to the look of worry she saw in Edward's face.

"Oh, well, you know. She told me pretty much what I expected to hear."

"So is she real or fake?" Elinor asked, wondering what he meant. Had what she told him concerned them? She'd referred to Elinor as *your girlfriend,* after all.

He hesitated before answering. "Perhaps a little bit of both."

"So what did she say, or are you oath-bound never to reveal her dark secrets, ha ha?"

Edward looked around, as if he thought other people might be interested in their conversation, which Elinor was sure they were not. "If you don't mind, I'd rather not say. It was mostly hocus-pocus, but like most of her kind, she hit a few balls home."

"I'm sorry," Elinor said, without being sure why she did.

But then Edward smiled and linked his arm through hers. "Come on, how about that lunch we talked about. I'm suddenly very hungry. My treat—lunch is on me."

"Okay."

The couple pushed their way back through the shop and out onto the street. The brilliant sunshine hit Elinor hard, raising her spirits as always. *Pah! to Lady Eliza,* she thought, mentally blowing her a raspberry. Edward had his arm through hers, and all was right in the world. Who cared what future the palmist had predicted for Edward? She was with him now, this very moment, and Elinor was determined to enjoy every second of it.

As they crossed the busy road, his hand slipped down to take hers, her stomach muscles trembled, and her soul filled with a delicious light that no shadow of the future could do anything to dispel. Especially one cast by a pretty fairground hustler.

Chapter Thirteen

AN INVITATION

ELINOR WATCHED AS THE WAVES WASHED GENTLY AGAINST THE GRANITE rocks below. At least they were peaceful, unlike Elinor, who was idly smashing a small pebble against the granite. *Marianne was supposed to have been here by now, for Gaia's sake,* she thought. Tomorrow was Yew Day, when dryads around the world played tribute to the trees in their keeping. Marianne had promised she would help her prepare, but where was she? Elinor flung the pebble high into the air and watched it land way out in the sea with a barely audible plop. Oh well, if it came to it, she would just have to manage on her own. As always.

Elinor dangled her legs over her favorite rock as she dreamed about Edward. If she was being honest with herself, it bothered her a bit that he had left so little time for her when his other friends in Bar Harbor had gotten a full two weeks with him. Still, she had no true claim on him—well, nothing had been said anyway. Not even a kiss goodbye. Did she just have a bad case of unrequited love? Maybe that was what this was. Well, if that were true, it totally sucked, because she'd never felt so elated and yet so miserable in her life.

Behind her, Elinor heard the roar of an engine and the heavy squeal of tires coming along the drive. Willoughby and Marianne had borrowed Elinor's Subaru, and from the sound of it, Willoughby had a ridiculously heavy foot. Her bile rising, Elinor jumped up from her rock and ran to meet them both on the drive. They were already getting out of the car, and both of them were laughing.

"I can't believe you almost rode old Mrs. Jennings off the road. Didn't you see her?" Marianne giggled.

"I could hardly miss her!" Willoughby grinned. "I thought she was going to chuck her handbag at us."

"I wish she had. It would have been so funny," Marianne added.

"What the hell way was that to drive my car?" Elinor exclaimed. "You'll ruin my tires, and what did you do to Mrs. Jennings? Are you crazy? You know, she could have us thrown out if she had a mind to. What were you thinking, Marianne?"

"We didn't do anything!" Marianne exclaimed, clearly peeved. "We were just having a little bit of fun. Why do you always have to be so serious and annoying?"

"One of us has to be," Elinor said, snatching the keys from Willoughby's hand. Of the two of them, he looked a little less recalcitrant, but not much. They both looked fit to burst out laughing some more.

"It's my fault," he said, feigning penitence. "I just took the corner a little too fast. The rest of the time I was being a very sensible driver, I promise you. Mrs. Jennings was never in any danger, I swear."

Marianne snorted into the back of her wrist, suggesting quite the opposite.

"Anyway," Willoughby continued, "I'd better go. See you tonight?"

Marianne nodded.

Elinor held in her anger as Willoughby pecked Marianne's cheek and took to the air. They both stood in silence as they watched him rise a few feet, then glide away. Even angry as she was, watching Willoughby fly never got old.

"Did you have to be so nasty?" Marianne asked as soon as Willoughby was out of earshot. "I swear, you're always ragging on him over something or other."

"I was not *ragging* on him, as you put it, but I have every right to be annoyed. That's my car, Marianne! I lent it to you both in good faith. Who would pay for the damage if he drove it into a tree? You? You haven't even begun to look for a job yet, as far as I can see."

Marianne inhaled defiantly. "Well, I've been too busy. I will soon enough. You're just mad at me because I've found Willoughby whereas you...."

Elinor stiffened. "Whereas I *what?*"

"Whereas you would rather wallow in misery and worry about dollars and cents. Who wouldn't want a bit of fun outside of this house? Sometimes you're intolerable, do you know that? No wonder Edward didn't stay more than one day. You're a pain in the ass."

Before Elinor could say another word, Marianne marched back to the cottage. Elinor didn't follow her. She was too full of rage and needed a moment to simmer down. Marianne had made her feelings regarding Edward clear enough. She thought his lack of interest was entirely Elinor's fault, because she gave him no encouragement. That was not true. She was guarded for a reason, and Marianne was too much of a wrecking ball to see it. The reserve was his; she'd given him plenty of opportunity, but for whatever reason he'd never taken the bait. What, was she supposed to throw herself at him? Where would that get her? Without a bonding ceremony her dryad power would fail, and her soul would diminish. That wasn't what she wanted. Not that he'd even asked that of her.

Now that Elinor had calmed down sufficiently to control herself, she turned to stroll back to the house. The offerings weren't going to make themselves. Just as she turned, she saw Chris Brandon wandering up the drive toward her.

"Good afternoon," he said warmly. "I was hoping to catch you and your sister. I thought I just saw her and Willoughby in your car?"

"Er, yes," Elinor replied, half-expecting his admonition for upsetting Mrs. Jennings, though he said nothing about it. "She just went inside. Do you want to come in?"

Chris gazed at the house, like he really wanted to accept her invitation, but instead he shook his head. "Actually, I can't stop. I just wanted to invite you over to a barbecue at my house on Saturday. It's partly in honor of Yew Day, and John's cousin and their family will be in town, so it should be quite a gathering. Would you all like to come? After your own observances, of course."

Elinor smiled. "I can answer for my mother, Margaret, and myself— we'd love to. As for Marianne, you'd have to ask her."

He stared at the house again. "Oh, just tell her Willoughby has agreed to come. That should do it, don't you think?"

Behind the lighthearted banter, Elinor could sense his pain. Gosh, he really liked Marianne, she could feel it. Instinctively, she wanted to comfort him, but what could she do? She couldn't make Marianne love him if she didn't.

"Yes, I'll be sure to mention that." She wondered if Willoughby might have told Marianne already.

"Very well, I'll see you Saturday then. My regards to your mother and sisters."

Elinor watched as Chris walked back along the drive toward their cousin's house. There was a slowness about his pace that had nothing to do with his age. Marianne didn't know how lucky she was to have a man such as that smitten with her. Elinor only hoped Willoughby would be worth it in the end. She'd seen nothing to believe it so far.

Chapter Fourteen

YEW DAY

MARIANNE'S BACK ACHED FROM LEANING OVER THE SEWING MACHINE for so long. In front of her was a basketful of brightly colored ribbons. Everyone had contributed, but with all her distractions of late, Marianne's offerings were the last.

Their mother was adding some last touches of henna paint to the back of Margaret's hand. At thirteen, this was her first official Yew Day, and their kid sister couldn't have looked more pumped. She sat perfectly still, her back straight, delighted to take her first steps into the giddy world of grownups. Marianne glanced at her own markings on the back of her hands, which her mother had painted on earlier. Had she ever been that eager, she wondered?

"There, that's the last one," Marianne said, flopping back in her chair. "Are we all set now? I need to get changed."

Elinor looked up from the basket she was working on, where she was neatly placing a small scoop of saffron in the center of her bowl of herbs and spices. Marianne was glad Elinor volunteered for the herb bowl. That stuff was expensive, and Marianne didn't fancy another scolding from Elinor if she messed up.

"Yes, I think so," Elinor said.

Thankfully, Elinor was never one to hold her anger for long. Even though Marianne believed Elinor had overreacted about the car—and shamed her in front of Willoughby—a tiny voice deep inside knew her sister had been right and that she'd been out of line. Marianne told her inner voice to be quiet and ran upstairs to dress for the ceremony, leaving Elinor to fuss around with the herb pots.

Marianne pulled her traditional Lincoln-green robe from her cupboard and slid it over the top of her jeans and T-shirt. She let her hair, held up in a loose topknot, fall to her shoulders and brushed it out. She applied a little gloss to her lips. Willoughby had said he would try to make their morning worship if he could, but if not, he'd definitely be at the barbecue. She might as well go prepared.

"Are you ready, Marianne?" her mother called from downstairs.

"Just coming!"

Marianne slipped into a pair of flats and skipped freely down the stairs. All thoughts of everything else jumped out of her head at the prospect of hooking up with Willoughby again. She even picked up the bowl of ribbons, ready to get going. Her mother smiled approvingly. Elinor was ready to go, the herb bowl in her hand, and Margaret carried a bowl of fruit and nuts.

"Ready, girls?" their mother said.

"I'm ready," Margaret said, looking cute as a button in her new robe, Marianne had to admit.

"Good." Their mother led the way with her ball of red and gold thread that she'd woven herself, and the girls followed her out—Elinor first as the elder, then Marianne, then Margaret. They followed her in procession along the north of the cliff, their mother stopping only when she reached the eldest tree, a great white pine. Sadly, they hadn't encountered a yew in the area, though that wouldn't stop them.

All their friends had come to share this time-honored dryad tradition. Mrs. Jennings was there, beaming and clearly having forgotten (for now) her recent transgression; Chris Brandon, looking very solemn; Uncle John, Gemini, and all their boys, who for once were well behaved and scrubbed. There were even a few faces Marianne didn't recognize, whom she assumed were the out-of-town relatives and no doubt would be introduced later. She thought she caught a hint of wing; succubi perhaps, or faerie—she would find out soon enough.

But the one face she truly sought was not there. Willoughby was nowhere in sight, so Marianne lowered her eyes, not wanting anyone to guess at her disappointment.

Mary began by kneeling in front of the tree, her daughters lined up behind her, waiting for their turn to approach.

"Sisters of Gaia," Mary said in a loud, clear voice so everyone could hear her. "We give thanks for your many blessings. For your beauty and your blossoms, for the food you provide to us and the air you clean for us. For the fuel you give to warm us and the timber you provide to shelter us. Sisters of Gaia, for all that you give us, please accept these humble tributes from your thankful daughters."

Then she stepped forward and, with the help of a friendly branch that had swooped down to hold one end of the thread while she walked around the tree, she managed to tie the whole thing to its mighty trunk.

Finally, she stood to one side and bowed her head.

Elinor was next, and after kneeling in reverence, she placed her bowl of herbs at the roots, then carefully smeared some of the saffron spice on the bark, painting it slightly orange.

Marianne followed, and forgetting her personal disappointment, she knelt before the great pine. As soon as she did, she closed her worldly mind to let the spirits of the trees embrace her soul. After accepting their gift of peace, the pine tree spirit lifted her up to its taller branches, allowing her to tie the ribbons she carried to its upper limbs.

Marianne felt safe and at peace, like a child returning to the secure arms of a beloved mother, as the tree moved her around its upper branches. Only when it returned her to the ground below and the connection severed did she think of Willoughby again. But she did her duty and stood beside her sister and bowed her head.

Last, but not least, Margaret knelt before the tree, and after praying, she placed her little bowl of fruit beside Elinor's bowl of spices.

Playfully, a branch swooped down, accepting the dryad child as one of their own. Marianne couldn't help but smile to see the joy on Margaret's face. This was her first ceremony and the first time a tree had carried her to its bosom. She remembered her first time and how wonderful that bond of magic had felt, and for a moment she could feel no sadness but could only share her sister's happiness.

When at last the tree carefully lowered Margaret to the ground, the youngest sister took her place beside Marianne. For a moment, all was quiet.

Then a faint cracking noise could be heard coming from below, and a few feet away a new sapling broke free of the ground and began to climb upward. Marianne saw at once that it was a new yew tree. This was the highest honor the trees could bestow, and the joy of the tree spirits filled her soul. Marianne stole a glance at the onlookers, who had gasped in awe. A slight breeze returned to the branches above. The ceremony was over.

"That was amazing," Margaret beamed, the first to break their ranks. "I want to do it again and again and again!"

Mary laughed. "You are a daughter of the tree spirits. You can do this now whenever you want. You have nothing to fear, they will protect you."

"I can do this forever?" Margaret gasped in awe. Marianne had lost track of the times they had told Margaret this. But knowing it and experiencing it were totally different things, so for once she didn't tease her.

"Until you are bonded," Elinor said. "It was amazing, wasn't it?"

"Then I'm never going to be bonded!" Margaret said. And everyone laughed. "It was like flying!"

Overcome with joy, Margaret threw herself into her mother's arms. Elinor walked over to the others, but Marianne hesitated, as she saw Chris was smiling directly at her and she didn't want to feel obliged to speak to him. Willoughby might come at any moment, and what would he think then? Anyway, talking to Chris only made her feel awkward, and she wasn't in the mood for that. Instead she turned away and pretended to straighten the thread around the tree. Only when she was sure Chris was no longer looking her way, distracted by her mother and Mrs. Jennings, did she dare to join the rest of the party.

As soon as she was close, Gemini stepped forward and gently took her by the arm. "Oh Marianne, I would like you to meet some of my family, Lucy and Anne Steele." She led her over to where the two girls in question were chatting to Cousin John and Elinor.

"Ah, there you are," John said. "This is Marianne, Elinor's younger sister. Marianne, these are the wife's relations, though I don't recall quite how. But they are lovely girls, and they were both anxious to meet you and your sister. My, my, all this beauty coming out of the blue, I can hardly contain myself. Well, this here is Anne, and this one is Lucy, or is it the other way around? I'm always forgetting."

"Oh John, you're such a tease, but then you men are all alike, I suppose," Anne said—or was it Lucy? "It's a pity you don't have any brothers, Marianne, but John tells me there's a heck of a lot of good-looking guys in town and, well, we've only just got here. I can't wait to meet some of them, isn't that right, Lucy? Not that you're interested in meeting someone, eh, Marianne? I heard Willoughby is here all the time, and he looks pretty all right to me. I wouldn't have minded a go at that myself, if you hadn't got in there before me! Ha ha!"

Marianne blushed at the mention of Willoughby—*Did she have to be so crude?*—and Lucy seemed quick to notice.

"Oh Anne," Lucy gasped. "Do you ever stop thinking about boys? You're a terror, I swear. We've only just met these girls. At least give them a chance to say hello."

Both girls were about Elinor's age, Anne perhaps look a little bit older. Though pretty, her open expression made her look a little stupid. They were dressed well, in very fashionable designer jeans, and now that she could see them up close, Marianne was sure they were succubi. Their strong leather wings were tucked tight behind them but were clear enough through the slits of their jackets. Anne couldn't stop looking around, and when her gaze fell on Chris, which it seemed to do every few seconds, she would giggle and nudge her younger sister.

Lucy, who was a shade taller than Anne, could only be described as stunning, with bottle-green hair and sea-green eyes. She wore a tight leather jacket that showed off her curves to perfection, but unlike her sister, she didn't seem interested in the company at all. That is, except for Elinor, whom she couldn't take her eyes off.

"Um, it's nice to meet you," Marianne said, wanting to change the subject and shaking each of the offered hands in turn. Anne's handshake was soft and squishy, and Lucy's was firm and pleasantly warm. Marianne found herself not wanting to let go but somehow managed to. "Did you enjoy the tree ceremony?"

"Oh we did indeed, didn't we, Lucy?" Anne replied. "I confess, I almost died when that tree swooped down and pulled you off the ground. I mean, me and Lucy can fly of course, but it doesn't stop us getting dizzy when you non-flying folk take to the air. Ooh, my heart was all a flutter, I tell you. Do they do that often in these parts? The trees I mean. Because I swear, I've never seen them act that way before."

"There's no need to be frightened," Marianne laughed. "Dancing with our tree friends is one of the most exciting things a dryad can do. Becoming one with the trees gives us all great pleasure."

"I can think of a few things that give us great pleasure, eh, Lucy?" Anne said, nudging her sister. "That Chris guy, is he single?"

"Anne, be quiet will you," Lucy exclaimed. "Why must you always be going on about men and things? You must excuse my older sister," she said to Marianne. "Sometimes she babbles on when she should hold her tongue."

Anne blushed, looking a tad goofy. "Oops, sorry Lucy." But she didn't say anything more.

"They just arrived this morning," Gemini said. "They bought so many toys for the children, I just don't know what to do with them. Thank you so much."

Lucy smiled, although Marianne noticed she smiled only with her mouth. "Oh, it was nothing, really. Anything for those lovely little boys."

"Ah yes, the kids are very thankful," John beamed. "You didn't have to go to any trouble on our account."

"It was the least Anne and I could do, given your hospitality to us."

Marianne stifled a sigh, not quite fitting in with the crowd today. Willoughby had said he might not make it, but that didn't stop her hoping he'd get here all the same. And worse, now she had to contend with the run-at-the-mouth sisters. It just wasn't fair!

"Well, it was nice to meet you," Marianne said, anxious to make her escape. "But I'm afraid I have a lot to do before tonight. I'll see you there, won't I?" Marianne said, knowing she would but wishing she wouldn't.

"Oh, of course, that's why we're here," Lucy said. "We'll catch up with you then. Oh Elinor, if you have time, would you come for a little walk with me?"

Elinor looked surprised at suddenly being addressed. "Er, okay, if you like."

Before Elinor could change her mind, Lucy linked her arm through

Elinor's and the two disappeared off on their own. What could they have to discuss, Marianne wondered? They had only just met each other. Ah well, she was sure Elinor would tell her later back at the house.

"See you later," Marianne said, eager to make her own escape before Anne or the others could speak again.

"Yes, yes, go pretty yourself up," John said. "Not that you need it. So many pretty faces, what is one to do!"

"See you later," Anne said. "Hopefully, with you-know-who next time! Ooh, she's so lucky!"

Before Anne could get too excited, Marianne waved goodbye and headed back to the house. She'd be seeing them later in the day anyway. Maybe Willoughby would show up before that, so she could stake her claim before Anne made a play for him. Taken or not, she wouldn't put it past the horny succubus to try. Wasn't that what they were famous for? Of course, incubi were famous for things, too, but Willoughby wasn't like that. He was a gentleman. He'd been so nice to her. Unlike creepy stalker Chris Brandon. Couldn't he take the hint? She'd made her choice, and he should respect it.

Willoughby, where are you?!

Chapter Fifteen

A PROMISE IS A PROMISE

NO ONE COULD HAVE BEEN MORE SURPRISED THAN ELINOR WHEN LUCY took her arm and led her to the cliffs. Elinor had been barely listening to the others. Her mind had switched off almost as soon as Anne Steele had begun her ramblings. She'd been thinking of Edward and of what he'd have thought of the ceremony. She'd sent him a text inviting him to join them, but though he replied promptly, he politely declined.

My apologies, I'm tied up. Maybe next time. Enjoy yourself. - EF

So odd. He was part-druid, so the ceremony would have been right up his alley.

The sound of her name brought her back into focus.

"You will probably be wondering why I wanted to talk to you, Elinor," Lucy said.

Elinor nodded. "Yes, I am rather curious."

Lucy smiled. "Well, what I'm about to tell you will definitely surprise you, but before I tell you what it is, I have to ask you to promise that you won't breathe a word of what I'm about to say to anyone else. Not ever. Not to your sisters, nor to your mother."

Elinor stopped dead in her tracks. That was an odd request from a total stranger. But as intrigued as she was, she was suddenly nervous. After all, she knew nothing about Lucy Steele and had no inkling of what she wanted to tell her. Giving such a promise might be foolish. "I'm not sure I'm comfortable making a promise when you haven't told me what it's about. Especially since we don't really know each other. Could you tell me a bit of what to expect before I give you my word?"

Lucy's smile faded, and she pulled away. "Oh dear, oh dear. That does put me in a bit of a quandary."

Elinor's instinct warned her this could be trouble, but Lucy looked so distressed she couldn't help but feel a little sorry for her. Even as a voice whispered in her head that she'd live to regret it, Elinor heard herself saying, "Look, I'm sorry. Tell me whatever you like, and I promise I will keep your secret if I can. That's the best I can do."

Lucy's smile returned, and Elinor thought she saw her wings jolt just a fraction. She wasn't quite sure what that meant, good or bad. But once again, Lucy linked her arm through hers, and they carried on strolling as before.

"You'll be surprised to hear, you're the main reason I came up to Maine."

Elinor was indeed surprised. For the second time, Lucy brought her to a complete stop.

"Me? I don't understand. We don't know each other."

"I agree, we didn't," Lucy said. "But we have a friend in common."

"Oh?"

"Yes. Edward. Edward Ferrars. Now don't play all coy and tell me you haven't heard of him?"

"Why, yes. Yes of course. We all know Edward. We're very fond of him."

Lucy smiled. "So I've heard. In fact, he talks about you—your family, that is—rather a lot."

"Does he?" Elinor smiled, thankful that at least he could share his feelings with others, if not with her directly. "What does he say?"

"Oh, this and that. That he values your friendship. Yes, that was it. Of course, he wouldn't say much more than that, would he, since you couldn't be any more than just a friend."

Elinor started again. "What makes you say that?"

They had reached a point near the cliff that afforded a most impressive view of the ocean. Elinor invited Lucy to sit down on her favorite rock, and once Lucy sat down, she sat beside her. She was desperate to hear more, but equally desperate not to show it.

"Well, because I know he couldn't be. Not to you nor to any woman for that matter. You see, Edward is bonded with me."

Elinor sat up straight. "Wait, what?"

"I met him when I was visiting my uncle up here, and well, there's not many men who could pass on *my* charms." She looked down at her own rack with evident satisfaction.

Elinor could barely get the words out. "You? Bonded with my...with Edward. How?"

"How? Oh Elinor, I'm sure your mother told you about the birds and the bees. As for that, I have to say he's very, um, very well...." Lucy's sentence trailed off. She wiggled her eyebrows suggestively. Elinor definitely got the message. Her cheeks burned with embarrassment. "Anyway, he talks about you often, and I thought, well, any friend of Edward is going to be a friend of mine. So here I am, eager to learn all about you so we can be the best of friends too."

Elinor felt nothing as Lucy put her arm across her shoulder and pulled her close. Edward was bonded. To Lucy. A succubus! Edward. Her Edward. Well, that's how she thought of him. The realization of what she'd heard began to sink in, and her heart grew heavy. She wanted to push Lucy away. Hell, for that matter she was half-tempted to throw her over the cliff, but that would never do. And anyway, Lucy had wings. But Elinor sure would feel better.

"The thing is," Lucy continued, "we have to keep our, um, love something of a secret. The goblin side of his family are very particular about him and his career, and if they found out he'd gone and bonded himself without their permission, then oooh." She mimed slicing her own throat.

"So what are you going to do? They're not likely to change their minds, are they?" The words were forced out, and they sounded strange to Elinor, like they weren't her own.

"We're just waiting for the right moment. Edward, dear Edward, doesn't know exactly when that will be, but he says when the time is right, he'll know. I trust him implicitly. As I trust you." Lucy grabbed Elinor's hands and held them tight inside her own. "Promise me you won't tell a soul."

There was a flicker of doubt in Lucy's eyes. It was subtle, but it was there. Or cunning, perhaps? Elinor wasn't sure. Whatever it was, her promise had already been given, and since Lucy's secret caused no harm to anyone but herself, she was bound to keep it.

"I promise," she said, though the words hurt her to say them. Then again, who could she tell? Or even discuss this with? It was such a private matter. She would not wish to embarrass Edward.

"I knew I could count on you," Lucy beamed. "Edward said you were the sweetest thing that ever lived, and he was right. Now, I suppose we should get back and join the others before they wonder what we're up to. My, my, what a morning. I hope your friend Chris is quick about this barbecue thing. I'm positively famished, aren't you?"

Elinor wondered if she'd ever feel hungry again. Or feel anything, for that matter.

"I suppose we ought to get back," she said, sounding more together than she felt. "There are things I need to do before we go."

They began to stroll slowly back to the cottage. Once more, Elinor could feel Edward's hand in her own as they crossed the road and his letting go as soon as they were safely across. She recalled the sadness in his eyes as he left her. His reluctant withdrawal whenever she'd drawn close to him. All these moments were now painted with their true meaning, and her soul was crushed under the weight of her sorrow. She had lost him forever. And yet, he did care for her. She knew this to be true in her heart, and she couldn't fault him for not taking advantage of her when he knew he wasn't free.

But he was bonded to another now. There was no doubt in her mind that Lucy was wrong for him, and she could only guess at how this might have come about. *Oh, Edward.* But there was nothing to be done for it. She knew that once his word was given, a druid could never renege on a bond oath, which meant he was bound to Lucy forever. That is, unless Lucy herself set him free, since, as a succubus, she wasn't bound by the same conventions of behavior. But somehow Elinor knew that was never going to happen. Edward was too good of a catch. And the Ferrars fortune was too much to pass on.

They were just outside the front door of the cottage now. Lucy looked like she wanted to be invited in, but Elinor wasn't quite ready for that. She yearned for the solitude of her bedroom, somewhere, in fact anywhere she could gather her thoughts without Lucy.

"I guess I'll see you later," Elinor said with her hand on the door. "I'd invite you in, but I have a lot to take care of between now and then. I'd better get on with it."

"Oh, yes, well if you say so. Until the barbecue. Bye for now."

Elinor didn't wait to watch as Lucy wandered back along the path. She didn't feel ill, but she was weighed down with the burden of Lucy's revelation and needed to rest.

Marianne was sitting on the sofa when Elinor stepped inside. "Oh, there you are," Marianne said. "What did she want?"

"Nothing exciting," Elinor replied, making straight for the stairs. "Just small talk, things about Yew Day and such."

"Oh, that's a bummer," Marianne said, biting into an apple she'd just selected from the bowl. "I thought she might have some juicy news or something. Any sign of Willoughby?"

Elinor shook her head and began to climb upward. "No, sorry. I guess he's still tied up."

"Yeah, probably. I sent him a text, but he hasn't responded. Er, are you okay?"

Elinor suddenly realized how slowly she'd been climbing upstairs. "Oh yeah, sure. I'm just going take a quick nap before we head over to Chris's. I didn't sleep too well last night. I might try for a few extra winks."

"Oh, all right," Marianne said, satisfied. "I'll see you in a bit then."

"Yeah. Be down in about an hour or so."

As soon as Elinor reached her room, she pulled off her ceremonial robe, kicked off her shoes, and flopped down on her bed. Sleep. If only she could. Unwanted images of Edward pinned to the wall by a sultry succubus came unbidden to her mind. Or maybe he had courted her. It wasn't fair to put this all on Lucy—after all, it took two to tango.

Assuming she was telling the truth. Lucy was a succubus, and succubi weren't exactly famous for their sense of honor. But everything Edward had done, all of his reserve—it all just made sense now. Even if Lucy was lying, Edward never would. The sad fact was that however this had come about, she had lost him. If she'd ever had him. What a mess. Elinor closed her eyes and prayed for the sleep she knew wouldn't come. *Oh Edward!*

Chapter Sixteen

A STRANGE EVENT

CHRIS WIELDED HIS BARBECUE TONGS LIKE A JEDI MASTER WIELDED A lightsaber. He had an impressive table, laden with all kinds of meats and fixings. Unlike John, who literally popped everything straight onto your plate, Chris had a remarkable lineup of cooked meats presented in heated chafing dishes, a small bar with all kinds of beer, cider, wines, and soft drinks, and a pretty little dessert table covered in miniature strawberry tarts, cheesecakes, muffins, and brownies. He had clearly gone to a lot of trouble. Marianne would have been quite impressed if she wasn't so distracted. Willoughby had texted and was on his way. Her gaze remained upward, scouring the sky and anticipating his arrival at any second.

"You picked a beautiful day for it," her mother said. Her plate was already filled with snacks and sandwiches, and she nibbled at the edge of a chicken drumstick. "This is very good," she remarked to Chris. "What did you marinate it in?"

"It's like a honey and Worcestershire sauce concoction," Chris said. "I'd be happy to give you the recipe."

"You did it all yourself?" Elinor asked. "I thought you'd hired caterers."

"No, not for this," Chris laughed. "I love to cook. I do it myself whenever I can."

Marianne caught him looking at her as he said this. She pretended not to notice and returned her attention upward. Out of the corner of her eye, she could still see him looking her way. Only now he wasn't smiling, he was frowning.

"This wine is excellent also," Elinor said, taking a sip.

"What? Oh—oh, yes. There are plenty of bottles in the cellar if we're out already."

"Willoughby!" Marianne cried. "There he is! At last, Willoughby! Over here!"

Marianne loved watching him fly. He never seemed to go too high, just a little over the trees, his great, powerful wings displacing the air around him. Then, feet first, he would descend slowly to the ground with the grace of a ballet dancer and the coordination of an acrobat. *Mmm, those thighs,* she thought. *How amazingly powerful and dreamy.*

"You missed a wonderful ceremony," Marianne said as he landed beside her and tucked his wings away. "The trees gave us a new yew, which is a great honor."

Willoughby smiled affectionately and kissed her on the cheek in greeting. Marianne noticed that both the Miss Steeles, busy chatting to Gemini and Mrs. Jennings, were watching him closely—especially the elder sister, Anne. Marianne linked her arm through Willoughby's and pulled him close, claiming him.

"I'm sorry, something came up I had to take care of." He whispered so close to her ear, she could feel the warmth of his breath on it. He smelled so good, she almost didn't want to let him go. What was this power he had over her? Whatever it was, she liked it. Oh yeah—incubus. She kept forgetting.

"Anything exciting?" Marianne asked, staring coquettishly at Anne as if she and Willoughby were discussing something naughty.

Willoughby frowned. He looked hot even when he was bothered by something. "Nah, nothing worth talking about." Then his face lit up with a smile. "Now, since I missed the fun, tell me all about it." His gaze fell on the two Miss Steeles. For a second, Marianne thought she saw a flicker of recognition, but then it faded. "Who are they?" he asked casually.

"Gemini's relatives. You don't know them?"

Willoughby shook his head and smiled. "No. Should I? Do you know every dryad?" Gaia, he was so cute.

"No, I suppose not. I could introduce you, if you like. The crazy-looking one is Anne, the good-looking biker chick with the leather jacket is Lucy."

He shook his head. "Not right now." He turned and put his hands on her shoulders, and for the briefest second, she thought he was going to kiss her. "I'm famished. Let's go get something to eat."

Marianne swallowed her disappointment, but seeing Anne and Lucy were watching, she smiled and led him over to where Chris was brushing extra marinade on some chicken.

"This all smells good," Willoughby said.

"Thank you. I'm sure you'll find something here to your taste," Chris said.

Though their conversation was polite enough, their voices were clipped, like it strained them both to make the effort. Marianne assumed it was due to rivalry, and thinking nothing more of it, she picked up a clementine from a bowl of fruit and began to peel it.

She had just popped a single segment into her mouth when a phone rang.

"Oh, that's me," Chris said. He downed the brush carefully on the plate and pulled his cell from his pocket. "Hello." His smile faded as the person on the other end of the call spoke. Chris didn't say a word until the very end. "Don't worry. I'll be there as soon as I can. Goodbye."

He swiped off his phone and turned to John, who was leaning over a chafing dish as he decided what to have. "Could you take over? Sorry, I have to go."

"Wait, what?" John looked decidedly confused. "Go? Go where, man? You're our host. You can't just go. There's all this food. Surely nothing's that important it can't wait."

But Chriswas already taking off his apron. "I'm sorry, but it can't. Look, as you say, there's no need to waste all this food. I'll leave you to look after everyone. Just turn everything off when you're done."

Before John or anyone could say another word, Chris ran off into the house. Marianne looked askance at her mother, who had come to join them, and even Elinor looked lost for words.

"How odd," John said. "I wonder what all that was about?"

Mrs. Jennings, who could pick up on trouble at a hundred paces, had practically run over to the table and now was breathless. "What have I missed?" she gasped, holding onto her cleavage as she tried to catch up. "Has something happened? Is everything all right? I don't think I've ever seen Chris move so quickly. Is he sick or something?"

"We've no idea," Willoughby said, "but Chris has decided to abandon us. Look."

Even as he spoke, Chris's garage door popped open. Chris sped out along the drive as if he were already on the freeway.

"He can't just leave like that," Mrs. Jennings said. "He's our host!"

"Well, it seems he just did," Willoughby said, not bothering to hide the contempt from his voice. "But that's Chris all over. Drama queen. Calm on the outside, train wreck on the inside."

"I don't think you like him very much," Elinor remarked.

"That's a bit strong," Willoughby said, helping himself to a small steak and adding a few spoonfuls of potato salad. "He's all right, I suppose. He's just so...so...*dull*."

"Willoughby!" Marianne retorted, but she couldn't disagree with him.

"Well, whatever it is, it must be important. I hope everything's okay," Elinor said.

Marianne, chastened a little by her sister's words, added, "Me too. I wonder what happened?"

"I'm sure he would have had his reasons," Mrs. Jennings said thoughtfully. "I've known that man for a very long time, and he's never been the crazy type." She shot Willoughby a glare, and Marianne felt sure she was remembering how he'd almost knocked her down in Elinor's car. "Suffice it to say, it must be something important."

"I'm sure you're right," Marianne said. "So, what are we going to do now?"

"Well, there's a ton of food, so I say we carry on as before," John said. "I mean, it feels a bit odd without our host with us, but let's all make the most of it and have a party anyway. It is Yew Day, after all!"

"Well said," Willoughby agreed. After grabbing a bottle of cider, he wandered over to one of the tables placed under the shadow of a tree. Marianne followed him.

"I wonder what all that was about?" she said, sitting down opposite him.

"I dunno," Willoughby said. "But let's not let him ruin the day for us. How would you feel about coming with me after we eat?"

"Coming with you?"

Willoughby looked up at the sky. "I'd like to take you for a little spin. There's someplace in particular I'd like you to see. If you don't mind flying with me again, that is?"

"Oh Willoughby, I'd love to," Marianne said, barely able to conceal her delight. "As long as you don't fly too high it should be all right. I don't want Mom to have a cow."

"Well, that's settled then," Willoughby said.

"Where are we going?"

A mischievous twinkle lit up his eyes. "That part's a secret," he said. "You don't mind secrets, do you?"

"Of course not," she said, finding herself unable to say no to anything he might suggest. Suddenly she wished the steak and potato salad on his plate would disappear. "I'm game for anything as long as it's fun."

The mischievous twinkle intensified. "I thought you might be."

Willoughby appeared as anxious to get going as she was, for he wolfed down the last of his food, and after dumping his trash in a can, he swept Marianne up in his arms, then with a great heave, he took to the skies.

"Wait, where are you going?" Elinor called from the ground.

"Come down, that's too high, it's dangerous," her mother shrieked. Gaia, did she always have to create a scene?

"I want to fly too!" Margaret cried.

But it was too late. Marianne heard nothing but the whoosh of the air around her as Willoughby's great wings climbed higher and higher, and she felt nothing but the beat of his heart as it pounded next to hers. Nothing on the ground mattered anymore. There was only Willoughby and her, and the protection of his arms as he held her close and carried her upward. If she felt giddy at all, it wasn't from the height or from how little she'd eaten at the barbecue. It was because she was with Willoughby, a man she would do anything for, whatever he asked of her, because Marianne Dashwood, as young as she was, was desperately in love.

Chapter Seventeen

SOUTHPORT

WILLOUGHBY LANDED SO GENTLY, MARIANNE MIGHT NOT HAVE KNOWN they were back to earth if he hadn't let her slide from his grasp. She was torn between the joy of being safe on terra firma and the sorrow of being released from his arms. She held onto him for a moment longer than she should have and enjoyed his gaze, which was both deep and playful.

In front of her was a beautiful Maine house with red cedar shake siding and freshly painted white trim. Behind it was a slight slope leading to a sand and shingle beach. The house was surrounded on three sides by trees, giving it almost complete privacy. They were on an island, that much she knew, but which island she couldn't say. "Where are we?" Marianne asked.

"We're on Southport Island, and this is my home—Allenham. I wanted you to see it."

She had guessed as much. "It's very beautiful."

"I'm glad you like it. I've been wanting to show it to you for a while."

He moved very close, then rested his forehead gently on hers. Marianne was spellbound, and she closed her eyes, breathing him in. Her heart raced. What if he took her inside? They were not bonded. Being alone with him could get her in a hell load of trouble. Would she have the power to resist him? Would she *want* to resist him?

"Come on down to the beach," he said.

She nodded, afraid to speak in case her voice betrayed her.

He took her hand. Her own felt tiny inside his, and she suddenly felt very small and vulnerable, but in a good way. She followed Willoughby along a gravel path that sloped down to the empty beach. They were completely alone—that is, besides the few gulls pecking for food between the sand and shingle, and a rock crab who was sitting at the water's edge and appeared to be admiring the view.

Willoughby led her over to some large rocks set a few feet from the water's edge. There was a towel draped over the larger rock, and he set it down on the shingle and ushered Marianne to sit down on it. Perhaps it would have been decent of her to hesitate just a little, but the little nook looked so inviting, and heck, she had to sit somewhere.

As soon as she was settled, Willoughby hunkered down beside her, crooking himself up on one elbow.

"The view is spectacular," she said.

"I'll say," Willoughby said, staring at her. She laughed and pushed him gently. "Seriously," he continued, "I think this is the most beautiful place in the world. I'm always sorry when I have to leave it."

"So why leave it?" Marianne asked. "What do you do when you're not swanning around at the beach chasing lobsters and running down little old ladies?"

Willoughby's smile faltered for just a second. "Like most people in the world, I have to work. I'd like to be able to afford to live here year-round, but that's not possible. I have to earn my living, same as everyone else."

"You have an employer?"

Willoughby's frown deepened. Then his face brightened again. "Hey, let's not talk about that now. It's a beautiful day, I'm here on a beautiful beach with a beautiful girl—let's talk about something else."

Curious, Marianne would have liked to learn more, but she didn't want to pry. He was right. It was a beautiful day, and the last thing she wanted to do was spoil the moment.

"Okay," she said, "what do you want to talk about?"

He thought for a moment as he kicked off one of his sandals and idly pushed his foot into the sand. "Tell me about this morning," he said. "I don't know many dryads. How does all that work?"

"Ha, what a way to put it," she laughed. "Well, as you know, dryads share a very special relationship with the trees. Our souls connect with them, especially once we reach maturity around thirteen." She thought about Margaret and smiled to herself. "That relationship changes again when we become a mother, and again when we die."

"What happens when you die?"

"Well, we come from the trees, and when we die, our spirits return to them."

He laughed. "You came from the same stork as the rest of us, I think."

"Yes, if you're being bluntly physical about it, but I'm talking spiritually. We have a special bond with the trees; we care for them while we're living, and they care for us once we're dead. The only thing that breaks that connection is if we turn our backs on them."

"Like how?" he asked.

"By giving ourselves to someone outside of the circle."

Willoughby snorted. "Isn't that being a bit judgmental?"

"Maybe. They don't mind who we love. All they ask is that we honor their ways."

Willoughby fell back on the towel and stared up at the clouds. "Love," he said, shaking his head.

"Why do you say it like that?" she asked. "Do you have something against it?"

"Love? No. It's just such a fickle thing, don't you think? I don't think two people ever understand the same thing by the word."

"What do you understand by it?" Marianne leaned over him and cleared a lock of hair from his eyes. He turned to gaze into hers. His were filled with such longing that it overwhelmed her, and she had to look away.

Willoughby must have felt just as uneasy, because suddenly he jumped to his feet and looked out at the ocean.

"Come on, let's go for a swim," he laughed. "The water here is excellent! Just watch where you step. The lobsters can be nasty!"

Before Marianne could say a word, Willoughby had stripped down to his undies and headed straight to the sea. She watched with awe as his powerful wings tucked behind him, and after wading in a few feet, he jumped into the air and dived majestically into the water, like a kingfisher after spotting its prey.

When he came back to the surface, he shook off the water like an excited puppy, then held his hands out to her, beckoning for her to join him. "Come on, come on. Don't be bashful. There's no one about to see you."

"I don't have a costume," Marianne called, trying desperately hard to remember what underwear she had picked this morning.

"No one will see you. Come in."

Willoughby fell onto his back, using his wings to back-paddle through the water; then he seemed to float on them, like a kid on a raft.

It was a warm enough day to want to swim, but Marianne hesitated at the water's edge. She wasn't afraid of the water but of what getting into it might lead to.

"Come on, scaredy-cat," Willoughby cajoled. "You're missing all the fun. It's not even cold!" He splashed the surface of the water as if to prove a point.

It did look fun.

Marianne made up her mind, and with a carefree laugh she began to strip. A minute later she was wading into the cold water.

"Agh, you brute, you lied! It's freezing!" she laughed.

"Only at the beginning. Just dive in, you'll be fine."

The shoreline was steep, and Marianne was soon up to her waist. Shivering, she took a deep breath, then following Willoughby's advice she plunged under the surface. *Might as well get it over with.*

The world was lost to her as the water whooshed around her ears. Her mouth was closed, but the saltwater teased her lips, consuming her.

When Marianne came up for air, she was laughing. Willoughby had already swum to her side and had a mischievous grin on his face.

"No, no, NO!" Marianne laughed, anticipating the great sheet of water as Willoughby splashed her with his wings. "You rotten beast!". She took a few steps back, anxious to put a safe distance between them, and though she fought back, her efforts were nothing compared to his, and she soon had to raise her hands in defeat. "Okay, okay, you win! But it's not fair. You shouldn't be allowed to use your wings. That's cheating."

"We all use the weapons Gaia gave us," Willoughby laughed. But he tucked his wings behind him and carefully waded through the water and was soon back beside her.

He took her hands in his and spread her arms wide so that she was drawn into his body. "Now I have to combat your primary weapon," he said, his voice suddenly an octave or two lower.

"Oh, and what weapon is that?"

The corner of his lips smiled as his penetrating gaze transfixed her. "Gaia made you beautiful," he said.

Marianne felt the rush of desire. She had never been in love before, but lately this new feeling had been whispering to her constantly, and she knew it for what it was. She closed her eyes and waited for his kiss. Yes, he was an incubus, and yes, his kind were deviants in the art of love, but none of that mattered now. All that mattered was the sun was shining, they were in a beautiful place, they were alone, and she loved him. She would bond with Willoughby, even if it meant being banished from her kind. Love was love. Let the world turn its nose up at her. As long as Willoughby was at her side, none of that mattered.

Her lips tingled as Willoughby's brushed against hers. Her whole body focused on that tiny space where the two of them connected in a beautiful intimacy, warm flesh against warm flesh, naked but for a couple of tiny pieces of clothing. Her instinct was to fling her arms about him and draw him even closer, but he still held her arms wide, controlling her andtaking the lead.

Willoughby lingered at her lips for the longest time. Yet the kiss, as soft and alluring as it was, went no further. He pulled away, and when she opened her eyes, he was gazing at her strangely. The desire was there—that she could see clearly—but there was more. His eyes held a question.

"What? What is it?" Marianne asked.

Willoughby paused before giving his answer. Then his smile returned. "Perhaps the water is a little cold. Come on. I should get you back before they send out a search party."

Still holding her hand, he began to lead her out of the water. Confused, Marianne followed, lost for words until they were back on the shore.

As soon as she felt the sand firmly between her toes, she stopped and put her hands on her hips. "Wait! Did I do something wrong?"

Willoughby bent down to pick up his clothes, but since he was still dripping wet, he just held onto them. "No, not at all. Why do you say that?"

"I thought...I mean, what happened back there?" She pointed over her shoulder to the sea. "Everything was okay, wasn't it? Did I do it wrong or something? I know I've never done it before, but I'm sure it wasn't *that* bad."

He grinned. "Trust me. You did it right. It's just we've been away longer than I intended, and I don't fancy getting an ear lashing from your mother."

Marianne had crossed the beach and was standing in front of him now. He looked sincere enough, and he was smiling—yet something still felt wrong. She just couldn't put her finger on it.

"You're sure?"

"Really," he said, putting his hand to her cheek. He bent down and picked up her clothes for her. "Come on, let's get you showered and dressed, and then I'll take you back home."

Marianne nodded. The emotions he had unleashed were still battling inside her, and she was at a loss for what to do. Perhaps going home now would be the right thing. Her head was spinning, and she didn't know up from down right now.

She followed him back toward the house, over the shingle, to a small deck overlooking the sea. Willoughby tilted a flowerpot and pulled a key from under it.

"It's not much," he said, "but I love it. To be honest, I'm hardly ever in it, but it has the most comfortable bed and could be really something if I spent more time here."

He pushed open the door and stepped inside. The back door led straight into a large, sparsely furnished room. Although Willoughby said he stayed here, the place smelled empty, as if it was never occupied for any length of time. She looked around at the old but comfortable chairs and the great fireplace that at this moment was unlit. Willoughby was right; she supposed it could be really nice, with a few carefully chosen female additions. And the view through the large windows behind her—well, that was something else entirely.

"I love it," she said truthfully.

"I hoped you would," he said. "Look, why don't you shower quickly, and then we can get going. Come on."

He led her out of the room to a guest bathroom on the ground floor. "There's plenty of clean towels and toiletries, and I think there's a hairdryer in one of the drawers. Throw me your undies, and I'll pop them in the dryer. Do you want a pop or something?"

"Ugh, sure," she said.

Willoughby smiled, grabbed a towel for himself, and closed the door. Still in a surreal daze, Marianne stripped out of her undies and opened the door just a crack, passing her wet things through. "Don't do anything naughty with them!"

He laughed and said, "No promises!" As soon as she closed the door, she turned on the shower and stepped inside once the temperature was right.

Everything was so weird—and she wasn't thinking of the strange peach blossom shower gel she was using to wash herself. Why had he stopped just as things were getting interesting? His kiss had been tender and full of promise, so why the sudden change of heart? Surely he must have felt she wanted him just as much as he wanted her. She liked to think she knew him well enough to believe he wasn't messing with her.

She washed and dried quickly, anxious to spend more time with him. She found him on the deck outside the back of the house, overlooking the sea. He had already dressed and was sipping a glass of something. He handed her a second glass as soon as she joined him.

"That was quick," he remarked.

"I'm a very low-maintenance girl," she said, trying to sound upbeat, though she was still confused as hell. "Thanks for the drink." Even as she took a sip, he brushed her cheek with his knuckles. Marianne felt that same surge within her, and Willoughby must have seen it too, because he immediately turned away, pretending to concentrate on putting his glass down.

Marianne drained the last of hers and handed him the empty glass.

"Thank you," she said.

"You're welcome," he said, taking it and putting it down next to his own. "Come on, let me get you home."

She nodded.

Her heart raced as once again he scooped her up in his arms and took to the air. The smell of the sea was still on him, and she breathed in deeply, loving his scent. How could Willoughby not know love, she wondered? Or perhaps he did but failed to recognize it. Had something awful happened to him, had something in his life forced him to shut love out? Or was it an incubus thing? No, she couldn't imagine that for a second. She knew him. They were like two peas in a pod, and he could feel things just as deeply as she did. So, what then?

Marianne nuzzled into his shoulder, not caring how high they were from the ground or what tomorrow may bring. He had her safely in his arms now and wouldn't let her go. Whatever had happened in his past, she knew he would never let her down. She trusted him completely, and nothing else mattered.

She wondered what her mother and Elinor would say when she told them she loved Willoughby and intended to be with him? She would have to phrase it in the most delicate manner. She'd give this some thought. But first, there was the little problem of making Willoughby fall in love with her. If he hadn't already.

Chapter Eighteen
SECRET THOUGHTS

ELINOR STOOD AT THE WINDOW, SCOURING THE SKIES FOR ANY SIGN OF Marianne. Her mother, beside her, was chewing the side of her finger, something she only did when she was worried or upset.

"I'm sure everything will be fine, Mom. Marianne's a sensible girl, she would never do anything foolish." Elinor hoped as much anyway.

Her mother nodded quickly but continued to chew. "He's a good man, I know he is."

Who was her mother trying to convince, Elinor wondered? He was also an incubus, and that could mean a world of trouble. She had been stupid to trust him. Perhaps her mother and sister, who never thought ill of anyone, could be forgiven for believing him to be sincere, but Elinor was supposed to have more sense. And yet she had seen them together, and Willoughby, though a little wild, had never been anything worse than a young man in love. Maybe she was the one judging him too harshly? After all, it had only been a few hours.

Elinor looked at the time on her phone. Mary noticed and asked, "How long has it been?"

"Four hours." And five minutes since her mother had last asked, to be precise. Elinor picked up the basket full of sprouting potatoes she wanted to plant and headed for the door. "I guess there's no point watching. They'll show up when they do."

As she opened the door, she chanced to look up just as Willoughby appeared through the trees, with Marianne in his arms.

"Mom, they're here," she said. Her mother turned away and closed her eyes. Her lips moved in a silent prayer. The two of them rushed outside, though Elinor wondered which of them would fire first—since one way or another, Marianne and Willoughby deserved a good butt-kicking for their inconsideration.

No sooner were Willoughby's feet planted on the ground, and Marianne safely released, than their mother burst into her angry tirade. "Where *exactly* have you been?" she demanded. "Have you any idea how long you were gone? I've been worried sick! Anything could have happened. Willoughby might be an ace flyer but you're not. Don't forget what you are and what could have happened if you fell! Really, all this flying about! You're giving me a heart attack."

"Really, Mom, I'm not twelve," Marianne said. She glanced at Willoughby, and Elinor caught the eye roll. This was getting out of hand.

Willoughby reddened. "Um, perhaps I'd better get going."

"No," Elinor said, her temper peaking. "You stay and listen. You're as bad as she is." Then to her sister she said, "Is there something wrong with your cell phone? I swear, I've sent you a hundred or more texts, and you haven't answered a single one."

"I turned it off."

"Why would you do that?" Elinor demanded.

"We were at the beach. I didn't want it overheating."

The flimsy excuse made her want to scream. Overheating, indeed! "And you didn't think to turn it back on?"

"I guess it slipped my mind. I was too busy flying. I was afraid I'd drop it!"

This time Willoughby stepped in. "Look, I can assure you all, you've nothing to worry yourselves about. Okay, maybe Marianne and I were gone longer than either of us anticipated, and I'm sorry for that. We may have lost track of the time, but we've done nothing wrong. Anyway, Marianne isn't a baby. Aren't you both being a little overprotective?"

"No—she's a dryad, not a human. Do either of you have any idea what people are saying about you both behind your backs?"

Marianne rounded on Elinor. "The Middletons? Mrs. Jennings? Chris Brandon. What do I care what those people think? They're not my keepers. And I hope you're not encouraging them. You're supposed to be my sister—you're supposed to be on my side."

"Of course I am!" Elinor said. "It's just...."

"That's enough," their mother interrupted. "Let's talk about this inside. Willoughby, perhaps you had better go after all."

To Elinor's surprise, Willoughby reached out and grabbed Marianne's hand. "I shall go, but listen, I'm coming back first thing tomorrow morning to see Marianne. It's very important that I do."

"What's up?" Marianne asked, looking puzzled herself.

"It's a surprise. But there's someone I need to see tonight, so you'll have to wait for tomorrow to find out what it is."

The two exchanged happy glances, and Willoughby refused to budge until Marianne nodded her understanding. "Remember! I'll be back first thing. Watch out for me."

And he took off. The second he was gone, Marianne stomped her feet like a petulant child, then stormed inside the cottage.

"I can't believe you two just embarrassed me like that in front of Willoughby," Marianne complained as soon as the door closed behind them. "You both made me feel like a total idiot. What do you take me for? We were both on our best behavior, and you two just went and ruined a perfectly marvelous afternoon. I almost died from embarrassment, the way you were talking out there."

"Marianne, you can't just run off with him like that. He's an incubus. You know they can't be trusted," Elinor said.

"Oh Elinor, what do you know, you've never known an incubus yourself, at least not as far as I know. Anyway, Willoughby and I are just friends. All we did was go for a swim, and you're making such a big deal about it."

"Swim?" Their mother raised her eyebrows. "Without a costume?"

"Oh, don't be such a prude, Mom."

Elinor was about to join the admonishment when Marianne shook her head in annoyance. "If you must know, I went into the sea in my undies. Willoughby did too. He was a perfect gentleman. He didn't lay a finger on me. Really, Elinor, just because you think a certain way doesn't mean that everyone else does. Just because I feel more deeply than you doesn't make me an idiot. Nothing. Happened."

Elinor exchanged glances with their mother.

"Marianne, that's not a nice thing to say," their mother said. "Elinor feels just as deeply as you do, she just hides it more."

"Don't worry about it," Elinor said, trying to appear casual about it, though she was annoyed as hell that Marianne presumed to know anything at all about what she was feeling. Elinor thought about Lucy. Ugh, if only she could tell Marianne what she had learned—that might shut her up. But Lucy had bound her to secrecy. Elinor could say nothing. Besides, how would Marianne react when she was in this defensive state of mind? She wouldn't believe a word; she'd just be even more angry.

"Well, the most important thing is you're home now, safe and sound," their mother said. "And that's an end to it. Elinor, would you mind running up to the Middletons' and fetch Margaret? It's time she was home."

"Sure."

Elinor put down the basket of potatoes she was still holding and went into the kitchen to wash her hands before setting off.

"I wonder what Willoughby wants to do tomorrow?" Marianne said distractedly, helping herself to an apple.

Elinor's back stiffened. In spite of his grand words, she still didn't trust him. But if she said anything to Marianne now, all hell would break loose again. "I suppose we'll find out soon enough. What beach did he take you to?"

"He has a place on Southport Island. Oh Elinor, I can't wait for you to see it. It really is beautiful there."

Southport Island. Elinor knew where that was, and after doing the math in her head, her mood softened. They wouldn't have had time to get up to too much mischief, given how far away it was. Then again, she had no idea how quickly an incubus could fly. But there had to be a natural limit.

"Maybe I can go with you sometime to look it over," she said, hoping to keep the peace.

Marianne beamed, their former argument already forgotten. "I'm sure you would love it."

Perhaps it was just as well. Elinor dried her hands on a cloth and headed for the door. Sooner or later, Marianne would find a way to throw Edward back in her face, and she wasn't sure she was strong enough to hide her hurt just yet. And in any case, Marianne would never understand. She would tell her it was a long way from a simple pledge to an actual bonding ceremony. But Elinor knew neither she nor Edward would feel that way. A pledge was a pledge, and if Edward had given his word to another, that was all there was to it. He was as good as bonded. Why couldn't she sweep him from her mind and have done with him? Why did it have to hurt so?

As Elinor passed by the dandelions and wildflowers on her way to the Middletons', she thought mostly about Edward. Was she being unnecessarily hard on Marianne because of her own disappointment? She hoped not. And yet a part of her couldn't help dreaming about another world, a world where it had been her and Edward alone on a beach, and where she could swim in the ocean with him, unseen by anyone else. Would she have turned off her own phone for a moment's privacy? Maybe. But no one would have worried about Edward ruining her; he wasn't a goddamn incubus.

She, too, wondered what Willoughby would have to say to Marianne tomorrow. What if he wanted to bond with Marianne? Would that be so terrible? Would the trees accept him? His kind were notorious for bad behavior, but Willoughby had done nothing to show that side of him, if he had a bad side at all. His eyes were only ever for Marianne and no other. Maybe things would work out just fine, despite her misgivings.

Yet the two of them had known each other for such a short amount of time. Not that it meant anything. After all, how long had she known Edward? Were her own feelings not just as powerful? What if it was Edward knocking at her door tomorrow, dropping to one knee, asking her to bond with him? Would she have the power to refuse him if he were free? No, definitely not. She wanted him so badly it was killing her.

She looked up to see Margaret waving to her from an upstairs window. She was glad Margaret had made friends with the younger Middleton boys. *Such friendships are much simpler when you're young,* she thought. *If only the same could be said for older friendships.* Elinor smiled, and putting away her secret thoughts for the moment, put on a brave smile and waved dutifully back.

Chapter Nineteen
HIGHLY STRUNG

"Ooh, do you think he will have asked her yet?" Margaret walked on top of a garden wall; her arms splayed like an airplane as she attempted to maintain her balance. She tripped, but a friendly weeping cherry pushed her gently upright so that she didn't fall.

"Get down from there!" Mary said. "You'll hurt yourself."

"And probably break the wall with your head," Elinor added for good measure.

Margaret had been asking similar questions all morning, usually with her kissy-kissy face, which Elinor found really annoying. On the fifth or sixth time, Elinor had shared one exasperated look with their mother, and seeing she was in total agreement, they had both marched her annoying kid sister out of the cottage on the pretext of going into town to do a bit of shopping. Margaret was never one to pass up on the chance of a candy bar, and now they were returning home. Marianne said Willoughby would be there at ten, and it was now almost eleven. Surely that was enough time for them to have discussed their business.

The consensus of all was that he intended to bond with her, and all that remained was the blessing of some guardian or relative, assuming incubi cared about such things, which it seemed they did.

So they were all surprised when they got near the front door and Marianne came running out past them, her eyes glistening with tears.

"Wait, what?!" Elinor exclaimed.

"Oh, just leave me alone, will you?" Marianne disappeared behind some trees. Their branches moved as if stirred by a breeze, but there was no breeze; the trees had sensed Marianne's distress and were calling to her. The replanted Norland Park shrubs were especially upset. For the first time, they shared their feelings with the tall, aloof Maine pines surrounding them. Their different branches reached out to each other and touched in a tender, almost human gesture. Elinor swallowed hard and looked away. Hell, too many feelings....

Margaret was about to go after her, but Elinor caught her in time and shook her head. Whatever was going on, Marianne clearly needed some time alone. "Give her a minute," she whispered. "Go inside. We'll find out what happened later."

Margaret frowned, but she knew better than to go against Elinor, so she stomped into the cottage and was soon heard running upstairs. Margaret's bedroom door slammed just as Elinor and Mary went inside.

Willoughby was standing in the kitchen. Though not crying himself, he looked upset.

"What's going on?" Mary asked. "What did you say to my daughter to make her cry?"

"I, um, that is to say, I, er, have to get out of town for a bit."

"Oh?" Elinor said, desperately trying to keep the cynicism from her voice. "Why's that?"

"My boss, um, well, he's given me anoth—I mean, a new assignment."

"Well, okay," Elinor said reasonably. "I'm sure Marianne will be happy to wait until you get back."

"Yes, well, the thing is—that is to say—I'm not exactly sure when that will be. It might be some time, maybe even a year or so. It's, um, down in the south."

"Well, that's a bit sudden," Mary said. "Still, I'm sure your boss is a reasonable man and will give you a few days to wrap up your affairs here in Maine. And you know, maybe Marianne could come and visit you in a few weeks? As you know, money's a bit tight, but as they say, where there's a will, there's a way. I'm sure something could be worked out. My daughter would be delighted, I'm sure."

"Yes, well, I see, actually, look—oh this is ridiculous. I'm sorry, I have to go." And without another word, he pushed past Elinor and made a dash for the door. Before Elinor or Mary had a chance to turn around, the door slammed shut behind him.

"Well, what was all that about?" Mary said, clearly trying to overcome her astonishment.

Sweet Gaia's mercy, Elinor thought, *had Marianne broken away from him and fled as he'd tried to paw her? What if she hadn't been able to run out of the house? What if they hadn't returned home when they did?* "Beats me," Elinor said. "I'm sure we'll find out more from Marianne when she calms down."

Perhaps it was something in Elinor's tone, but her mother looked at her suspiciously. "I can tell you're thinking the worst."

Elinor shook her head. "I'm trying not to, but Mom, he's an incubus. Perhaps we should never have encouraged this friendship in the first place. It was only ever going to lead to trouble. We all knew that."

"Did we?" Mary said bitterly. "Maybe you did, but the rest of us believe in giving people chances. It wouldn't hurt for you to hope for the best once in a while!"

This time it was her mom's turn to storm off, and Elinor found herself alone. With a sigh, she wandered over to the kitchen and shaking the tea kettle, she discovered it was empty. As she poured cold water into it, she wondered how much of what Willoughby had said was true. It was a small world these days, and what was the inconvenience of a few miles to people who were genuinely in love? As her mother had just pointed out, Willoughby would be just a plane ride away. And yet her sister had looked inconsolable. Sure, Marianne was a little highly strung at the best of times, but there had to be something more behind this than what met the eye.

Perhaps the two had a little lover's tiff? If that were the case, then in a few hours or days, all would be well again. But in her heart of hearts, Elinor knew there was more to it than that. Willoughby was leaving, and from the sound of things, he had no intention of coming back. Naturally, Marianne would be upset, but maybe this was a good thing. If she was right, and Willoughby was going to prove to be a total lemon after all, then maybe his leaving would be for the best. Not that Marianne would see that. Not for a while anyway.

Elinor lit the burner under the kettle and stared at the wall. Love. What a crazy business it was. Did anyone ever really understand the ways of it? She sure as hell didn't, but each to their own. Elinor pulled clean cups from the upper cupboard and pondered such things as she fixed them all a cup of tea. Maybe she would make lemon ricotta cake to cheer everyone up. She realized she could do with a bit of cheering up herself.

Chapter Twenty

DILL PICKLE

ELINOR WATCHED MARIANNE AS SHE SAT HUDDLED IN THE WINDOW seat, lost in a book of woeful verse. It was mid-afternoon, yet she still wore a pair of pink pajamas. A potted bonsai tree kept pressing her arm, trying to draw her attention, but Marianne merely sighed and swatted it away. The tiny tree gave up, and its branches drooped in sadness. Her sister was a healthy girl, but this falling-out with Willoughby had left her pale and peaky. She'd hardly said a word the past couple of days.

"It's just not like her," Elinor whispered to their mother. "She usually bounces back by now."

"Do you think we should text him? Maybe see if we can get a little bit more out of him?"

Elinor shook her head. "No, I don't think so. I hate to say it, but I think the less we have to do with Willoughby the better." She raised her hand in placation as her mother looked ready to make an argument. "Look, I know you want to think the best of him, and believe me, so do I. But really, look at Marianne. If he was truly a good soul, would he have left her like that? She looks awful."

"You don't think she's...that he got her...?" Mary couldn't bring herself to say the words.

Elinor stared at Marianne thoughtfully. Then she remembered the trees and how they'd embraced her when she'd sought their protection. "No. I don't think so. The trees would know if something had changed, and they didn't act strangely. I'm pretty sure whatever went on, Marianne is entirely blameless."

They were interrupted by a knock on the door. Elinor began to get up, but Margaret sprang from nowhere and beat her to it. She flung the door open to reveal their cousin John, carrying a sickly sapling in his hand but with his usual happy grin fixed firmly in place.

"I hope you don't mind," he began without preamble, "but a friend showed me this sorry-looking thing, and I told him I knew just the girls to make it better. Will you take a look at it for him?"

Mary got up at once, and after taking the sick plant out of his hand, she took it into the kitchen and examined it in the stronger light. "Yes, I know, baby," she cooed to the sapling, tickling its fragile bark. It barely responded. "Don't you worry. We can make you right." She smiled at John. "Just leave it with me for a few days. I think this poor little thing just needs some TLC. Thanks for bringing it to me."

"Oh, you're very welcome," he said. "Although that wasn't the only reason I came. We're having a bit of a dinner party up at the house, and I'd like you all to come. Seven sharp, mind you. Gemini hates it when people show up late for her dinners. Nothing too formal, so no need to dress up. In fact, it was Gemini who insisted I come down here and round you all up. Between you and me, I think she misses her friend's company." He nodded none-too-discreetly in Marianne's direction. "A little party will do you all the world of good. What do you say?"

"Of course," Mary replied for everyone. "We'll be there, don't you worry."

"Is there anything we can bring?" Elinor asked. "I made a lemon ricotta cake yesterday—would you like me to bring it?" She was pleased someone would get to eat it, since the others had brushed it off yesterday.

"Sure, why not?" John beamed. "You can't have too much cake now, can you? I'll be off then, but I'll tell Gemini to expect you all tonight. My, my, she'll be pleased, I promise you. Lemon ricotta is her favorite. See you in a bit."

With that, he turned on his heels and let himself out. It was beautiful outside, and Margaret ran out with him to go play.

Elinor glanced over at Marianne. She had barely looked up when John arrived, and she didn't acknowledge him when he left. Thankfully, he didn't seem to mind, but that wasn't the point. Marianne could be thoughtless, but this was extreme even for her.

"I wonder how many people will be going?"

"Where?" Marianne said, only half-listening.

"To John's do tonight. Really, Marianne, didn't you even hear his invitation?"

"What? Oh, no, sorry, I was miles away. What did he want?"

"He's invited us all to dinner up at the house."

Marianne pulled the blanket out from under her and huddled inside it. "Yeah, I'm not up to that. You all go."

"Marianne!" Elinor said. "Gemini expressly asked to see you. Anyway, it's too late. I said we'd all go. And you can't lollop about like this all day. It just isn't healthy."

The old Marianne would have spat out a sarcastic retort, but the new one picked up her phone, only to stare sadly at it.

"Has he answered your text?" Elinor asked.

"No," Marianne sighed. "Not to any of them."

"How many have you sent?"

"Oh, I dunno. A few dozen or so?"

"A few dozen!" Elinor gasped. "Don't you think that's a bit excessive?"

"No. I don't. Anyway mind your own business. Maybe if you'd sent Edward a few texts, you might have heard from him by now. He's probably forgotten you exist, since you do nothing to remind him of you."

Elinor shook her head, then turned away, not wanting Marianne to see her misery. Maybe Edward had forgotten her, but she couldn't say the same about him. She thought about him every minute of every hour of every day. Not that pining did her any good. But she could hardly help herself.

"Whatever. Just get your butt out of those jammies and be ready for six-thirty. They're expecting us at seven."

"Whatever yourself."

Marianne turned away, and a minute later, she was lost in the woes of some lovelorn poetry. Elinor shook her head again, and preferring distraction to indulgence, got on with her chores.

There were quite a lot of cars parked on the drive. John liked a good party, but for some reason Elinor had expected a much smaller gathering.

Elinor knew that underneath the makeup, Marianne was still a little peaky; but to be fair, she'd done a good job of hiding it and now looked as pretty as ever. Elinor hoped that Chris would be here; now that Willoughby was safely out of the picture, maybe he'd finally have a chance with Marianne. Even though this was as unlikely as Edward appearing out of thin air and asking her to marry him—but one could hope. His car wasn't on the drive, but that meant nothing; it was still early.

Her heart sank when she heard the unmistakable giggle of Anne Steele, which meant Lucy would be about someplace also. Perhaps she should have listened to Marianne after all and stayed at home. Marianne, who walked a few feet ahead of her, must have heard it too, because she turned around and rolled her eyes. Their mother and Margaret remained happily oblivious and hurried on inside.

"Ah, there you are," John said the moment they walked into the house. "I was getting ready to send out a search party." His gaze fell upon the cake carrier Elinor had brought with her. "Ooh, is that the cake? That does look nice. Let me take it to the kitchen. Come on. What would you like to drink?" He whipped the cake carrier from Elinor's hands and marched off, leaving them all to follow.

"I think we know who's going to get the biggest slice," Mary said, chuckling.

Lucy, who was sitting alone and scrolling on her phone, looked up and smiled at Elinor. Elinor smiled back, but seeing Lucy was about to get up, she pretended not to notice and dutifully followed John into the kitchen, grabbing a bottle of water from the selection on the counter. She was inches from making her escape out the back door when she heard a light cough behind her.

"Well, hello," Lucy said. "I was looking forward to seeing you again. How have you been?"

"I'm doing well," Elinor said, with more politeness than she felt. "How about you?"

"Oh, just fine. Missing our mutual friend, of course, but getting by.

Shall we go for another little walk together? I could tell you all the latest news. It really is rather exciting."

As desperate as Elinor was for news of Edward, she wasn't quite ready for another smug fest from Lucy just yet. "Maybe later. We've only just got here, and it might seem a little rude to wander off already." She smiled at Gemini, who was a few feet away, stirring something that looked like gravy in a great, red cast-iron pot.

Lucy's wing twitched just a little, then she shrugged. "Oh yes, well I suppose you're right," she said, dropping her voice so only Elinor could hear. "Poor darling. You know he misses me dreadfully whenever we're apart. He stays away for weeks on end just to avoid putting himself through the torture of a fresh separation. So thoughtful. And so sexy. Ha ha, you know what they say about the quiet ones."

"Yes, well." Elinor didn't want to hear any more of *that* and pretended to be interested in the plates of appetizers laid out next to the drinks. She turned her back on Lucy as she loaded her plate with anything within reach—she didn't even like dill pickle—but Lucy still wouldn't take the hint.

"You don't worry with him being away all the time that you might grow apart?" Elinor asked, since Lucy was clearly determined not to budge. "Don't they say that absence doesn't make the heart grow fonder, or some such?"

"Hmm, whoever *they* are, they don't know what they're talking about. He's a rock, is my Eddy. An absolute diamond. And I think the expression is it *does* make the heart fonder. I'm sure I'm right."

Elinor cringed. She didn't like to think of Edward as an Eddy. But then she checked herself, since she really had no right to think about him at all. She wished Lucy would just find someone else to torture.

She was saved from further comment by Marianne, who chose that moment to burst in the kitchen, a huge grin fixed on her face.

"What is it?" Elinor asked, wondering what on earth could have happened in the last three minutes to bring about this change. Surely it could mean only one thing. "Have you heard from him?"

"No, no," Marianne said, barely able to catch her breath. "But oh Elinor, it's the next best thing, it really is!"

"Come on, tell me," Elinor cried, her curiosity getting the better of her.

"Betsy. You won't believe it, but she's just invited us all down to Florida. Oh Gaia, I'm so excited I can hardly breathe."

Elinor was bewildered. "Really, is that all? I thought maybe you'd won the lottery or something. That's very kind of her, but what's the big deal?"

"You don't get it. There's a big conference down there. Anyone who is anyone will be there, and she reckons that's where Willoughby went. Oh Elinor, if he's down there and I could get to see him, I think everything would work itself out."

The snide look on Lucy's face suggested she thought otherwise. Elinor fought the urge to stick the dill pickle in her stupid mouth.

Still, the annual Magic-Con Florida conference was a big thing—it was little wonder her sister was so excited. "What did Mom say? Will she let you go?"

"Not just me, silly, all of us. You, me, Lucy, and Anne. Mom said I could definitely go if you went with me."

Astonished, Elinor turned to Lucy.

"That's what I wanted to tell you," Lucy said. "I found out earlier that Edward will be down there at the same time. He always goes for the annual Magic-Con! We could all hook up and go out together. How exciting is that?"

Elinor thought otherwise. The last thing she wanted in the world was to see those two loving it up in front of her. And the idea of Marianne chasing after Willoughby didn't sound like a good time either. For the first time in her life the Magic-Con gathering didn't sound like fun at all.

"I dunno," Elinor said. "Can we even afford it?"

"Afford what?" Betsy wandered into the kitchen and joined their little circle. "Don't you worry about that. Your mother and I have worked it all out. It will barely cost you a thing. My late husband was on the board of Para-Air, and I get free tickets for life. All it takes is a call to book seats in advance. Plus I have a huge house down on the beach where we can all stay. Freddy and I had planned to snowbird, but then he popped his clogs, so he never got to use it, poor dear. And of course, now my girls are all grown and have families of their own, I have no one to enjoy it with. So please, make me happy and say you'll come. It'll be such fun. I love being with young people. It makes me feel so young myself!"

Elinor felt cornered. Marianne and Betsy were a force not to be denied.

She could have done without Lucy's smugness, but if it would make her sister happy, well, it might be worth it just for that. And she had always wanted to go to the Magic-Con. She'd heard wonderful things about it, lots of dryads networked down there, and the weather would certainly be nice.

"All right, if Mom says yes, then I suppose so."

Marianne was so excited she began to squee. Elinor bit her lip. She wished that sometimes Marianne could rein her feelings in just a little. But go she must, and if Elinor's suspicions were right, at least she would be there for her sister if the axe fell. As for Edward and Lucy, well, there was nothing she could do about that. Maybe she'd get lucky and not have to see either of them at all.

At that moment, Chris, arriving late as usual, wandered into the kitchen and quickly caught onto the excited mood. "What's going on?" he grinned.

But his smile soon waned as Betsy filled him in on her latest plan.

"Ah, yes, the Magic-Con. I'm going there myself to meet up with some old army warlock friends."

Elinor perceived that he deliberately avoided looking at Marianne and felt a pang of sympathy for him.

"Well then, why don't you come with us?" Betsy said. "These young women are wonderful to be around, but they're so independent these days. I'm a bit more old-fashioned and would love to have a big old warlock along for the ride to protect us." She fluttered her lashes. "Come on, Cuh'nel Brandon, suh. What do you say?"

Chris threw back his head and laughed at her playfulness. Elinor smiled too, because even though Marianne was clearly ignoring him, Elinor could tell he was concealing his true feelings. In fact, she decided that if she did run into Edward at the Magic-Con, she hoped she could be half as cool and not give Lucy the satisfaction of betraying her emotions.

"Right, I'm off to tell Mom you said yes, see you in a bit." Seemingly with a much lighter heart, Marianne ran into the other room in search of Mary. Chris watched until she was out of sight and then looked thoughtful. Elinor couldn't help but suspect he might be sharing some of her own misgivings. But if he did, he didn't breathe a word, and Elinor didn't think she had the right to ask him about it. In any case, it might upset him if she did. And if Elinor knew anything about anything, it was about the misery of an unfulfilled love. She wouldn't wish that pain on her worst enemy.

As she pondered these events, she absentmindedly picked up an appetizer from her plate, and without thinking, chomped down on the vinegary dill pickle and almost choked to death.

Betsy patted her back while Elinor gasped for breath. "There, there. I love a big dill pickle in my mouth, but they can take some getting used to."

"I wish people wouldn't eat just before dinner," Gemini said, her eyes huge. "It spoils your appetite."

Elinor wished she'd given that advice ten seconds earlier. She gratefully accepted the glass of water Gemini offered her and chugged it back. It washed away the hideous taste, and she was able to breathe again. She nodded her thanks.

"And now, perhaps you can all go through and sit at the dinner table and get ready for dinner," Gemini added. Elinor remembered Cousin John's warning: *Gemini hates it when people show up late for her dinners.* Or spend time talking about things that could have waited until after dinner.

"Sorry, Gemini," she said sheepishly, and hurried out of the kitchen.

Chapter Twenty-One

MAGIC-CON

WHETHER SHE HAD LOST HIM OR NOT, THERE WAS A CHANCE ELINOR might see Edward, so she dressed carefully. She knew she didn't have Marianne's flair for fashion, but she could still hold her own. Today she looked really pretty, with her hair loosely braided and wearing a crisp, white shirt and her best figure-hugging jeans. If she couldn't have him, she sure as hell wanted him to feel what he was missing.

Marianne was on the same page and wore a gorgeous blue sweater that made her eyes pop. The Dashwood sisters were set to turn some heads, that was for sure. Elinor had a good feeling. Surely dressed like this, nothing could go wrong.

Elinor was the last out of the Uber. Anne had rabbited on throughout the whole journey, but at least that kept Lucy quiet, which suited Elinor just fine. The only thing she had whispered of interest was that she'd texted Edward earlier and had high hopes of seeing him sometime in the afternoon, though she was kind of vague about when. Elinor hoped she could find a way to be elsewhere if that came to pass.

Though she kept her gaze fixed out the window of the car, Elinor could feel Anne's close examination, taking in her appearance. *Ha, take that, succubus. My dump truck ass brings all the boys to the yard, it's better than yours.* Elinor tried not to smirk.

The Magic-Con was buzzing; paranormals from all over the world had come, some in regular clothes, some in traditional dress such as full wizard robes or dryads in plantwear. Elinor was already regretting she hadn't brought hers. It looked so much fun, and apart from holidays like Yew Day, she rarely got the chance to dryad up. But whatever they wore, one thing was clear—everyone at Magic-Con was there to have fun.

There were bursts of flames and screams of delight as mages showcased their more dramatic magic; stands showing new innovations such as magical cell phones where you didn't just Skype with your friends, you could literally sit in a room in cyberspace with them; and vacation tours where for a few magic bucks you could transport to the destination of your dreams without leaving your sitting room, so you could still take care of your cat while enjoying the sun in Hawaii.

They stopped at a stand decorated with some robust saplings, where a very sharp-looking dryad in a woven plant-fiber business suit was handing out flyers.

"Well, hello," he cried. "My kinda people at last! How are you? Did you just arrive?"

Elinor, who hated being sold anything, instantly stiffened.

"Yes, thanks."

He handed her a flyer, and she noted his perfect smile and the high-end vulcanized plant leather on the soles of his shoes. From the look of them, she suspected he was very good at what he did. For a moment she imagined him in tight swimming trunks on the beach, dribbling sun cream over her back and massaging it into her skin with his strong hands.

The flyer had a picture of a glass vial decorated in sparkles, with a test tube vial next to it. It read:

The Amazing Magical Grow Tube
Accelerate your saplings' growth by 333%!
Only $39.99
Plus shipping and taxes.
Limited Time Offer!

It looked interesting, but Elinor was against messing with nature and preferred to grow her trees the old-fashioned way. In any case, she had read about this, and though these saplings did well, they tended to be weaker as they aged. She smiled politely, and though she held onto the flyer, she moved pointedly on.

Unperturbed, the young salesman turned his charms on the next passerby.

"Well, hello," he cried. "My kinda people at last! How are you? Did you just arrive?"

Her fantasy about tight swimming trunks and a sun cream massage evaporated. Elinor tossed the flyer in the first available trash can.

There were stalls showcasing practical magic for its use in the kitchen to miniaturized solar systems showing how magically generated forcefields could help with global warming. Elinor smiled at the simulated glacier that looked perfectly cold and frosty, not melting one bit as a blazing purple field arced over it.

Marianne and the others were a little ways behind her, still fascinated by the wares on a simple herbal stand. Just ahead was a stand for ParaWand, the global paranormal bank chain of which Fanny's family were major stockholders. It was decorated in purple and gold banners, each one depicting a leprechaun waving a wand over his pot of gold as it sparkled, filled to the brim, overflowed, then started over. As well as the banners, there was a large cut-out of several uncommonly attractive goblins standing in front of some impressive houses and exotic-looking flying carpets. It read:

Finance your dream today!
Failure to repay may result in forfeiture of your soul.

Elinor spotted Fanny and John at once, who were inspecting the stand and talking softly to the young goblin attending it, so she surmised they were talking shop. Fanny's figure was back to normal, though there was no sign of a wee goblin-snotling or a buggy or anything. Not that Elinor would have called the child a snotling out loud; John had told her goblins hated that name.

"Oh gosh, I didn't know you two would be here or I'd have phoned to say we were coming!" Elinor said. "Where's the new, um, baby?"

"Well, hello!" John said, smiling warmly and treating Elinor to a stilted hug. "How lovely to see you. I had no idea you were coming either. The little demon child is back at home with the nanny. We thought he was little too young to travel just yet. And Fanny said she needed a break, so here we are. Look at you, all nice and suntanned. The cottage life seems to agree with you. Are you here all on your own?"

"No, no," Elinor said. "I came with some others." She pointed behind her.

Fanny looked neither pleased nor annoyed to see Elinor there, though she did arch her eyebrows in surprise. No doubt she was wondering how Elinor could afford it, since her brain was wired solely for dollars and cents. Fanny looked around her, as did Elinor, and she pointed out Marianne and the others who were still a little ways off.

"Who is that with Marianne?"

"That's Betsy Middleton—she invited Marianne and me down. The two younger ones are Lucy and Anne Steele. They came down with us too. The wizard is Chris Brandon, a friend of the Middletons."

A strange look came over her brother's face, like someone had hit him over the head with something heavy and he was waking up dazed.

"I've seen that succubus girl before.

Oh, for an hour alone with her, or more!"

As soon as the words escaped his lips, he clamped his hand over his mouth looking guilty.

Fanny gave him a sharp, threatening look, so John looked away in case his mouth should get him in any more trouble.

"Lucy?" Elinor asked. "You know her?" She wondered what kind of spell must have been placed on John; was it succubus magic? Where could he have met Lucy, and more importantly, why would he have met her? No doubt Fanny was wondering the exact same thing. Her sister-in-law looked positively fit to explode.

At that moment, Marianne must have spotted them, because she dashed over and greeted them warmly. "Well hey, fancy meeting you all here. Let me introduce you to Anne and Lucy Steele, our new friends."

Elinor looked behind her to where Betsy was talking animatedly to the dryad salesman. She looked happy enough, though the salesman looked like he might fall asleep at any moment. Chris, bless his heart, remained at her side, patient as ever. Still, Elinor had to conceal a grin. Poor Chris.

Lucy locked eyes with John, but before she returned the greeting, she took his hand and seemed to hold it for a little longer than was socially polite. As she did so, the funny, dazed look returned to his face. Elinor braced herself, not sure how Fanny would react if....

"Are you well?" she asked, still not letting go.

"I, um, yes, I'm fine," John said. "Um, nice to meet you."

"Have we met before?" Lucy asked.

"Um, I don't think so," John said.

Thank Gaia, he's dropped his embarrassing rhyming couplets, Elinor thought.

Fanny was critically looking Anne and Lucy up and down, and Elinor suspected she was checking out how affluent they were and whether they were worth getting to know.

"Nice to meet you all," Fanny said. "Where are you staying?"

"At the beach. Betsy has a house right on the ocean," Marianne explained.

If little dollar signs could have popped into Fanny's eyes, they would have. "Oh, very nice. Anywhere near Cocoa Beach?"

"Slap bang in the middle of it."

From her tone, Elinor knew Marianne had enjoyed that, just to see the look on Fanny's face. But then a thought seemed to occur to her, and she was suddenly less cheeky.

"Lucy says your brother is supposed to be coming to the Con," Marianne said, stealing a glance at Elinor. "Is he about?"

The superior, smug smile returned to Fanny's face as she said, "Why, yes! I saw him just a minute ago. Let me see." She stood up on tiptoe, looking over the heads of the other visitors. "Why, yes. There he is, over by the bar. Figures."

Her brother must have felt her gaze because he looked over. Fanny began to frantically wave. Elinor stood frozen, her heart pounding like a drum, yet ever conscious of Lucy, whose eyes were boring into her like daggers.

Be calm, be calm. Don't let her get to you, Elinor thought.

"Why, hello," said a friendly male voice. It wasn't Edward's. Masking her surprise, Elinor took a deep breath and turned. She had never seen this other man in her life.

"This is my *other* brother, Robert," Fanny said with some delight. "You won't have met him, Elinor. Robert is just back from Europe and wasn't at my wedding, naughty fish. Robert, these are my sisters-in-law, Elinor and Marianne Dashwood."

Robert's ears pricked up at their names, and his smile faded a little.

"Oh yes, I've heard of you, um, ladies." He glanced at Fanny as if confirming something, and Elinor caught a discreet nod pass between them. "Um, very nice to meet you both." His weak smile wasn't reflected in his eyes.

"Nice to meet you, too," Marianne said. Elinor didn't respond. She could not bear people who thought themselves above others. She treated him to a frosty smile instead and didn't much care how he took it.

"Oh? And exactly what have you heard of us?" Elinor asked, trying to sound as upbeat as she could.

"Oh, nothing bad, I assure you," Robert greased.

"And these," Fanny interrupted, "are...um? Sorry, please remind me again. I'm afraid I have a memory like a sieve."

"I'm Lucy Steele, and this is my sister, Anne," Lucy said, putting herself forward and shaking Robert's hand eagerly.

Hmm. Elinor was surprised Lucy didn't look the least bit sorry this was Robert and not Edward. But who knew what she was thinking or feeling? Elinor was pretty sure Lucy would make full use of any chance to ingratiate herself with the family. She felt a little pang of jealousy that Lucy was the favored one, and not her.

"Ooh, at last, a handsome beau come to join us," Anne said. "I was beginning to despair of meeting anyone good-looking at this Magic-Con. Really, what's the point of coming all this way if there are no men to play with. It's been all rush, rush, rush since we got here, not that I'm complaining, mind you, oh no. I'm sure it was very kind of Betsy to invite us, yes it was. Is my hair straight? He-he."

"Anne! Hush now, you're babbling," Lucy exclaimed. "Please forgive my sister. She gets overly excited when she meets new people."

"Not at all," Robert said, his eyes transfixed on Lucy as she smiled demurely. "Have you been here long? I'd be more than delighted to show you around. Both of you, that is. My, my, two succubus sisters together. Now there's a wicked thought." He chuckled to himself.

Whatever that wicked thought was, Elinor was not destined to find out, because without another word, Robert linked his arms to both sisters and led Lucy and Anne off into the crowd. Elinor thought she ought to feel slighted; however, he'd done her a favor of sorts. Any time spent without the luscious Miss Steeles in tow was a bonus. She felt as if she could breathe again. They really were a pair of sour dill pickles.

Fanny smiled her approval, though Elinor suspected that came more from the snub to Elinor and Marianne than from any particular like for Lucy or Anne. But then Fanny caught sight of her husband, who once again was staring all googly-eyed after Lucy, and she elbowed him sharply in the ribs.

"Ow!" he cried. "That hurt."

Fanny's smile returned.

"Is Edward not here?" Marianne asked as soon as the others were gone. "Lucy said he would be."

"Yes and no," Fanny said. "He was here when we set up the stand this morning, but he didn't hang around. He got a text from someone and decided to cut out short. Probably a friend or something. Edward has soooo many friends. Anyway, he went back to the hotel as soon as he was done. From what I gather, we probably won't see him for the rest of the day."

Poor Edward, Elinor thought. Had he gone and bound himself to a woman he didn't love? Is that why he'd made a quick getaway? She would be heartily sorry if that were true. Lucy, she didn't give a fig about, but the thought of Edward being miserable for the rest of his life cut her to the quick.

"Well, well, must mingle," Fanny said. "We're here to network, after all. Maybe we'll see you all later?"

She wandered off without another word.

"We're staying at the Cauldron," John said over his shoulder as they were leaving. "I'll text you later."

Elinor nodded.

Marianne, who had been looking about for Willoughby ever since they'd arrived, suddenly froze solid and clutched Elinor's arm.

"Oh Gaia, Elinor, look! He's here."

"He is? Where?"

"Over there, just ahead. Has he seen me? Is he looking this way?"

Elinor scanned the sea of faces, but it took her a while to spot Willoughby in the crowd. She saw him at last, standing a little farther along the bar where they had first seen Robert. But he wasn't alone. He was drinking with some companions, and Elinor froze. Was that...a demon? From where she stood, she couldn't see his features too clearly, but there was no mistaking those horns and that aura.

Whoever it was, Willoughby had his head bowed and was laughing. But there was something affected in his laugh; it didn't sound like him at all. He looked like quite another incubus altogether.

Marianne looked like she was going to bolt over to him, but Elinor grabbed her arm, stopping her just in time. "Wait, Marianne, think. Did you send him a text this morning, telling him we'd be here?"

"I did." Marianne wrenched her arm free but couldn't take her eyes off him.

"Did he answer it?"

"No."

"Has he answered any of your texts?"

"No. You know he hasn't. And dammit, Elinor, I have a right to know why, don't you think? You can't just shut people off like that. Something awful must have happened, and I deserve to know what it was. Maybe it was a misunderstanding. Whatever it was, I need to speak to him now. I didn't come all this way just to look at him."

"Oh Marianne, I just don't want to see you hurt any more than you already have been. He's an incubus, dammit. I know you hate me bringing that up, but it's what he is. You could never have been a couple. You're too different, like...like cosmic and elemental magic. Like the stars and the earth. Don't hurt yourself anymore, please?"

But she saw her words had fallen upon deaf ears. Her sister was too emotional, too distressed to think straight. This time when Marianne set off, Elinor let her go. Elinor was wise enough to know there was no stopping her. And Marianne did have a point. To abandon her like that was just plain cruel. If Marianne could get some sense of closure from this, then good luck to her. She was entitled, after all. What was the worst that could happen?

Hating every step, Elinor followed her. Marianne was marching into battle against the unknown and needed a friend at her side. Oh Gaia, if only this could have been handled privately, that would have been Elinor's choice. But that was never Marianne's way.

As soon as Marianne was close, she called out. "Willoughby!"

The excitement in her voice was unmistakable. For a split second, when Willoughby turned to see her, Elinor thought he looked just as excited too. But then he seemed to remember the company he was in, and his face hardened.

"Hello, Marianne. Elinor. I didn't expect to see you here."

"Willoughby, by Gaia! Didn't you get my messages? I sent enough. I told you we were coming."

"I read a couple."

Elinor's attention drifted to the demon by his side. Now that they were this close, she could plainly see the demon-slit eyes and the red hair. More annoying than anything, he had a dry smile on his face, like he was enjoying himself. And beside him was a young nymph. She looked perhaps a little older than Marianne and Elinor, but not by much. She oozed money. Was that what this was about? Had the slimy SOB gone and better-dealed her sister?

"Why aren't you answering them?"

"Come on, Marianne," Elinor said. "I think we'd better go."

"No, wait," Marianne said. Her face had turned a nasty shade of pale, and suddenly Elinor remembered her sister hadn't eaten a thing all day. Elinor took her hand, and it was trembling. This was not good. "I want him to answer me."

"I've been rather busy," Willoughby said.

"Busy?" Marianne repeated. "I thought we were...friends. I don't understand. Did I do something wrong? What did I do? Tell me!"

Marianne could contain herself no longer. Her emotions got the better of her, and she began to sob violently. And it wasn't the delicate kind of polite, dainty weeping Elinor sometimes saw on the Hallmark channel. This was full-on, body-racking convulsions. People began to turn their heads to watch and wonder what on earth was going on.

The more upset Marianne became, the more the demon smiled. He was just lapping this raw outpouring of emotion up. And then Willoughby did the nastiest thing. He turned his back on Marianne, dismissing her from his thoughts. Right there, in front of everyone at Magic-Con, he left her sister dangling and in tears.

Elinor wanted to grab Willoughby by his wings and turn him around and demand he explain himself. No way could Marianne have done anything to deserve this. But before she could do anything, Marianne began to hyperventilate, and she would have fallen to the floor if Chris hadn't come out of nowhere and caught her in his arms. Chris and Elinor exchanged worried glances, and with a hostile glare at Willoughby, Chris gently walked her away, back toward the exit. Elinor gave Willoughby a final scathing look, just catching his eye as she did so. He had been chuckling, but when he saw Elinor's look, his smile faltered a little and was replaced with something like shame. But not enough of it. After what he'd just done to her sister, Elinor wished he would rot in hell, along with the demon now laughing beside him.

"Trust me, you can do a lot better than these two, sweetie," she said to the nymph, whose eyes widened in shock. Elinor turned, and as quickly as she could, hurried after Chris and Marianne.

Chapter Twenty-Two

THE CONFESSION OF COLONEL CHRISTOPHER BRANDON, USMC

ELINOR SIPPED HER TEA AND STARED AT THE BEAUTIFUL VIEW overlooking the beach and the blue waters of the Gulf of Mexico. She'd enjoy it more if she had someone she could share it with. Her thoughts wandered to Edward, as they often did, and she wondered where he was and what he was doing now. It was odd she hadn't seen him. Lucy had been darn sure he was coming, and if she didn't know better, she would have said he was ignoring her.

Her gaze wandered to the clock. It was almost eleven. Lucy and Anne had gone shopping, and Betsy was out visiting friends. Elinor wished Marianne would get up. Marianne hadn't said a single word since her tussle with Willoughby yesterday, and she had gone straight to her room the second they were back at the house. She'd skipped dinner, and when Elinor later knocked on her door, Marianne was either sleeping or just ignored her.

She didn't want to enter her sister's room uninvited, but if Marianne didn't come down soon, she felt she might have to. Fortunately, there was no need. She was just thinking these thoughts when she heard footsteps on the stairs, and looking up, there was Marianne. Her dryad skin was cracked from weeping, and the first thing she reached for was a box of lubricant tissues sitting on the side table.

After blowing her nose half a dozen times, Marianne handed her phone to Elinor.

"What?"

"Just read it." Marianne sat down across from Elinor and turned her nose up at the cup Elinor nudged in her direction.

Elinor shrugged and read the text on Marianne's phone.

M. I didn't want to be blunt, but you forced my hand yesterday. You might as well know, I'm with someone else now. I wish you well but please stop texting me. It's embarrassing for us both. W.

"What a total bastard," Elinor said, shaking her head even as she read it. "I can't believe this is even the same Willoughby."

"I know, right?" Marianne said. "I mean, that wasn't written by the man I knew. He sounds like a whole different person. All right, maybe he could jerk around at times, but he was never a total bastard. Not like that."

Elinor agreed with Marianne's assessment. She'd seen them together, had heard them talking and laughing, had seen the love shining in their eyes. The two had been besotted and inseparable. This latest text and yesterday's bewildering behavior made absolutely no sense to her, and she didn't know him half so well as her sister. No wonder Marianne was a mess. She looked up to find Marianne watching her, hoping perhaps Elinor could explain it, when clearly, she couldn't understand it herself.

"I'm sorry, I really am. I don't know what to say." She slid the phone across the table.

"I do." Marianne bit her lip and looked out the window. "I want to go home. Now. How long do we have to stay here?"

"You know how long. Another week."

"Maybe Betsy can call in a favor at the airline and book an early flight home? I think I'll die if I have to stay for much longer."

"You can ask, but I doubt it."

Marianne slouched a little in her chair. "I suppose it would be a shitty thing to do. After all, it's not Betsy's fault, but still."

Marianne dabbed carefully at the side of her eyes. Elinor knew herself how delicate their skin was when destroyed by sorrow. Her purse was by her feet, and she reached in and pulled out a vial of special lotion she kept for such occasions. "There, put a dab of that on your fingers and rub it in. It will stop it from flaking."

Marianne stared at the prettily wrapped lotion. "How is this doing online?"

Elinor smiled. "Still my best line. My customers say it's the best anti-aging cream ever. And it will stop those cracks in their tracks. Go on. Dab it on."

"Thanks." Marianne did as instructed.

While Marianne massaged the cream into her temples, Elinor's phone buzzed. Looking down she saw it was a text from Chris. He wasn't one for casual communication, so this was probably important. She picked it up and read it.

"Chris is on his way over," she said. "Looks like he'll be here in a few minutes."

Marianne looked glummer still. "No, sorry, I'm not in the mood right now. Can you tell him I'm ill or something? I'm going back to my room to lie down."

Elinor shrugged. "All right, if you say so, but at some point, you need to thank him for last night. He didn't have to come to your rescue, you know. He's just concerned about you, that's all."

Marianne nodded. "I know—just...not yet." She slipped quietly from the room, staring dejectedly at her phone.

Elinor was worried. She hadn't seen Marianne's skin as bad as that since she'd caught flora measles at eight years old. If only there was something she could do. She'd go and have it out with Willoughby herself if she thought it would do any good, but she knew instinctively it wouldn't. Screw him. He didn't matter anymore. Only her sister's heart did.

She sat there thinking until the doorbell rang. True to his word, Chris had been just around the corner when he'd texted.

As soon as she opened the door, she could see he was worried about Marianne, even before he uttered a word.

"How is she?" he asked as he crossed the threshold and wiped his feet on the doormat. "Is she any better?" Elinor tried not to smile. As ex-military, Chris typically liked to dress formally, so she was a little weirded out by his khaki shorts, sandals, and bright Hawaiian shirt. He looked very different, younger even. It was funny what the warm Florida weather did to people.

"A little. I think last night was a shock for her more than anything. Can I get you something to drink?"

"Um, no thank you," he replied. "I won't be staying long. I just wanted to be sure she's okay."

"I think so," Elinor said. "But I don't think she's up to seeing anyone right now. I hope you understand."

He paused for a second, and Elinor could see that he did, though he looked disappointed just the same.

"I was about to make myself some more tea?" Elinor said. "This warm Florida weather can be exhausting to a dryad. We have to stay moist," she said, stifling a giggle.

Chris shook his head, but she ushered him into the kitchen and invited him to a chair at the table, which he gratefully took. After she pulled a cup from a cupboard, she turned around and asked, "Are you sure you don't want one? It won't be any trouble to pour a second cup?"

"Oh, go on then, you twisted my arm," he said. "I'm surprised you're here all on you own. Where are the others?"

"Oh, Lucy and Anne are out shopping. I'm sure you're surprised by that news. I don't know if they do anything else. My brother is taking us out to dinner tonight at some posh place, and they wanted to find something nice. I'm not sure about Betsy. She said she had some friends to visit, but she didn't say how long she'd be. It's fine though, I like my own company— I mean, I wish Marianne was feeling up to doing something, but it's okay that she's not. You know what I mean. I was thinking of catching up on my reading or something. I never have time up in Maine, not with my potion business and everything."

"I can believe that. You girls are always running about doing something or other. Can I help you with that?"

Elinor pulled a gallon of milk from the fridge and poured some into a small decanter. She grinned before setting it on the table in front of him. "No, I think I can manage. I am strong like a bull. Sugar? Milk?"

"One, please."

They sat in silence for a moment as the tea brewed in the pot.

"Um, you know, I made this tea myself. Well actually, Marianne and I both did. But this is my favorite blend."

He nodded admiringly.

Elinor wondered what exactly he was here to say, but she sensed he was shy by nature, and she didn't want to press him too hard. Whatever it was, if he wanted to say it, she trusted he would find a way.

After a little while, the tea had steeped enough, and she poured some from the teapot into both cups.

"Thanks," he said as Elinor nudged over the sugar bowl. "I, um, actually, there was something I've been thinking of saying, although I've been on the fence for a while, not sure whether I should interfere or not. After all, your sister's affairs are none of my business, and well, she's made it perfectly clear at times that she doesn't...well, in any case, I want to tell you now."

Elinor stirred her tea, letting it cool, but didn't interrupt him.

"Do you remember the day of my barbecue—no, wait. I should probably go back further than that. Elinor, do you mind if I share something that's totally private? I don't ask for myself, but I share this secret with another."

"You don't have to tell me anything, not if you don't want to."

Chris shook his head. "It's not whether I want to or not. But I think if I tell you this, well, I think it might help Marianne. Maybe not now, but in the end—at least I hope it will."

Elinor blew on her tea, and Chris did the same as he organized his thoughts.

"As you know, I'm a very private man. I'm not one to gossip, and I don't like it when people do it to others."

Elinor simply nodded. She could see that. Chris had never spoke ill of anyone, not in her hearing. He barely ever practiced magic in front of them, which was odd, since most wizards and warlocks loved to strut their stuff every chance they got. Chris just wasn't showy like that. She liked him all the better for it.

"I have no family, not now, but I was in love once. So much so that I wanted to marry her and was delighted when she said yes."

That was a surprise. "Oh. I never knew."

"It was quite a while before you came to Maine. Two years, I think. I'm not sure even Betsy knows. Lord love her, she's a good soul, but she loves a good gossip, and well, you know my feelings on that." He took a sip of his tea. "This is excellent," he said, tipping his cup toward her.

"Thank you."

He was lost in thought for a while.

"Her name was Eliza. She was a bit younger than me, not that I mind. And no, don't look at me like that. I just found her charming, very much like your sister Marianne. She, too, was a dryad and had a thing for music, and she had a voice like a lark. I could listen to her talk night and day."

Elinor laughed. "I wasn't looking at you *like that*. I was just laughing."

"Anyway, everything was going great—at least, I thought it was. But as the date of our wedding grew closer, she grew more and more distant. Her skin began to look, ugh, sounds awful, but like, um...."

"Flaky?" Elinor finished for him. "Like dry tree bark?"

"Yes, I suppose, for want of a better word. I didn't realize that was a dryad sorrow thing. I mean, I do now, I looked it up. But at the time, I had no idea what was going on with her."

He took another sip of his tea, and she sensed he was close to the point of his story.

"A few days before we were due to be married, she disappeared. There was no note, nothing. I didn't know what happened and feared the worst. We put out a missing persons alert, but I heard nothing from her from that day until the date of the barbecue, when out of the blue she sent me a text.

"It said she was in trouble. I was bewildered, totally in shock to tell you the truth. At that point I never expected to hear from her again. But then suddenly, there she was."

"So that's why you ran away from us that day."

"Exactly," Chris said. "I didn't know what else to do. It had been my first communication in forever, and I didn't want to risk losing her again. She was in trouble with the police, and I was afraid she might make a run for it. I had to go to her."

"I can't blame you," Elinor interjected. "I'd have done exactly the same."

He smiled warmly. But then his smile faded.

"She was in such a state when I found her. Her once-beautiful skin looked more like the bark of a tree than the youthful bloom I had loved. Not that I wouldn't have married her just as she was; I still loved her, after a fashion. But life had been cruel to her, brutally so. I won't bore you with the details, but when I found her, she was so broken the doctors didn't think she had all that long. All her friends had abandoned her, and I was the only person in the world she thought she could turn to."

Elinor shuddered.

"Believe me, I did everything I could, got her the best care and found her the best comfort money could buy. She's on the mend now, but her spirit is gone. Eliza is not the girl I fell in love with, and we both know it."

A shadow crossed his face, and he finished the last of his tea with a grimace. When he returned his cup to its saucer, it rattled. "Now I suppose I should come to the point. While I was with her, she confided in me what started her troubles."

Elinor was no fool. She could guess the rest. But she kept silent, thinking it was probably important for him to say it—not just to hear the name, but so Chris had the chance to unburden himself.

"I'm sure you guessed it, but that bastard Willoughby set her on the path to destruction. He seduced her before we were bonded and delighted her with the bright lights of the casino life, staying with her until all the money ran out. In the meantime, he got her into all sorts of crap, drugs not the least of them, and before she knew it, she lost control of everything."

Ugh, drugs. With their plant-blended genetics, dryads were incredibly intolerant of commercial human drugs. Their reactions were swift, and the results could be devastating. *Foolish, foolish girl,* she thought. A dryad ought to know better. "She never thought to reach out to you? To ask for your help?"

"I asked her that. But she said no. She was too ashamed. In the beginning she thought she could handle it. When the time was right, she thought she could turn things around again. Isn't that the addict mantra?

"So." He took a deep breath. "That morning when I visited you, and there was a knock at your door and Willoughby walked in? It was all I could do to stop myself from murdering him there and then, and to hell with the consequences. If not for the fact I have fully committed myself to ensuring my dear Eliza regains her vitality, your mother would have had a dead incubus on her rug. And who knows? Perhaps that might happen still. It's a question of timing and opportunity. I swear I'd...."

At last, Elinor could see it. Funny she hadn't noticed it before, his boiling-hot hatred of Willoughby only *just* kept under control. Every time he spoke his name, Elinor noticed his hands curl into claws, as if he was imagining them tightening around Willoughby's throat, throttling the life out of him.

She reached across the table and gently rest her hand on his, letting him know it was okay, that she completely understood his feelings.

Chris sighed. "Anyway, I wanted to tell you this, not that I give one jot about that idiot, but because, well, I thought perhaps in time, Marianne might come to see this not as the beginning of the end, but as a lucky escape. I'll leave it up to you whether you think she ought to know or not. But personally, I think it would help her in the end."

Elinor agreed. "Thank you. I think you're right. I'll give it some thought. So what's going to happen to Eliza now?"

His smile returned a little. "As I said, she's doing much better. She agreed to go into a program. The doctors are hopeful they can help her, and I'd like to believe them. If she gets a little better, I'll maybe help her get back on her feet, if she'll let me. I'd like to help her. But the rest is up to her."

Chris pushed his chair back and stood up. He looked a little relieved, and Elinor was glad he'd shown enough trust in her to confide so much. He was a good man. Maybe, when all this business with Willoughby was over, her sister might come to appreciate him more, in time.

"Thank you," Elinor said as Chris prepared to leave. "We're lucky to have you as our friend. You've been very kind."

Chris shook his head, a little uncomfortable as ever with a compliment.

"Give my regards to Marianne," he said. And with a final kind smile, he made his goodbye. Elinor was left alone again to pour herself another cup of tea as she gathered her thoughts.

Wow, that had been unexpected. Deep down, she had always known Willoughby was a douche, but that was way beyond anything she'd ever imagined. And Chris, too. If she were honest, she'd always thought of him as something of a wuss—nice, sure, but he had always kept his feelings hidden from view. Not today. Today his anger was plain to see. She admired him for it.

Oh, if only Edward were here and he were free. It was so unfair to be in such a place of beauty but to be stuck in this house with a sister who just would not listen and would not believe anyone who said anything bad about Willoughby—a goddamn *incubus,* for Gaia's sake. Boy, she wanted

Edward so bad right now. She needed someone who would listen to her feelings, and who she could just be herself with. Elinor walked to the window and stared out across the ocean, and just like Marianne had done a little earlier, Elinor wished with all her heart she could put this place behind her and go home.

Chapter Twenty-Three

TATTOOS AND PIERCINGS

THE LAST THING IN THE WORLD ELINOR WANTED TO DO WAS GO TO THIS dinner tonight. She'd been cooped up on her own all day, and though getting out would be a good thing, spending the evening with her sister-in-law, Fanny, was something else. She wished there was a way to get out of it, but she couldn't think of a damned thing.

Betsy was lying down with a headache, so she could hardly use that excuse. She wished she'd thought of it first.

The house was madness. Anne's high-pitched screeches could be heard through the walls and doors, and more than once Elinor wondered what on earth the two sisters were up to in their bedroom. If Betsy really did have a sore head, she'd be suffering right now. She wondered why the succubi weren't being a little more considerate. Perhaps being self-centered little bitches was a succubi trait.

On the upside, Marianne had come down at last. Her skin still looked a little rough around the eyes but was much improved from earlier.

"You look nice," Elinor said, admiring Marianne's choice of a wish-grey all-in-one dress that showed off her figure perfectly. "I don't think I've seen you in that before?"

"No, it's new. I treated myself. I bought it for Willoughby with the last of my savings, but…" Her voice trailed off, and she sat down across from Elinor at the kitchen table.

"Well, you look amazing. It's his loss."

Elinor's heart was heavy with worry. "Was I stupid to tell you what Chris told me earlier? I thought you should know, but I suppose I could have waited until we were back in Maine."

Marianne shook her head. "No, no. I'm glad I know—well, not glad. At least I know what Willoughby's like now. He's just a stupid incubus after all. I thought, well, I thought maybe he was better than that. Oh well."

Elinor hated how flat Marianne sounded. It wasn't like her at all, and if she hadn't hated Willoughby before, she totally hated him now.

"You look nice," Marianne remarked. There was a fresh round of stomping, and her gaze turned to the ceiling. "Anything new from the slut sisters?"

"Marianne!"

Marianne shrugged and stroked the skin on the back of her hand. That, too, looked a little better.

"Keep rubbing my lotion in for a few days, and you'll be fine," Elinor advised. "And no. They came in earlier with a truckload of shopping bags, but they ran upstairs and haven't been down since."

Marianne looked as if she couldn't care less. "I just hope this'll be quick. Don't let Fanny start on me. I'm not in the mood for her snideness."

"I'll do my best."

Upstairs, a bedroom door burst open, and the two succubus sisters came bouncing down the stairs. They were giggling and laughing, and Elinor checked the time. The sooner the Uber came and they were out of here, the sooner Betsy's head could get better.

"Well, we've made a day and a half of it, to be sure," Anne chuckled. "And what do you make of this? Isn't it amazing? Lucy said I probably shouldn't, but I thought I might as well as not, and now I really love it. What do you think?"

At first Elinor wasn't sure what Anne was talking about, but then she saw the glint in the light. "You pierced your wing?"

"Yes! It's all the rage in Europe, the man said. Everyone's getting them done. Course, it being my first time I just had the one. But now I know how easy it is, I might have him pierce me all over. Go on, Lucy, show 'em your new tattoo!"

Intrigued, Elinor stood up to take a look.

"Oh Anne, shush! I told you it was meant to be a secret. I swear, my daft sister can't keep her mouth shut about anything." Still, Lucy looked pleased to be the center of attention, and she turned around. Elinor had already seen the saucy images on her arms and shoulders, but was still quite surprised when Lucy turned around and pushed the waist of her leather pants down so they could see the top of her butt crack. Elinor tried not to stare at that perfect heart-shaped succubi butt; it took all her willpower and several calming breaths before she could wrench her gaze away and concentrate on the tattoo instead. "Well? What do you think? Don't you think it looks awesome?"

Elinor wasn't sure what she was seeing at first; the tattoo site was still red raw. When she cocked her head to one side, she saw it was a dying rose with the initials E and L laced around it.

"I'm sure it'll be very pretty," she said, trying not to show her dislike. "Once it's all healed up and everything. Would you like some of my balm? It will take some of the burn out."

Marianne barely glanced at the tattoo. "Nice."

At least her disinterest kept her from wondering about those initials. Lucy hadn't said it was okay to talk of her relationship with Edward yet, and Elinor had kept her lips zipped as promised, as hard as this was.

Lucy shook her head. "Nah, thanks, but I'm used to it. The pain doesn't last for long."

Elinor wondered what Edward would make of it. It hardly seemed his thing, but perhaps Lucy knew him better than she did. Perhaps he was secretly into sexy goth succubi with tats and piercings? Elinor felt positively plain by comparison and hated the feelings of inadequacy that washed over her. What chance did a dryad have alongside a succubus? Small wonder Edward had lost interest in her so quickly.

"The crazy things we all do down at the beach, eh!" Anne beamed. "I can't wait to show everyone. It's a real diamond, you know. Do you think it'll look tacky if I have more all along the length of my wing?" She flexed one, almost knocking a glass off the shelf. "Whoops! Silly me." She reeled the wing back in. "I can be a klutz sometimes, can't I? What time is that Uber coming? I don't know about anyone else, but I'm starved and if you dryad girls weren't here, I'd fly there directly, I swear I would."

"They should be here any moment," Elinor said, standing over by the window and pouring a glass of water. A car drew up at the bottom of the driveway, and the driver leaned forward to look at the house. Elinor waved to him, telling him she'd seen him. "In fact, here they are. You all go on and jump in. I'll just run this up to Betsy and make sure she's all right. I'll be right behind you."

"All right, but don't be long," Anne said.

Elinor bit her lip. It was bad enough having one succubus sister rip her heart out, but to be ordered about by the ditsy second sibling was more than a mortal dryad could bear. *Just a few more days,* she thought to herself, *and I will be back among my beloved trees in Maine.*

"You go on," Lucy said to the others. "I'll wait for Elinor."

Better and better. After climbing upstairs, Elinor knocked on Betsy's door, but there was no answer. She put her ear to it and heard a reassuring snore on the other side. Ever so gently, she opened the door, tiptoed across the room, deposited the glass on the bedside table, then turned and tiptoed back out.

From the top of the stairs, she saw Lucy waiting at the bottom. She steeled herself for yet another of the gazillion comments Lucy tried to make sound innocent, but which she knew came with poison barbs.

"How is she?" Lucy asked, feigning a concern she hadn't thought of just a few minutes ago.

"Sleeping soundly. I didn't want to wake her."

"You're such a sweetie."

Elinor braced herself for the punch.

"So, do you think Edward's gonna like my tattoo? I'm surprised Marianne didn't comment on the initials. I didn't think when I showed her, but I could've given the whole game away."

Elinor chose not to answer the first question. "I suppose she had her mind on other things."

"Oh my, yes. The Willoughby thing." She rolled her eyes in feigned sympathy. "The poor girl. To be *so* humiliated like that, and in front of *everyone*. I think I'd have died if that were me, though to be frank, I'd never let him get away with anything so wicked."

"Yes, well, perhaps we'd better get a move on before Anne starves to death."

They headed for the door, but Elinor had the distinct feeling Lucy was deliberately trying to slow them down.

"Do you think Edward will be there? I mean, Fanny will be, and they're all supposed to be in town for this Magic-Con thing. Oh Gaia, and we're going to meet his mom. What if she doesn't like me? Sweet heavens, if she doesn't, I think I'll die."

"I dunno," Elinor replied. "I'd have thought if anyone knew if he was coming, you would. It's not like he writes to me." *Much.* "I can't say about his mom. She's a funny old thing." Elinor opened the door and stood aside so that Lucy was forced to walk ahead of her. "Anyway, I suppose the sooner we get there, the sooner we'll find out," Elinor said.

Pulling the door closed behind her, she waited until Lucy was squeezed into the back seat with the others before strolling purposely to the front of the car and sliding in next to the driver. Anything rather than get in the back with her.

It turned out that Fanny had a thing for raw food, and though her tastes were often extreme, they could all happily meet her halfway and eat sushi. The Gnawing Gastronomic—*GG* on its napkins—was an upscale, experimental sushi and Japanese dining experience that overlooked a private lake filled with hungry alligators, which the guests could feed while they were dining.

The place was packed solid with goblins, lighter-skinned half-goblins, and their larger hobgoblin brethren. There were a few other magical types, but this was a favorite hangout for their kind. The arrival of non-greenskins drew some curious glances, but none were hostile. Even goblins had a thing for succubi apparently, and Elinor shuddered as a few fish-slickened black tongues ran over their pointy teeth in appreciation. *Gross.*

Elinor knew they could never afford something so posh on their own, so she was glad their brother, John, had offered to foot the bill. That said, she didn't much care for the handfuls of live goldfish the diners were tossing over the banisters so they could watch the alligators snap and hiss. She hid her disgust, not wanting to appear too gauche—but boy, did it bother her.

The hostess led them through the open-air round tables to a very nice spot overlooking half a dozen alligators or so, happily climbing over each other to get to the food.

"Well, thank goodness you made it," John beamed, giving each of the girls a warm hug. "I was about to send out a search party." As he pulled back, he stared oddly at Lucy. "You both look fit, really swish—wanna know what I wish?"

Lucy snapped her fingers, and the rhyming stopped.

"Oh, you know us girls," Anne laughed. "I don't know about the others, but it took me forever to decide what to wear."

"Well, you're all here now," he said, resuming his seat and inviting them all to sit down.

Elinor took a seat by the solid fence overlooking the alligators. She tried not to knock over a bowl of goldfish as she sat down and took care that her limbs were tucked safely on the right side of the fence.

"Well, we're glad you made it," Fanny said, popping some raw salmon in her mouth. When she was mostly done chewing, she said, "So sorry, we couldn't wait for you. I was positively famished so ordered some appetizers. I hope you don't mind."

"Not at all," Elinor replied.

"We ordered wine and water for everyone, so please, help yourselves," John said kindly.

As the other girls squeezed around the large table, Elinor smiled politely at Fanny's mother, Mrs. Barbara Ferrars. They had met only on a few occasions—the wedding of course, and a couple of holiday get-togethers. She was a pure goblin, though she had married someone outside of her species, which was kind of intriguing since goblins were so proud. She didn't return the smile, but then Elinor never expected her to. So instead, her shrewd eyes narrowed, and when she looked away, Elinor and Marianne exchanged knowing glances. Mrs. Ferrars had made it plain from day one that she considered the Dashwood family inferior, tolerating John merely because of her daughter.

"You two must be the Steele girls," Barbara said pointedly to Lucy and Anne. "I've heard so many good things about *you*." She indicated her son Robert, who was sitting by her side and chomping down on some raw eel. He smiled warmly at Lucy and Anne, and Elinor tried not to be peeved he hadn't even said hello to her or Marianne. Elinor wondered whether they'd screwed Robert senseless the other night. Or at least, whether Anne did. Lucy might be saving herself for Edward, but with their kind, who knew? Perhaps she was being unkind. She lowered her eyes, hoping no one could guess what she was thinking.

"Why, thank you," Lucy beamed. "You're very kind." Lucy shot Elinor a furtive glance, and Elinor smiled and picked up her menu, desperate to hide behind it. It was all she could do to stop herself from telling them all to go get stuffed. She didn't give two monkeys what these idiots thought about her and her family. Who the heck did they think they were, constantly flaunting such meaningless fake superiority in her face? There was no difference between Barbara's family and the gators. Except the gators only take bites out of people when they're hungry.

"Not at all. You might as well know, I'm known for speaking my mind. Perhaps, if your schedule will allow, you and your sister will join us for tea at my hotel tomorrow morning? I could use a little young company while the others are working at the Magic-Con, seeing to our bank business."

Elinor knew the old bat was snubbing her on purpose, and she suspected Fanny had told her something of how things had gone on with Edward when they were together at Norland Park. That would put the old harridan's nose out of joint, that was for sure.

"We'd love that, wouldn't we, Anne?" Lucy beamed, delighted to be the center of attention.

"Ooh yes, indeed we would," Anne replied. "Though I don't suppose you have any nice men about the place? There's been a shocking lack of flirtation on this trip, I must say. Everyone said to me, 'Anne, go to Florida. There are hot men dripping from the ceiling down there. You're sure to meet up with lots of them.' And men there might be. But flirting? No, not a one. I might as well be back in the north for all the action I'm seeing down here. Do you think it might be the weather? I think it's the weather. All that sweating and dripping probably puts them off thinking about women and all that. Who knows? Do you think it's the weather?"

"Anne, hush now. You don't want Mrs. Ferrars thinking you're man-mad now, do you?" Lucy smiled awkwardly, though Elinor suspected she was more worried about what everyone would think about her by association.

"Well all right, but I'm just saying. What's a succubus supposed to do?"

The conversation was interrupted when a tall, hooded wraith hovered over them. His arms were folded before him, and Elinor noticed he had a few fingers missing from both hands. Clearly, he'd had some unfortunate dealings with the restaurant's pet alligators.

He said nothing, and Elinor wondered what he wanted, but without losing a beat, Fanny reeled off what she wanted from the menu, and the others quickly followed suit.

"Um, I'll just have the seared chicken wrap with a side of Krystal rolls," Elinor said. Raw fish wasn't her thing, but a walnut and avocado roll sounded pleasant enough.

When everyone was done with their order, the wraith, who hadn't written a thing down, bowed then turned transparent and floated off.

The table fell silent. Elinor covered her part of the awkwardness by reaching for the wine and pouring herself a glass. She passed it on to Marianne, who shook her head and passed it on to Lucy.

"Well, I must say, you're all a glum-looking lot," Barbara said, staring pointedly at Marianne.

Fanny leaned into her mother and whispered, "Willoughby," though they could all hear it.

"Ah."

Robert had no such scruples. "You have to admire the man. He knows how to live it up but is always one step ahead of the ladies. They all make a play for him, but he hasn't been caught yet, and I doubt he ever shall. He's too smart for that."

Marianne looked fit to burst into tears, and Elinor wasn't the only one to notice.

"Er, how is your mother?" John asked, trying to avoid a situation. "And Margaret? I imagine she was peeved to be left behind."

"A little," Elinor said. "But she has school."

"Ah."

"What about you?" Lucy asked, treating Robert to what Elinor assumed was her most winning smile. "I kind of got the impression you were a bit of a tease yourself. There hasn't been a woman to trap you?"

Robert put down his chopsticks and smiled saucily. "If there is, I haven't found her yet. Anyway, I'm not the real catch in the family. If you want a real winner, you should make a play for my brother, Edward. He's the real catch, and to be honest, I don't think it'd be that hard to nab him. He's more of a sucker for a pretty face, and he's going to inherit the lion's share of the family fortune. My portion is a mere pittance compared to his."

Elinor tried not to color at the mention of Edward's name. She was more than a little aware of Fanny and Barbara's scrutiny at this point, and if nothing else, she didn't want to give them the satisfaction of seeing her suffer. *Just a few more days, just a few more days,* she repeated in her head. Feeling a stab of hunger, she looked about for a breadstick. "Hell. Fanny, you ate all the breadsticks too? Couldn't you have had a snack before you left the house?"

"Oh well," Fanny said. "I'm sure we can order some more when the waiter comes back."

"Where is he?" Anne asked. "Edward, that is. I thought he might be coming tonight, on account of Lu—ow!"

Elinor felt the full force of the jolt as Lucy kicked her sister under the table. "On account of—losing—track of the time and missing a thing with his, um, friends."

Good recovery, Elinor thought.

"Eek no," Fanny said, looking about impatiently for the waiter. "We invited him, of course, but when we told him who was coming, he seemed determined to make other plans."

Fanny wasn't looking at her now, but Elinor didn't need telepathy to know who that was aimed at.

"Pity," Anne said. "I like Edward. He's always been good for a laugh."

"You know him then?" Barbara asked, an eyebrow dangerously raised.

"Oh, just a little," Lucy jumped in. "Not, um, well."

Satisfied, Barbara took a long sip of her wine. "I suspect my Edward will settle down soon enough. It is expected. He is my eldest, after all. I've been checking out a few suitable candidates. Heiresses of course, from the most noble goblin houses. I expect he'll do very well when the time comes."

"But surely you would want him to marry for love," Marianne said, speaking up at last. "I mean, money's all very well, but we know Edward. He has a good heart. I don't think he'd be happy with someone he didn't care for."

"Ha, love! What do we goblins care about that?" Barbara snorted.

"He's a half-goblin," Marianne said. "And half-druid, no? From what I've seen, he favors that side more than his goblin heritage. His sensibilities aren't that different to ours."

"More's the pity if he does," Barbara said. "I suppose he does rather take after his father. But I would have hoped a childhood full of thrashings and beatings would have cured him of any of that nonsense. Still, I would pity him if it didn't."

"Why's that?" Lucy asked.

"Because I would cut him off without a penny if he ran off and married the wrong sort. I've always been clear on that. But I'm not worried. Edward is a good boy, and he knows his duty. He will do the right thing, I am sure of it. At least, he'd better."

The conversation was interrupted by the return of the wraith and a few other servers. It was time to eat. Elinor watched with admiration as, despite his mutilations, the waiter was able to balance multiple plates at once.

Fanny and her mother were less enthralled. As the servers went about plating, their goblin hands dipped freely into the bowls of goldfish left for the guests on the table. Elinor watched in disgust as they alternated between gnawing on the little live wrigglers themselves or tossing their brethren to the snapping jaws of the alligators below. She shuddered, weighing which of the two fates she found more distasteful. Deciding her sympathies were with the alligators, she took a sip of her wine and wished they were all back in Maine, away from this dreadful circus.

She owed Fanny and her mother and brother nothing, not even lip service. They were rude to her and rude to her family, and she could not overlook this. The thought of chucking them all into the alligator pit after their food was suddenly very appealing. Although the gators would probably spit them out again—too chewy, especially Fanny. She sniggered at the thought, and Marianne smiled at her.

"What's so funny?"

"I'll tell you later," Elinor said, enjoying her seared chicken wrap. Her only regret was that she couldn't have shared it with Edward.

Chapter Twenty-Four

SEE YOU LATER, GATOR!

FOUR MORE SLEEPS BEFORE THEIR FLIGHT HOME. ELINOR HAD BEEN SLOW to drag herself out of bed this morning, but even though it was already ten, she still appeared to be the first of the girls up. Betsy was in the kitchen, fussing over something rather delicious-smelling on the stove.

"Good morning," Elinor said. "Are you feeling any better?"

"Ah, there you are, sweetie," Betsy said, barely turning around. "Much better, thanks. Though I must say, I woke up this morning famished and thought I'd make us all something sweet. I hope you're hungry. I'm making French toast."

Elinor thought about her meager meal the night before and had to confess that she was. "Totally. I could eat a horse. Can I help you?"

"No, no, just sit there at the table, or if you want, help yourself to some coffee. It won't be long. Lucy and Anne went out earlier. I offered them some breakfast, but it appears succubi don't like French toast. Who on earth doesn't like French toast? Anyway, they didn't want anything so off they went on one of their little strolls. I suspect you all had a good time last night. How's your brother and his family? Are they well?"

"He and Fanny are good. And yes, I suppose the wine flowed a little freely last night. I know Anne was blotto. I'm surprised she could get up so early."

Elinor pressed the button on the Keurig and waited as the machine gurgled and percolated. "You want some?" she asked.

Betsy motioned toward a mug on the counter by the stove. "No thank you, dear, I'm all set."

When it was done, Elinor tossed the hot K-Cup in the trash and opened the fridge to grab some half-and-half.

"I heard about Marianne's little ding-dong," Betsy said, lowering her voice though there was no need. No one could hear her upstairs. "I'm sorry to say, it's all over town. That's the trouble with having a permanent place down here. Everyone knows everyone's business. That's why I had to go lie down last night. My poor head was spinning with all the gossip, I didn't know what to think."

"Oh, what are they saying?" Elinor asked, annoyed that people had to be so darned nosy. Couldn't they mind their own damned business?

"That he's running after some little faerie with her own software company in Baton Rouge. I didn't believe it at first. I mean, we all saw him and Marianne together. 'No,' I said, 'you must be mistaken.' But no, it's true. I never imagined he was a gold digger. But then he *is* an incubus, and their sort can never be trusted, I suppose, can they? But it's such a shame. I really thought he was different, didn't you?"

Betsy flipped the toast over in the pan and, satisfied it was perfect, set it on a plate and slid it in front of Elinor.

"Thank you, this looks amazing." Elinor dusted her toast in the powdered sugar already on the table, then poured a generous amount of maple syrup over the top. "Yes, and although I don't know anything about the woman, I can assure you it is true. I was there and heard him myself. He fooled us all, and I will never forgive him. Poor Marianne is heartbroken."

"I bet she is, poor little darling. I suppose she's pining to get home?" She turned back to the stove and turned it off, since Marianne wasn't moving upstairs.

"A little bit, maybe."

"I can imagine. And I would rebook our flights immediately, I promise, but I do have a little gathering tomorrow that I must go to."

The doorbell rang.

"Oh," Betsy said, pulling her dressing gown close and putting her hand to her bed hair. "Are you expecting anyone?"

Elinor shook her head. "No. Shall I get it?"

"Do you mind? I'm sure I look a total fright. I'm not really dressed yet."

Elinor put down her knife and fork. "No, not at all. I'll let you know if it's for you."

"Thank you, dear."

Betsy left in a hurry, disappearing up the stairs as Elinor walked along the short hall to the front door. To her surprise, it was Lucy standing on the doorstep, fully dressed and rummaging insanely inside her purse.

Elinor looked behind her. "Where's Anne?"

"Never mind Anne, where's my goddamn key? Oh, she wanted to pick up a few things, so I said I'd meet her at the hotel a bit later." Lucy followed Elinor back to the kitchen and helped herself to a bottle of Evian from the fridge. Seeing Elinor's plate, she sat in the seat beside her. "Anyway, I've had such a lot on my mind this morning. Last night was amazing, don't you think?"

"You want some?" Elinor said, pointing to her plate.

"Nah, a moment on the lips, a lifetime on the hips," she said, glancing at Elinor's hips.

Elinor thought about her brother's flesh-eating family and her overpriced chicken sandwich. "It was all right, sure."

"All right? Just all right? I thought a lot more of it than that! Barbara was very nice to me last night, don't you think? I almost wondered if she knew about me and Edward, she was being so nice and attentive. Surely you must have wondered the same thing yourself?"

"She was polite, sure," Elinor said, picking up her fork and helping herself to a bite of French toast.

"You think she was just being polite?" Lucy snorted and chugged down a little of the Evian. "I think it was more than that. I didn't see her inviting you or Marianne over for tea."

Elinor wondered if Lucy knew she was being rude or if she was just plain ignorant? As she had often done before, she found herself more than a little astonished that the man she loved could have in any way ingratiated himself with this little twerp. To her dying day, she would never understand it.

Elinor was just pondering how best to answer without coming across as either jealous or snooty when the front doorbell rang again. And since Lucy made no move to go and answer it, she put down her fork again and got up herself. The girl really was too much.

Consumed by these thoughts, she opened the door. Her heart almost stopped. She hadn't been expecting anyone and was wholly unprepared to see the man standing on the other side of the door.

Elinor gasped, her mouth wide open. She remembered to close it.

"Hello, Elinor," Edward said, a hesitant smile on his face. Like Chris, he looked rather odd in his khaki shorts, sandals, and T-shirt.

"Edward...I...well, I wasn't expecting you at all."

"I hope you don't mind. I heard the family were all meeting up for tea this morning, so I thought I'd steal the chance to come and see you. My apologies, I should have come much sooner, but I've been, um, tied up, and there's something I really want to talk to you about."

Elinor shook her head, as if shaking an illusion. "Oh, right?"

She wondered if he'd made a mistake and was here to see Lucy, and it was just bad luck that she opened the door.

"Are you going to leave me standing on the doorstep all morning, or are you going to invite me in?"

"Oh yes, of course, sure."

She stood aside. Edward, probably thinking he should take his chance when he could, moved quickly inside. As he passed, her thoughts shifted. What if he was here to see her after all, and this wasn't a mistake? *Oh Gaia, Lucy!* "Um, Edward!"

But it was too late. Edward was no sooner in the kitchen than Lucy was on her feet, smiling at him.

"Um, oh," Edward faltered. "I thought you were expected at Mom's hotel this morning?"

"I am, well, in a little while. Not until noon, I believe," Lucy replied.

"Oh. They told me eleven."

Lucy glanced up at the clock. "No, I'm sure I'm right. My sister, Anne, said she might go over a little early, but I came home to change first. I do want to look my best when I see your mother."

Elinor was shocked at the transformation in him. A moment ago, he'd been all smiles and ease, and now he looked like he'd been punched in the face.

Edward looked back to the kitchen door, clearly thinking of making an escape, but then it opened and Marianne walked in.

"Edward! Oh sweet Gaia, Edward! I thought that was your voice I heard. Wow. What a lovely surprise. Elinor and I expected to see you long before this. Where have you been hiding?"

"I...I..." But Edward had no answer.

Elinor ached to hear him falter like that. It was as plain as the nose on his face that he hadn't expected to catch Lucy at this hour, and that he wasn't thrilled that he had. Something didn't quite add up.

"Has anyone offered you a drink?" Marianne asked. "We have coffee, tea, a few sodas I think?"

"Um, no thank you, but I think I really should get going. I just remembered some place I need to be. I should head over to our hotel and get changed."

"But you just got here!" Marianne said, bewildered.

"Well, if you are going over the to the hotel, perhaps we can go together?" Lucy suggested. "I was going to change, but on second thought, this is a nice dress. Not too sexy, I think. I don't think your mom will mind it. What do you think, Elinor? Do I look too saucy? Too hot?"

Elinor gave Lucy the once-over. Lucy's cold shoulder blouse was cut a little too deep for Elinor's taste, but it was fairly conservative by Lucy's standards and probably served her well with her wings. "You look nice," she said. "I don't think you need to change." She reluctantly tore her gaze away. She would give anything to have Lucy's sex appeal—especially now, in front of Edward. If only some devil would spring up and offer her a deal, she'd take it in an instant. Having Edward enfold her in his powerful arms and tell her that he loved her and no one else would be worth her soul. Well, maybe not her soul, but something.

"Just nice?" Lucy said, preening. "Edward, what do you think?"

Edward's cheeks turned almost the color of Lucy's red top. "You look great," he said. His voice was hurried, and he clearly wanted to go. "Come on, let's hit the road. Both my mom and Fanny hate it when people show up late."

"Well, we'd better scoot then," Lucy said, grinning at Elinor. "See you later, gator!"

A moment later, they were both gone.

Elinor hadn't a moment to gather her thoughts before Marianne rounded on her.

"Well, Elinor! Sometimes I don't understand you at all. Why didn't you ask him to stay? The poor guy must have felt really unwelcome, the way you were ignoring him."

"Wait? What? I wasn't ignoring him."

"Well, it sure looked like it to me," Marianne whined. "And that Lucy has her eye on him now. After what Barbara said last night about his fortune, I'm not surprised. Those dirty succubi are all the same. Gold diggers."

If nothing else, Elinor was glad to hear her sister's anger. Perhaps she was finally coming to her senses after all?

"Maybe. Who knows?"

She wandered over to the kitchen window that looked out over the beach. But it wasn't the view that caught her attention. In her mind's eye, all she could see was Lucy with her scheming arm linked tightly through Edward's. She had no doubt now that Lucy had ensnared him. And there was nothing to be done, because like her, Edward was a person of honor and would stand by his vows, regardless of the manner in which he had made them.

Behind her, her sister made ignorant jibes, condemning her for her incivility and coldness after not having seen him for so long a time.

"It's bad enough I lost a man, but you could have had yours if you'd only exerted yourself. Really, Elinor, where is your heart? I think you don't care for him at all, because you're not acting like you do. You're acting like an idiot. And they say *you're* the one with all the sense."

Elinor wanted to turn on Marianne and tell her to shut up. What did her kid sister know of her suffering? The little twerp had been so blindsided by Willoughby, she didn't have the slightest clue what was going in Elinor's heart.

But none of it mattered now. Marianne's comments couldn't touch her. Indeed, how could any dagger destroy a heart that was already broken? Edward was lost to her forever, and there was no amount of polite words or warm greetings that could do anything to change that now.

Chapter Twenty-Five
A HEART OF STONE

BARBARA FERRARS HAD BEEN IN LOVE ONCE. SHE REMEMBERED THE feeling well and worked hard to keep the sensation alive. Not, as anyone would imagine, due to any romantic sensibility—no, quite the reverse. Her reason not to forget her feelings for her long-dead husband was born of anything but sentimentality.

No. She wanted to make sure that if anyone dared stir those feelings in her ever again, that she'd be ready for them and could cut them dead in their tracks. Her late husband, Miles, had brought nothing to their marriage but heartache and shame. Despite early promises, he hadn't increased her fortune by a single dime, and though he had given her children, the sad truth was she was ashamed of them.

She'd seen the snide, half-sneer glances the other goblin mothers had given her. She'd endured the poor math grades and was troubled by their artistic excellence, which had no value for her at all. Luckily, there was enough goblin in two of them to overcome this rough beginning. Fanny and Robert took to the banking business like ducks to water. She could say the same of Edward, too, though he was a little gentler than the others, taking more after his father. He often displayed a more sensitive, considerate side that she'd worked hard to thrash out of him. Thankfully, he had come around at last and was toeing the family line. She would make a ruthless banker out of him yet.

Her daughter, Fanny, was sitting on their suite sofa playing with her smartphone, while Anne, the less pretty of the two succubus sisters, jabbered away to her about nothing in particular, as least as far as she could make out.

She had invited the two for tea yesterday just to snub John's snooty sister. Oh yes, she'd heard everything about the girl making ooey-gooey eyes at her son, and she wouldn't tolerate it. Who did she think she was anyway? But now that one of the succubus girls was here, she was already regretting it. She had asked them over for tea—not the whole day. Who did they think they were? And they smelled. What might be pleasant to the men was offensive to her goblin nostrils. She shivered and pulled a bottle of alchemy musk from her purse, spraying it around her face to alleviate the stench.

"Will your sister be much longer?" she asked, as the droplets lingered in the air, masking the girl's scent.

"Oh, sure, Lucy won't be very long," Anne replied. "She just had to go back to Betsy's for something or other. 'Lucy,' I said, 'I don't think Mrs. Ferrars will care one bit whatever you put on. She's a nice lady.' And I said she looked nice enough, I really liked the blouse she had on. But she would go, though I expect she had her reasons for wanting to look her best, I'm sure she had."

"Are you looking forward to getting back home?" Fanny asked. "I know I am. I find this Florida heat unbearable, and I long for the cold of the north. It's too humid, don't you think?"

"Well yes, you're right about that. I've gone through more bottles of deodorant than you could ever believe! And where are the men, I say? I mean, what's the point of being a succubus if there are no men to drool over, know what I'm saying? I mean it's all right for my sister, Lucy. She's got Edward—but me, I've got no one. It just isn't fair."

Barbara felt her body go rigid and even Fanny sat more stiffly in her seat. "What was that?" Barbara asked.

"You know, Lucy and Edward. I mean it's all right for them, they're in love. But what about me? No one's offered to bond with me. At this rate, I don't think anyone ever shall."

Fanny suddenly lost interest in her smartphone, dropping it on the sofa cushion.

"Are you telling me, your sister is bonded to my brother?"

At last, the penny must have dropped, because Anne's mouth fell open and she raised her hand to cover it. "Shoot. I wasn't supposed to tell anyone that. It's supposed to be a secret."

Slowly, Barbara rose from her seat. Then, though she was of advancing years, she crossed the room with uncanny speed. She took the girl's chin in her twisted goblin fingers and brought her face close to her own.

"Now let's be absolutely clear. Are you telling me my son Edward has bonded with your slut succubus sister?" She could see Anne was trembling and rightly so. Barbara was of a good mind to poke a sharp nail into one or both of those fearful eyes of hers. "Well?"

Anne was crying, and her words came out a jumbled mess. "I wasn't supposed to tell anyone," she repeated. "Lucy is going to kill me!"

"I will kill you if you don't answer my question," Barbara hissed.

She turned to find Fanny standing right behind her and looking just as horrified. "Call Edward. Call him and tell him I need to see him here at once! Do you hear me?"

"Yes, Momsie," Fanny said, jumping right to it and snatching up her phone.

But there was no need. In the adjoining room, Barbara heard a door opening, and a moment later, both Edward and Lucy were standing in the sitting room.

"Hello, Mother," Edward said politely. Then his gaze fell on Anne, who could not hide her fright. "What's going on?"

"I was just about to ask you the same thing. This...this *thing* has just informed me you've attached yourself to this succubus. Do you dare deny it?"

Edward turned a ghastly shade of white, and to her horror, he took Lucy's hand in his own and squeezed it. "Yes, Mother, I have. We are bonded."

"Yes, we are in love," Lucy said, as if it were the most wonderful thing in the world, completely ignoring her simpering sister. "We think we'll be very happy."

Barbara's blood boiled just beneath the surface. Her fingers began to tingle, and her skin turned a deeper shade of green. "Have you performed the actual ceremony?"

"Not yet," Edward said. "But we have exchanged vows, and my word is unbreakable. We are as good as bonded. But we would like your blessing."

Barbara was so incensed she'd forgotten she was still holding onto Anne's chin. She thrust it away now and could smell the blood she'd drawn with her sharp claws. Anne turned away, which was good, for Barbara couldn't bear to watch her sobs of embarrassment. Weakness repelled her, and this succubus was as weak as they came.

"My blessing?" Barbara smiled, but her smile was born of cruelty, not joy. "My blessing? Heed this. I don't care about your word at all. What is such a thing when offered to a slut like this one?" She fixed her cold gaze upon Lucy Steele. "I don't know what arts and allurements you practiced on my son but know this. YOU WILL NOT HAVE HIM. I would rather see my son dead and in his grave rather than shackled to such as you."

"Mother, watch your words!"

"Hush, Edward. You have had your say. Now let me have mine. You must give up this ridiculous fling at once. I will not have you make my family look ridiculous. Give her up, and everything will be forgiven." Barbara stared hard at her son, wanting to be sure he understood her completely. "If you do not, have no doubt I will cut you off without a cent. Not one cent. I'll rewrite my will and leave everything irrevocably to your brother, Robert. Have I made myself clear?"

From the ashen look on her son's face, she could tell he understood her completely. "Well?" Barbara pressed, needing to hear his words of submission.

Edward took a long breath, then clasped Lucy's hand firmly. "Mother, I gave my word. I cannot and will not go back on it."

Fanny stood bewildered and looked afraid to speak, no doubt fearing to draw any of this venom her way. Yet despite her daughter's shock, Barbara could see the wheels turning behind her eyes, calculating how this would turn to her advantage. At least one of her offspring showed some spunk.

Barbara's heart turned cold. "Then so be it. And may your decision bring you much happiness."

Anne, who had been weeping nonstop, jumped up and ran from the room, her wings drooping miserably behind her. Unlike her sister, Lucy was not sniveling, but she stood dumbstruck. Good. She deserved to suffer the miseries of hell, because she had cost Barbara a son. "Now leave us. All of you. And Edward?"

Edward turned as he was about to walk out the door.

"I never want to see your face again. You are dead to me."

The goblin who had once been her son nodded solemnly. She hated his weakness and his foolish pride in his sense of honor. How pathetic he was, how easily led astray. And how very much like his father. Edward had held a place in her heart for a while; after all, he was her firstborn son. But no longer. He was dead to her now, and unlike him, she would never weaken. She took a deep breath, and focusing on the love she'd had for her son, she turned that part of her heart to stone.

Chapter Twenty-Six

FOOTPRINTS

It was the talk of the town. Well, certainly of their little circle. Edward Ferrars and Lucy Steele! Who would have believed it? The first Elinor got wind of it was yesterday afternoon, when Anne came back surprisingly early from the hotel, her face awash with tears.

"Oh Elinor, what shall I do? Lucy won't even talk to me now!" she cried, collapsing onto the couch. "I couldn't help myself. I opened my mouth and bleh, it all came out. I mean, it was mean of her to expect me to hold onto such a big secret, though I did my best for ever so long. But she won't thank me for that now, I suppose, not Lucy. Oh Gaia, what am I going to do?"

Elinor had guessed the rest, and though like Anne, this development had released her from her vow of secrecy, her heart was still heavy. After all, this was hardly going to bring Edward closer to her. Quite the reverse.

That was yesterday. Today, Elinor was sitting on the low stone wall that led to the beach, pushing her feet into the dry sand as she tried to control her emotions. She had to face the truth now. Until this latest news, a little part of her heart had refused to believe Edward had tied himself to that succubus—but that he had more sense and would have been more guarded. In secret she had hoped it had all been some colossal lie, some tease, and that Lucy had made it all up as she'd gone along.

No. Now even that hope was stripped from her. The word was out. They were a couple. Edward could never be hers, and she had to learn to live without him.

The pain in her heart was physical as well as emotional. Whereas Marianne could give vent to her feelings, her own suffering had been silently eating away at her. It was a real thing, a hole, a chasm bereft of everything but heartache. She longed for the north, for their home, and for the comfort only the trees could bring her. Around them she could feel solace, she could be comforted, she could be helped to forget. But not here.

Familiar steps approached from behind, and turning slightly she saw Marianne, dressed similarly in a willowy dress adorned with wildflowers. Marianne sat down beside her, and for a while she said nothing, but kicked off her sandals and slid her feet into the sand just as Elinor did.

"How long have you known?" Marianne asked at last.

Elinor caught the lump in her throat, determined not to cry. "For a while now."

"And you never told me?"

Elinor heard the reproach in her sister's voice. "It wasn't my secret to tell. Lucy asked me not to breathe a word of it. She made me swear to secrecy, to give my word. Otherwise, I would have told you, of course. I'm sorry, it killed me that I couldn't tell you."

"I don't think I could have kept such a secret for so long. Maybe you weren't as much in love with him as you thought."

There was no need to hold back her feelings any longer. Weeks of hurt and suppressed disappointment bubbled to the surface in a single moment. "You don't think I loved him? Marianne, I—can you not have any inkling of what I've been going through?

"Almost from the first day we met those stupid sisters, I've had to crush every feeling, every desire, every hope I ever had. And worse, because I've not only had to endure the disappointment of losing him, Marianne, but I've had to put up with the incessant gloating of the very woman who took him from me. I might not have wailed and whined like a tormented banshee, but believe me, if I could show you my heart, you'd see enough sorrow there to satisfy the both of us. Don't love him? Who died and gave you a monopoly on feelings? Did you ever wonder at my silence? No, you didn't, because you were too self-absorbed with your own damned misery. Well, that's fine, Marianne, but don't you dare make any judgment about mine, don't you dare!"

Marianne's eyes filled with tears, and Elinor couldn't help feeling a little sorry for her. She was who she was after all, and nothing would ever change that. Not regretting one word, since it was good to get it off her chest at last, she still had enough grace to wrap a big sister's arm around Marianne's shoulders. The poor girl's dryad skin had taken enough of a beating. She didn't need to shed any more tears on Elinor's account.

"Oh, shush now, let's have none of that. We're both idiots, going after men who were unobtainable. How stupid must we dryads be?"

"Pretty stupid," Marianne sniffed, and they both chuckled.

More steps behind them made Elinor turn, and Marianne dried her eyes. To Elinor's surprise, it was their brother, John.

"Oh, hello. We didn't expect you here. Aren't you supposed to be over at Magic-Con?" Elinor asked.

"Yes, well, I was on my way, but I just thought I'd drop by for a little chat."

Elinor waited as John sat behind them and kicked off his shoes and socks, setting them neatly on the walkway behind them. After he rolled up his pants, he pushed them into the sand, just as his sisters had done.

"It's been a while since I've done anything fun like this," he said, wiggling his toes.

Elinor didn't doubt it. Fanny wasn't exactly the bucket and spade type.

"You should make a point of visiting us when we get back to Maine," Marianne said. "We do this sort of thing all the time."

John nodded and said, "Yes, I really should."

Elinor knew Fanny kept him on a tight leash and was unlikely to give him permission. His dryad sisters were dangerous. Who knew, the poor man might start having some fun again.

"So what did you want to talk to us about?" Elinor asked.

John turned his face to the sun and took a moment to enjoy its rays. "I'm pretty sure you've both heard about the, um, little fracas over at the hotel yesterday?"

"Who hasn't?" Marianne answered. "We heard it from Anne first, and then Betsy came bursting in with the news the moment she came back from her walk this morning. I think everyone knows. Poor Edward!"

"Yes, poor indeed. My mother-in-law didn't waste any time cutting him off. She canceled all his credit cards and wrote to her lawyers first thing this morning. I tell you, it's an ugly mess. I'd help him myself if that wouldn't put me directly in the firing line, but you know what Barbara and Fanny are like. I'd never hear the end of it."

Elinor's heart sank. Edward must be going through hell. She didn't know to what extent he depended on the family money, and she wondered if he had anything put by of his own. If she had indeed cut him off without a dime as rumor had it, what was he going to live on now? Part of her said this was none of her business, that he'd made his own bed with Lucy and now he had to lie in it. Another part of her ached for his situation.

"So what is he going to do?"

"I don't know. Fanny tried texting him this morning, but he didn't respond. But that's not what I came here to talk about."

"It's not?" Elinor asked, her curiosity aroused.

"No, it's not. I just wanted to say that when things had calmed down a bit, Barbara had been kind enough to mention that had Edward's choice fallen in another, um, direction—if you understand me...."

Elinor nodded. She could hardly pretend that she didn't, since everyone and their dog (apart from Marianne) seemed to have guessed at her feelings.

"Well," John continued, "then she wouldn't have reacted quite so strongly, and everything might have turned out all right in the end. Anyway, I thought you ought to know. She really isn't that bad a person once you get to know her."

Elinor wasn't so sure about that. She didn't think that Barbara had a kind bone in her body. If such a thought gave her brother comfort, then so be it, but being a slightly better alternative to the succubus sluts was hardly high praise. Especially since she'd seen firsthand how much Barbara regarded her. Oh well. Let John have his little illusion if it made him feel better.

In any case, Elinor had no desire to know her brother's mother-in-law any better. But she knew John was trying to be kind, and she was grateful for that at least. "Thank you," she said, wiggling her feet about in the sand. "It's nice of you to tell me."

John nodded. "I hope I will get to see you when we head back north. Perhaps, when things settle down, you could come and stay with us at Norland?"

Elinor pictured Fanny's face if she could have heard her brother now. She smiled to herself. "We'd all like that, John. Just name the day and we'll make it happen."

Appeased and looking as if he'd done his duty, John brushed the dry sand off his pants. "Right then, I suppose I should be off. I'd better get back before they send a search party out for me."

Elinor pulled her feet from the sand, and while John put his shoes and socks back on, she picked up her sandals, intent on going for a walk along the beach. There was a lot on her mind, and she needed some alone time.

"Well, goodbye then," John said, once his shoes were back on.

Elinor hugged him warmly. "Goodbye. And thank you."

Marianne hugged him also.

He nodded, and as soon as he was gone, Marianne picked up her sandals. "I'm going in," she said. "I think Betsy said we could check in online after one."

"Yes, you're right. Do me too? I want to walk along the beach for a bit."

"Sure." Marianne headed back inside.

Elinor turned and wandered down to the water's edge. After gazing out to the horizon for a few moments, she turned and started to stroll through the surf, stopping occasionally to watch as her feet sank into the wet sand. Then she would dream of another set of footprints that even now might have been walking beside her if things had been just a little different. And if she'd met Edward Ferrars before he had the misfortune to bump into Lucy Steele and her succubus charms.

Chapter Twenty-Seven

HOME

IT WAS GOOD TO BE HOME. THE FLIGHT HADN'T BEEN TOO BAD, APART from Anne's constant sniveling, which didn't stop from their departure in Florida to their arrival in Maine and all the ride home from the airport. Lucy hadn't boarded with them. Indeed, no one had heard a word from her since the big to-do. Not even Anne knew where she was, though Elinor was secretly glad to have dodged more gloating looks and comments—presuming there were any, since being cut off financially by Edward's mother was no small thing, she imagined. For once, Lucy might have kept her mouth shut. Still, she would have liked to have seen Edward one more time, if only to find out how he was doing.

They dropped Anne off on the way home and watched as she traipsed into her apartment with her head bowed and her wings drooping. Elinor looked at Marianne to see what she was thinking, but Marianne was lost in a world of her own.

Finally, the taxi pulled up outside their lovely house, and they got out. Elinor paid the elf driver and thanked him. He gave her a wide grin as he backed up the drive. As shadows played over his face, she thought she saw Edward smiling at her, but that was just a trick of the light. Damn her stupid thoughts. She said hello to the trees, then followed Marianne inside.

"Oh, my girls, you've no idea how much I missed you!" Mary said as they dumped their cases just inside the front door. As she squeezed Marianne, their mother looked over her shoulder at her eldest daughter. Elinor had kept her up to speed on developments. Elinor shook her head but gave a little half-smile and a shrug, too. Marianne's heart wasn't healed by any means, but at least she hadn't sniveled all the way back like Anne had.

Mary pulled away and held her middle daughter gently at arm's length. "What's this? All this time in Florida and no tan?"

"I didn't like the sunshine, it was drying me out," Marianne said flatly. She picked up her case and headed for her room, leaving Mary and Elinor to watch as she disappeared.

"Did you bring me a pressie?" Margaret looked just as pleased as their mother had to see her sisters return home. "I'm glad you're back. It's been so booooring without you. And Mom said if you go again, I can go with you!"

"That's not quite what I said." Mary smiled and tussled her youngest daughter's hair, making her scowl. "I said maybe next time you can go."

"That's just as good as a yes," Margaret said. "So what did you bring me?"

"Let me get in!" Elinor laughed. "There *might* be something in my suitcase for you. You'll just have to wait and see, won't you?"

"Please!"

"Let me get a cup of tea first, will you? That was a long journey, and I'm parched."

Elinor pushed gently past her excited baby sister and went straight into the kitchen. She longed for a cup of tea made with home water; theirs was much harder than the soft water down south, and she missed that special zing. A dryad needed her daily mineral nutrients.

"Mom, can I go play for a bit?" Margaret asked, still bursting with energy.

"Sure," Mary said. "Just make sure you're back in time for dinner. I don't want to have to come looking for you."

As Margaret scuttled off, Elinor set out two mugs and turned on the kettle.

"So, how is she?" Mary asked, lowering her voice and raising her eyes to the ceiling.

"I'm not sure," Elinor said, truthfully. "She has her good moments, but then she goes all quiet again. I mean, it's a little early to expect her to forget him, but I've never seen her this down in the mouth before, and it worries me. She spends almost all her time with her nose in the phone, though I don't think she's texting him anymore."

"We just have to be a little patient with her. She'll come around soon, I'm sure of it."

Elinor hoped she was right. "Talking of texts, I got one from Chris earlier."

"Oh?" From the look on Mary's face, Elinor could guess what she was thinking. "Oh Mom, it's nothing like that. We're just friends."

"If you say so."

"Mom!"

"I just don't know what's wrong with you young 'uns. I'd have snapped that one up in a heartbeat."

"Don't let me stop you," Elinor laughed.

"Cheek. So, what did Chris want?"

"He wanted Edward's contact info."

Elinor had told Mary about Lucy, and her mother was wisely keeping her thoughts to herself on that subject. She took the mug Elinor offered and blew on the tea. "I wonder what for?"

"Dunno, I didn't ask."

"Huh. Well anyway, on to more important things, I want both you girls in dryad robes tonight. I offered up a prayer to the trees for your safe passage, and we ought to give thanks straight after dinner before it gets dark. As soon as you're done with your tea, go and change—oh and tell Marianne to do the same."

Elinor nodded and turned, spotting the herb and spice basket Mary had already prepared sitting in the corner. Good. She had planned on a little tree time anyway. It wasn't the same in Florida; she didn't have the same rapport with the local trees, and she wouldn't feel truly at home until they had welcomed her back.

When Elinor looked up, Mary was studying her. She reached across the table and placed her hand over her daughter's. Elinor knew what she was thinking.

"I'm all right, Mom, really I am. Or I will be. I won't say it's not hurting because it is, but I'll get over it. Just give me a little time."

Mary sighed. "None of this would ever have happened if your father were alive. He would have protected you, or at least gone after the stupid boys to make them suffer. Or make good on their promises."

Elinor pulled her hand out and laid it over her mother's.

"It's okay, Mom. We're doing okay. It's nobody's fault. No promises were broken, it's not as bad as you think. Hey, do we have any of those nice lavender biscuits? You know how much you love those."

Mary laughed. "Um no, I think I ate them all while you were away. I have some gingersnaps though. Do you want some?"

"Sure," Elinor said, knowing dunking cookies would make her mother feel bucketloads better.

She rose from the table, and while she rummaged through a cupboard, Marianne came down from upstairs. She hadn't changed from her travel clothes and looked like she might have been lying down on her face, it was so flushed.

"Want some?" Elinor asked, pointing to her mug.

"Not right now."

"Actually," Mary said, "I'm glad you've come down. I want to give thanks for your safe return."

Marianne glanced over to the corner and saw the basket. "Sure, if you like."

Elinor put an opened packet of cookies in front of Mary and noticed Marianne had her nose in her phone, yet again. *What on earth could be so interesting?* she wondered, but she didn't dare ask in case Marianne bit her head off.

"Well, I'm going up to change," Elinor said, grabbing her mug to take it with her. As she passed Marianne, she took a sneak peek over her shoulder and noticed Marianne was looking at a map. Hardly exciting. The print was too small to see what it was a map of, but at least her sister wasn't brooding over some text or hapless love letter. Sensing Elinor had stopped, Marianne turned, and Elinor pretended to be waiting for her. "Are you coming?"

"In a minute. You go ahead."

Elinor nodded, and after taking another sip of her tea, left her mother and sister to it. She needed to prepare mentally for the trees, which meant a little quiet time. That was something she couldn't get down in the kitchen, worrying as she always did about everyone else. When she got to her room, she placed her mug on the bedside table, laid down on her bed, closed her eyes, and cleared her mind.

Elinor dreamed of her phone. Only it wasn't a dream. She opened her eyes and reached over to grab her cell phone. Still half-dreaming, she swiped without checking to see who it was.

"Hel-lo," she said, her voice broken.

"Elinor? Uh, hello. It's, it's Edward."

That woke her up quickly. She rubbed her eyes and checked the clock beside the bed. She couldn't have been asleep for more than five minutes.

"Edward, oh hey. Sorry, I must have dozed off. How are you?"

"I'm good, thank you." He gave a little sigh. "Probably doing better than I deserve. How was your flight?"

"Oh, you know, nothing special. Not even one hijacking to spice things up. We complained to the airline manager." *Oh Gaia, why had she said that?* "I'm glad to be home. Are you...still in Florida?" She couldn't quite bring herself to say "you and Lucy." She wondered if he caught the pause.

"Yes, until tomorrow. It's the only flight we could get at short notice. Everything was fully booked."

He fell silent for a moment, and Elinor stared intently at the screen, wishing she could think of something relevant to say.

Edward took a sharp intake of breath. "I wanted to thank you for what you said to Chris Brandon."

"What I said?"

"Yes. He called me a little bit ago and offered me a position in his company. I won't be arrogant and assume it was down to my own merits. I presumed he must have spoken with you, but it was nice of him all the same. I confess, I do find myself in a bind now that Mom has cut me off, so I really appreciate your help."

Elinor sat up straight in her bed. "No, you're mistaken. Whatever you and Chris discussed had nothing to do with me at all. If he made you an offer, it was entirely down to his assessment of you and your experience. I didn't even know about it."

"Hmm, well, I'm sure on some level he must have done it because of you. I'd never spoken to him before today."

"I couldn't say. But I'm happy for you. I'm glad something has worked out."

"Indeed. Er, he said he might drop by later to see you all got home safely. If he does, can you tell him thanks again?"

"I will."

The line went quiet again. Another sigh. Was he feeling regret, or did he have asthma?

"Elinor, I wanted to tell you—"

But he couldn't finish. Elinor heard Lucy's hurried voice in the background. She sounded a little irritated, but she was too far from the phone to be heard distinctly.

"Yes, yes, I'm coming." When he returned his attention to Elinor, his voice sounded a little lower. "Um, look, I'm sorry. I have to go. I just wanted to call to say thanks."

"You're welcome, I guess," Elinor said, intently listening to catch Lucy again. Did she know who Edward was talking to? She could hear nothing.

"Goodbye," Edward said.

It sounded so final. Suddenly, Elinor felt empty. "Bye."

And then he was gone. Elinor kicked herself for not telling him that they saw Anne home okay, and that she was still upset and apologetic for her blunder and wanted to tell Lucy she was sorry.

Even as she went over their conversation in her mind, there was a knock on her door and someone rattled the handle. It was Margaret.

"Mom said to come down. Soup's on the table and then we need to get started."

"Oh, okay," Elinor replied. "Tell her I'll be down in a minute."

"Don't forget my pressie," Margaret said and ran off.

Elinor slid off the bed and changed from her travel robes to her dryad dress. Her head wasn't as clear as she wanted it to be, but that couldn't be helped now. At least she knew Edward was all right, and that things were working out for him.

As she pulled her hair back into a braid, she tried not to think of Lucy being with him and what they might be getting up to even now. Such thoughts gave her no comfort, and as if to tear them from her mind, she pulled hard on her braids, seeking forgetfulness in the pain. Dammit, she would beat this heartache, she would rise above it, and all would be forgotten and go back to normal—in time. Though maybe not just yet.

She opened her suitcase and took out Margaret's present, then put on her best smile and went downstairs to join her family.

Chapter Twenty-Eight
BROKEN-HEARTED

MARIANNE SAT AT HER DRESSING TABLE MIRROR, BUT SHE SAW NOTHING reflected there. In her mind's eye, she wasn't back in Camden at all, but far away, in another part of Maine. Outside in the hall, she heard a door open and close and realized Elinor must be on her way down.

Reluctantly, she got up from her chair and followed her.

They were all changed into their dryad dresses. Mary stood ready by the door, basket in hand, and Margaret, who looked eager to start her second ceremony, was right behind her. Elinor was tidying up their discarded shoes by the door. Her sister was so OCD at times. Marianne, who was barefoot, slipped into her flats, accidentally knocking a shoe out of place and earning a low growl from her elder sister.

"Sorry."

Elinor didn't reply.

"Ready, girls?" Mary asked, passing the bowl of herbs and spices to Elinor.

They all said yes. Mary led the way out of the house, past all the blooming flowers, and over to the trees. It was glorious outside; the mature, early autumn sun caressed Marianne's cheeks, soothing the edges of her sorrow.

Ahead of them, a soft breeze stirred the leaves of the trees, as if calling to the dryads, anxious for the ceremony to begin.

As custom dictated, Mary, as the head of the family, knelt in front of the white pine, her head bowed. Her daughters lined up behind her in order of age, but then on impulse Marianne turned around.

"You go ahead of me," she whispered to Margaret. "My head's not quite ready yet."

Margaret didn't need to be told twice and shuffled forward to take her new place. Mary looked back, but seeing the new order, said nothing. Satisfied they were all ready, she turned and brought her hands together in supplication.

"Sisters of Gaia," Mary said, "we give thanks for the safe return of my daughters. For the love you show us, for your constant protection, and for all that you give us, please accept these humble tributes from your thankful daughters."

She stepped forward, the ribbon in hand, and once again a friendly branch swooped down to hold one end of the thread while she walked around the tree, securing it to its trunk.

Mary bowed her head and stepped aside.

Elinor stepped forward and bowed her head, then approached the pine, where she dabbed saffron down close to the roots. A moment later a branch descended, carrying her aloft and passing her joyfully from tree to tree. Elinor looked delighted, and Marianne was happy for her. She longed for the same sense of peace that only the trees could give her.

Margaret was next. She picked up the bowl Elinor had left near the tree's roots, then walked regally (if a little awkwardly) over to the growing baby yew tree and dabbed a little of the saffron at its roots. She then returned to the eldest pine, and like her sister before her, was carried lovingly up into its arms.

Now it was Marianne's turn. She tried to close her mind to worldly things, to allow the spirits of the trees a window to her soul. Try as she might, images of Willoughby tormented her. The white pine lowered a branch, which circled around her waist. But as it pulled her high into its limbs, Marianne struggled, fighting their union, unable to bond.

The probing spirits tried to calm her, whispering through their leaves, calling to calm her heart, but she would not listen.

"No!" she cried, and as the tree limbs flailed, she wrenched herself from their grip and fell, cutting herself on the limbs beneath her as she tumbled to the ground.

The others ran to her, anxious for her safety.

"Gaia, Marianne!" Mary cried. "Is anything broken? Are you okay?"

"What happened?" Elinor asked. "I've never seen that happen before!"

Marianne pushed herself up from the ground, the bases of her palms grazed and dirty. She didn't know what just happened, and she didn't have answers for anyone. All she knew was her heart ached more than her bones right now, and she needed to get away, to run and be free from this shroud of misery. "Oh just leave me alone, will you!"

With her eyes full of tears, Marianne ran back to the house, needing right now to be as far from everyone as she could possibly be. She didn't understand what had just happened, not one bit. She had never rejected or resented the tree spirits, and now that she had, she wondered if they'd ever embrace her again.

Confused, bitter, and with a strange determination she'd never experienced before, she snatched up Elinor's car keys, and picking up her phone, she ran out to the car.

The driver's door was unlocked, and she scrambled in, anxious to get away before the others returned to ask questions she had no answers for. She started the engine, and without looking back she zoomed away, her focus on one thing and one thing only. She set her phone on the dash, and through unchecked tears, pulled up Willoughby's address.

Thankfully, Elinor never let the gas tank fall below half-empty. Marianne calculated there would be plenty to get her to Southport. As the crow flew, her first journey with Willoughby hadn't taken that long. But it was a different matter getting there by road. Or maybe it was his magic that had made it seem much shorter. Due to the craggy shoreline, she had to go inland to Route 1 before she could head south. It would be an hour at least before she got there, but Marianne didn't care, just as long as she got there.

Perhaps it was the shock of coming home without him, but everything was finally sinking in. She had lost him. Forever. And though they had not bonded—at least she couldn't reproach him for that—she had wanted to with all her heart and soul. No vows were spoken, no promises made, but she had as good as given herself up for love. Now she was unwholesome, broken, and utterly alone.

Tears streamed down her face as she thought of how foolish she had been, how unguarded, and to someone she had thought of as noble, but who turned out to be nothing more than a bastard in the end.

She hit the gas a little harder, careless of the speed limit. All that mattered was she get to that beach, needing to relive what she'd felt there, longing, at least for a while, to be able to pretend.

She followed the signs and left Route 1. The landscape around her changed, becoming vaguely familiar. The road became a winding track leading down to the shore. A bridge extended across the lapping waters to a tree-locked island, her destination. She pondered whether the rickety-looking bridge would support the weight of Elinor's car. She drove over it and, thankfully, it didn't collapse. She followed the line of the trees, slowly circling around the island. And then she was there.

There were no lights on to indicate the house might now be occupied and no other cars in the drive. Not that she cared. If someone was inside, let them come for her. Even Willoughby. Better to fight with him and be thrown off his premises than to have no contact with him at all.

In her haste she left the driver's door open as she ran from the car and around the house to get to the beach—and back to the beloved memory.

The scene was just as before, the water as calm, the sand as hot under her feet. Even the birds flying in the air above were the same, perhaps curious at this new arrival come to interfere with their solitude. And yet it was not the same, because she was different.

Marianne wandered over to their rock. The towel was still draped over it, and she snatched it up and put it to her face, breathing in the scent, desperate to catch something of Willoughby's aroma. But all she could smell was the sand and the salt of the ocean. Perhaps other bodies had lain on this towel since then. Perhaps there had been other promises, or other whispers of love. She let the towel fall to her feet.

Her heart ached to feel what she had felt before, if only for a moment. Each step was heavier than the last as she sauntered down to the water's edge. The waves ebbed and flowed gently at her feet, as if trying to bring the comfort she could not feel.

Only Willoughby could bring her that. And he'd betrayed her, in the worst way a man could ever betray a woman. He had taken her heart, given so freely, and he had stomped on it. The pain she felt was real, and it was more than her dryad soul could bear. She put her hand to her face and felt the tell-tale lines of sorrow etched into her flesh. Perhaps her beauty would be gone forever. Well then, so be it. Perhaps to die for love would not be so terrible. Let Willoughby come home and find her broken body on the shore. Maybe then he might feel some remorse.

She sank down at the water's edge, not caring that the water pooled around her, soaking her ceremonial dress. She just wanted this to be over. The pain. The heartache. All of it. And to sleep. As the waves lapped over her weary body, she closed her eyes and prayed her suffering would end.

It was dark and cold. Marianne couldn't feel anything and could barely move. How long she'd been lying there, she couldn't say, but the sea sounded a way off now, so the tide must have gone out at some point.

Somewhere in the distance she could hear voices. And car doors slamming. Who it was didn't matter now. She closed her eyes, wanting to sleep some more.

A pair of warm, strong arms enveloped her, and she felt herself being carried.

Willoughby? she wondered.

"Hold onto me. You'll be okay soon, I promise." The voice that spoke was deeply masculine, kind, and reassuring. It wasn't Willoughby. Marianne's rescuer adjusted his grip, and she nestled into his shoulder. She suddenly felt safe, and though she kept slipping in and out of consciousness, she didn't mind.

He was going to take her home.

"Is she okay?"

She recognized her sister Elinor's voice.

"No, she's half-frozen to death. There are blankets in the trunk, can you get them for me? We need to get her warm, and quickly." She recognized Chris's voice this time.

"So reliable," she whispered.

There was a commotion and more slamming. Then some wool blankets were draped over her, and she felt herself being lowered into a seat. A belt lock clicked.

"I'll follow you in my car and see you back at the house."

That was Elinor. She was always so practical. Practical Elinor. Nice.

"Okay."

More doors slammed, and then they were moving. Marianne closed her eyes. Lulled by the motion of the car, she soon fell into a deep but dreamless sleep.

Chapter Twenty-Nine

INCUBUS FEVER

THE DOCTOR LEANED OVER MARIANNE AND TOOK HER PULSE. ELINOR watched her closely, for as well as being a very able physician, Doctor Yount was also a vampire, and right at this moment, she looked suspiciously close to her sister's jugular. The doctor sniffed, then cocked her beautiful head to one side.

Elinor wished they could have called Doctor Ramirez, who had been the family physician for years, but he was just too far away. Still, apart from the occasional disconcerting hint of fang, Doctor Yount appeared to know what she was doing. She certainly looked very professional, with her sharp suit and detached manner. She also was incredibly attractive, as vampires generally were, with her slick, blonde hair and perfectly pale vampire skin.

She set Marianne's wrist down gently, then removed a small plastic-wrapped kit from her bag. After popping on a pair of gloves, she propped Marianne's mouth open and dabbed at her cheek with a cotton bud. After a quick swipe, she dipped the bud into a little tube that came out of the kit. When she removed the tube, the bud had turned blue.

"It's just as I thought," the doctor said, slipping the bud and the tube back into the wrapping, dropping it into her bag, and snapping the bag shut. "Incubus fever. Pretty bad too. It has a particular odor. If you get close you can smell for yourself. She has a faint aroma of musk about her. Unmistakable."

Elinor leaned over, but the only scent she caught was more like rubbing alcohol. She wanted to weep for the state of her sister's skin, which looked much worse than before.

"Is it dangerous?" Mary asked. She was sitting in a chair on the other side of her daughter's bed. She reached out and took hold of Marianne's hand.

Doctor Yount's face remained expressionless. "Her temperature is dangerously high. Pray that the fever breaks this evening. I'll give her a shot of berry penicillin—but if I'm honest, I'm shooting in the dark. I've never known a dryad to catch incubus fever before. The drug has worked on satyrs, so let's hope it does the same for Marianne. I would give you something for her skin, but I don't think anything works better than your salve, Elinor, so keep applying that. I've used it myself."

"Is it infectious?" Elinor asked.

"No. You can only get it from having your heart broken by an incubus. Doesn't seem to work with succubi, possibly because they're less focused on love, but no one knows why for sure. So don't fret. Other paras can't pass it between them." She picked up her bag and headed for the door. "Call me if it gets any worse before dawn, and I'll come back to see her again. I'll let myself out."

She left, and Elinor watched her from the window. She had exited the house with the speed of vampires and was already climbing into her Austin-Healey Sprite sports car, which leapt away as if on wings.

"Oh Marianne," Mary said as soon as the doctor was gone. "My poor angel. If I ever see that Willoughby again, I'll snip off his wings with my fabric scissors, I swear I will." She leaned forward and kissed the back of her daughter's hand. "I'm going downstairs to see if Margaret's okay," she said to Elinor. "Can I get you anything?"

Elinor shook her head. It had been hours since they'd had soup, but Elinor couldn't think of food now. All she could think about was Marianne. Heck, Gaia knew how annoying her younger sister could be at times, but imagining a life without her was unthinkable. Her heart felt like lead in her chest as she contemplated this.

She sat in the chair her mother had just vacated and took Marianne's hand in her own. "Fight, dammit, Marianne. Fight!"

But Marianne didn't respond, and Elinor lowered her head to the bed and prayed to the trees to help her.

"Gaia, protect your beloved daughter, who needs your help this night. Please break the fever, please! I cannot live without my sister."

She felt their spirits move within her, like a whisper through her soul reaching out. She mentally thanked her mother for tonight's ceremony, which had renewed and reinforced their bonds. At least, for her they had.

Mary came back upstairs carrying a cup of hot chocolate. She put it down on the table nearest to Elinor. She also carried a garland of wildflowers she must have gathered from the forest floor and placed them around Marianne's head.

"Our magic," Mary said softly. "It will do as much as that berry penicillin, if not more, I am sure of it."

Elinor agreed and wished she had thought of it herself, but she was glad her mother had. "Oh Mom, I was thinking about the ceremony and how Marianne fell to the ground. What do you think it means?" With more than a little worry, she stroked her sister's hair. "Marianne fought the connection and rejected them tonight. What if running away severed her ties with them? What if they won't help her now?"

Mary took a place on the other side of Marianne's bed. She closed her eyes, and Elinor knew she had turned her thoughts inward to communicate with the white pine.

"They never rejected Marianne. She rejected them. They would never turn on her, Elinor, have no fear. They know about Willoughby—or at least, the turmoil in her soul over him. Marianne must find the strength to turn to them. That is her best hope." She stroked her daughter's face affectionately. "My baby is strong. She will beat this, I am sure of it." Then she sat up. "Now drink your chocolate. I don't need you losing your strength as well. I'm going to send word to Chris about what the doctor said. It's the least we can do for him, given all his trouble earlier."

Elinor nodded. "I'm just grateful he came when he did and that he had an idea where to look. I would never have found her."

"Oh, Gaia, yes," Mary agreed. "She might have died if he hadn't come in time."

Elinor lowered her eyes, frightened she would betray her latest thought that Marianne might have wanted to do just that. From the way her mother was avoiding eye contact right now, she wondered if she was doing the same.

Her mother stood up and kissed Marianne on the forehead before leaving her.

Elinor picked up her chocolate and took a little sip, just to appease her mother, but the second she was out of the room, she put it down again. She had no desire to eat or drink. Instead, she picked up the little vial of lotion and began rubbing it into her sister's skin. And she prayed.

Elinor woke up with a start. She had no idea what time it was. All was silent in the house. Her face itched from the imprint of the blanket she had lain on, but that didn't concern her. Something had changed. It was too quiet.

Marianne.

With a fear she had never known in her life, Elinor reached for her lamp by the bed.

"Please, Gaia," she whispered before turning to look at her sister.

The fever had broken, and her skin looked a little better, but Marianne did not move. She looked too peaceful. In fact, with garland around her neck and her hands crossed on her chest she looked....

Elinor couldn't even think the word. Now, more than in any other moment in her life, she realized just how much she loved her sister. Her crazy, headstrong, soppy, and passionate Marianne. They were both so different, and yet Elinor wouldn't have her be any other way. The thought of life without her was unbearable, and she stifled the lump in her throat, not yet ready to cry.

She touched her hand, expecting to find it cold. But it was not. It was dry and warm. Normal even. As she touched it, Marianne inhaled sharply and began to open her eyes.

"Oh Marianne!" Elinor cried, as relief coursed through her. "Marianne, Marianne!"

Too weak still to respond, Marianne just blinked and stared up at the ceiling. Elinor didn't care. That was enough of a response for her. She would have jumped for joy if she could.

Her commotion must have alerted their mother, because a minute later she came into the bedroom, wearing her dressing gown in readiness for her turn to watch Marianne. She looked like she hadn't slept at all.

"Oh Mom, she's beaten it!" Elinor cried. "She's awake."

Relieved, Mary came into the room and sat beside her daughter. "Oh darling, you look so much better. Can I get you something? Some water? Or tea, perhaps?"

Marianne shook her head ever so slightly. "What time is it?"

Elinor glanced at the clock, a glass of water already in her hand. "It's four in the morning. You should take a sip at least, even if you don't feel like it. You haven't had anything to drink for hours."

Marianne nodded in a rare show of obedience and took the drink.

Mary exchanged a delighted glance with Elinor and held her hands together in prayer. Marianne was alive. She had survived. She had beaten it.

Elinor watched as Marianne raised her hand to the garland about her neck. Her sister's fingers carefully touched the dying petals, and she smiled.

Everything was going to be okay.

Chapter Thirty
A LUCKY ESCAPE

THERE WAS A GENTLE KNOCK AT HER BEDROOM DOOR. ELINOR TURNED to look at it, her body still paralyzed from sleep. Whoever it was knocked again. She glanced at the clock. It was two in the morning. *Crap!*

She pushed herself up off the top of the blanket—she'd been too tired to crawl under it—and after indulging in a good stretch, she shuffled over to the door.

It was Margaret, still in her pajamas, the sleep still on her eyes. The frightened look on her kid sister's face put Elinor on alert at once.

"Margaret, what is it?" she asked. "Is Marianne okay? Has she gotten worse again?" Marianne had been better for over twenty-four hours now. Maybe this was a relapse. Who knew how incubus fever worked?

Margaret shook her head. "No, I don't think so. There's someone at the front door asking to speak to you."

Confused, Elinor stepped out of the room. Who on earth would be calling at this hour? And why did Margaret look so guilty? "Who is it?"

"Willoughby."

Elinor stood up straight, shocked. That was the last thing she expected to hear. "Willoughby? Here?"

"Yes. He says wants to speak to you. He's downstairs waiting for you in the kitchen."

Elinor shot a glance over to their mother's room, remembering what Mary said she'd do to him if she got the chance. "Where's Mom?"

"She just fell asleep, I think. She only left Marianne a little bit ago."

"Okay. Go and tell him I'll be down in a minute. I just need to get dressed." Margaret scurried back downstairs, and Elinor slipped back inside her bedroom. Willoughby! She couldn't believe he had the balls to make an appearance. Especially now. Did he have any idea about Marianne's state of health? Or how delicate she was even now? If he had come to rub it in, she might do for him herself.

Elinor brushed her hair and pinned it loosely up. She wasn't about to make an effort for a piece of scum such as this.

As soon as she was decent, she braced herself for confrontation and left her room. The idea of seeing him again was grossly unpleasant to her, and she prayed she'd have the strength to rein in her temper. Indeed, if she were a man, she would march him outside and punch him in the face. And might do even yet.

Willoughby sat at their kitchen table, his hands hidden beneath it. He looked as uncomfortable as sin, and Elinor was glad of it. She hoped it was due to remorse. If it wasn't, it ought to have been.

Margaret was standing by the kitchen sink, her eyes bright with excitement.

"Go to your room, Margaret."

"But Elinor!"

"Please, do as I say."

Margaret opened her mouth to argue but something in Elinor's tone must have touched her. Her mouth dropped in a sulk, but she did as she was told. As soon as her baby sister was out of the room, Elinor turned on their visitor.

"Willoughby. You know you're unwelcome here. Why have you come?"

"I—"

The incubus's wings twitched uncomfortably, and he stared upward as if he could see Marianne through the ceiling. He was as handsome as ever, though there was just the hint of a few dark rings under his eyes, suggesting sleepless nights. Good. He deserved to be plagued with restlessness forever.

"I wanted—I came to explain."

"There is nothing to explain. Anyway, Marianne can't see you. She isn't well right now." Elinor didn't tell him what was wrong with her. She didn't want to give him that satisfaction.

"Yes. There is. Marianne doesn't know any of it."

Elinor noticed he hadn't asked what was wrong with her. Perhaps he'd heard it on the grapevine. Or maybe he just didn't care. "She knows you broke her heart. What else is there for her to know?"

"That I love her," he blurted. "That I haven't known a moment's peace since she left me."

Elinor wanted to slap him in the face for that. The cheek of it! "Love. What does an incubus know of love? All you know about is seeing to your own pleasure. Love. It makes me sick just to hear you say it."

"And yet I do love her," he protested, sliding a little forward across the table. "You have no idea the pressure I was under. I have an employer. Well, employer might be the wrong word. I owe a debt of honor to a demon. I had to do what I was told."

Elinor scoffed at the word demon. In the back of her head, she remembered the one she had seen sitting with him at the bar down in Florida. Reluctantly, Willoughby now had her attention. "What does that have to do with Marianne?"

"Everything. All right, I confess. When I first met Marianne, it wasn't an accident. She was an assignment, nothing more."

"An assignment? What kind of assignment?"

"I had to—he wanted me to—" For some reason Willoughby had difficulty saying the actual words.

"Go on." Elinor folded her arms impatiently in front of her. "You came here to explain. So explain."

"Making women fall in love with me is what I do. As you keep reminding me, I am an incubus after all. I owe the demon a debt, and he makes me repay it by targeting the women of his choice. Usually they're extremely rich, and generally they're associated in some way with his gaming in Ocean City—I don't usually ask him questions about it, I just do it. Together we bleed them dry until they're broke, or ruined, or whatever retribution Angus sees fit to call my marker paid, I dunno. I don't get involved on that side of his business. I just do my job."

"Bully for you. You must be very proud." She thought about Eliza and wondered just how many lives Willoughby and the demon had ruined.

"I'm not supposed to fall in love with them," Willoughby continued, ignoring her quip. "And usually, I don't. I was supposed to make her miserable, steal her happiness. That was my mission."

"Well whoopee-do, mission accomplished, well done you." Elinor didn't even try to check the sarcasm in her tone.

Willoughby shook his head. "No. You don't understand. Most of the demon's targets are broken women, often older than I am, and I just go in and do what Angus asks me to do. But with Marianne, it was different. I felt a connection to her. Suddenly, I saw a different life, a simpler one, a life I wanted for my own. She touched emotions in me I never knew I had, and I fell in love with her."

His bleeding heart story only increased Elinor's irritation. If anything, what he had just told her made his betrayal even worse. Her gaze flicked around the kitchen, taking in the rack of knives, a frying pan, a meat tenderizer.

"Anyway, Angus got wind of how I felt about Marianne and gave me an ultimatum. Either give her up or he would take my soul. If I had refused him for Marianne's sake, he would have destroyed us both. I couldn't let that happen. I had to give her up. For both of us."

Elinor was shocked. Her anger remained but was suddenly softened a little by understanding. No one should be expected to surrender their soul to a demon. No one. But that didn't excuse what they did to women.

"So you just upped and left Marianne without even a word of explanation? You say you love her. That doesn't sound like love to me. That sounds like selfishness, or worse, cruelty. And I was there, remember? Willoughby, you humiliated her—and in the worst possible way, in front of all those people. You can't expect us to ever forgive you for that."

He bowed his head in shame. Or was it self-pity? Elinor didn't know and didn't want to know. He was an incubus, an expert at manipulating the emotions and senses of others. How did she know he wasn't messing with her now? No, he could not be trusted again. Not ever.

"Elinor, please. I didn't know what else to do."

He looked up and she saw directly into his eyes. Yes, perhaps there was a little remorse there. She hoped so, for his sake. Whatever he owed the demon, he would have to pay for it in time. Maybe even a lifetime. But that wasn't her concern now. Only Marianne's happiness and well-being mattered. Willoughby would have to look out for himself.

Still, perhaps she did feel a little sorry for him, but she did not forgive him. He had put her sister in an untenable situation she could not win, however it played out, and she hated him for it.

"You've given me your explanation and now you can go."

"Elinor, what was I supposed to do? This was my soul. Have you no pity? One way or the other, I was going to lose."

"Perhaps. All I know is your soul wasn't worth one-thousandth of Marianne's. Willoughby, you need to accept you have lost her forever. You've come and said your piece. Now, if you don't mind, I would like you to leave. And please don't ever come back. You are not welcome here anymore."

Willoughby sighed and rose from the table. She didn't know whether his sigh was for Marianne or himself, and frankly, she didn't care. She just wanted him gone.

Elinor was standing in front of the door, and Willoughby paused as he reached her. A bitter glint entered his eyes. "You only know the half of it," he hissed. And he left, slamming the front door behind him. She heard a flap of leathery wings. She hoped she would never hear them again.

Elinor closed her eyes and tried to compose her thoughts. Had that really just happened? She was still recovering from the shock of him being there at all. And from trying to guess what his parting words meant.

While she mulled all he had said over in his head, she looked up. Marianne was crouched down at the top of the stairs, her hands clinging to the banisters, her face void of any emotion.

"Did you hear it all?" Elinor asked.

Marianne nodded but said nothing.

"I'm sorry," Elinor said. "Should I have let him talk to you?"

Her sister shook her head. "No. I wouldn't have known what to say to him. At least I know everything now."

"I think you had a lucky escape," Elinor said, climbing the stairs and sitting on the top step next to Marianne. She wrapped her arm around her. "From what he was saying, things would only have gotten worse and worse as time went on."

"I think so too. But at least I know he loved me now. I heard him say it. And I'll always be able to tell myself that he did, whatever happens now. It was good to hear the words."

Elinor thought his confession was hollow, but if it gave Marianne comfort, so be it. Maybe that was the most love an incubus could give. Willoughby wasn't a dryad. Maybe he had given his best after all. But now they would never know. All that mattered was his coming here had made a difference to Marianne. Elinor could at least give him credit for that. "Yes, yes I suppose it was. Now I need you to get up and get back to bed. You've been very unwell. We don't want you sick again, do we?"

Elinor helped Marianne to her feet and walked with her back to her room. She tidied the blankets and re-fluffed the pillows, then made sure Marianne was comfortable in the bed. She was about to leave when Marianne spoke up.

"Elinor. I need you to do me a favor."

"Yes? What is it?"

"It was you and Chris who came for me, wasn't it? He drove me home in his car."

Elinor nodded.

"Send Chris a message for me, please. Tell him, tell him thank you. And tell him..."

"Yes?"

"Tell him I would like to see him. As soon as you think I'm well enough."

"I will. Now go to sleep."

Elinor switched off the light on the bedside table. It wouldn't be hard getting a message to Chris. The man had been texting Elinor for news practically every hour of every day. Even now he was probably staring at his phone expecting some kind of update. She left the room and closed the door softly behind her, smiling.

Chapter Thirty-One

THE GARDEN

WITH EVERY DAY THAT PASSED, MARIANNE FELT A LITTLE STRONGER. She sat on a rock by the cliff edge, wrapped in a checkered blanket as she stared out to sea. It had rained hard last night, so hard that they'd needed to close the shutters on the windows to secure the house. There had been some damage in the grounds; most of it was superficial, like fallen branches and an upended fence post. A few yards from where Marianne sat, a tree had fallen and slipped down the rock face. She stared at it now, wedged halfway down between the sheets of granite, stuck fast. She was sad to see it go, but it had been an old tree, and this was its time. Gaia knew what she was doing, and Marianne and the others had said a little prayer for it and left it at that.

In contrast to last night, this morning was peaceful. Above her, the sun beamed gently down, kissing her upturned cheeks and soothing her mind. Below her, the waves rolled slowly back and forth over the rocks, steady and dependable as always. She thought of Willoughby and Chris. If Willoughby was the tempest, Chris was promise of peace restored. He had come every day for her since her illness. Some days he would read to her. Other days they would just talk of poetry, or her love of trees, or how she missed playing the piano.

She held out her hand before her. The dryness was almost all gone, and her nails grew strong and shiny. Perhaps, now that she was feeling more herself, she might try playing a little. Chris had played for them all while she was convalescing, and she wondered how he'd feel about them playing a duet?

The gentle tread of feet on stone announced his arrival. She turned, and there he was, carrying a small book of sonnets he had promised to share with her. As he drew near, she shifted a little along the rock, patting the space beside her, inviting him to sit down.

"Shouldn't you be inside?" Chris asked. He adjusted the top of her blanket, which had slipped when she'd made room for him.

"No, I've been inside enough," she said. "It's a beautiful morning, and the fresh air makes me feel better."

"Well, in that case, I approve." He handed her the small book, and she opened the front cover. Chris had written something inside it.

To Marianne, With Fondness, Your friend, Chris.

She traced her fingers over the inscription. There was no mention of love, Chris was too considerate for that. But a part of her looked for the words, just the same. She frowned and lowered her head.

"Is something the matter?" he asked.

Marianne shook her head. "No." Then she smiled. "Thank you for the book. We left our copy of his sonnets up at Norland, and I've missed reading them. And things have been so hectic of late, I've had no time to buy a copy of my own. So thank you."

Chris nodded and stared out to the sea. Chris was awesome at quiet. She'd never realized before how much she appreciated the time to digest her own thoughts. With Willoughby it had been all go, go, go. There had been no time for reflection, and every sensation and feeling was experienced with a violence that threatened to consume them both. Perhaps in time, their love would have burned out as quickly as it had been kindled. Perhaps.

Everything was so different with Chris. But was this love? She had been so sure of herself with Willoughby, wouldn't it be madness to make the same mistake twice? And so soon after her...disappointment? She wished she understood herself better. She thought of Elinor. Maybe Elinor could help her understand more.

"It's a pity about the tree," Chris said, pointing to it.

"To everything there is a season." Then she added, "I have never said I was sorry."

"What for?"

"Oh, for me being so stupid about Willoughby. For all the things I said. For being so horrible to you."

"You weren't horrible."

"Yes, yes I was. I've caused you nothing but grief, and you would have every right to despise me if you wanted to."

Chris smiled. "I could never do that. I...well, why don't you just worry about getting better? That would make up for everything, don't you think?"

Marianne smiled. She didn't deserve such kindness, and she knew it. There was a slight flutter in her tummy, and fearing she might have overdone it, she took a deep breath. "You know, perhaps I should go in. I'm feeling a little tired after all. Would you like to come inside for coffee or something?"

Chris shook his head. "Thank you, but no. I have some business I need to attend to." He stood up and offered her his hand. "Can I walk you home?"

His hand was strong and well-shaped, and when she took it, she felt something pass between them, something new. She lowered her eyes again, not to conceal anything but to examine her feelings, which were anything but calm now. She wondered if Chris had felt it too?

Once again, Chris adjusted the blanket around her, and for a brief moment their eyes locked. His eyes were so gentle. For the first time she noticed something stirred behind their calmness, and she was glad of it.

"Thank you," she said again, and as she savored her new discovery, the couple walked slowly back toward the cottage.

Marianne found Elinor busy in the kitchen, peeling potatoes. She sat down at the table, feeling a little anxious and not sure where to begin.

"Whatever it is, Marianne, you'd better spit it out before I'm done with these potatoes. I really don't think I can bear the suspense much longer."

Marianne was amused by the humor in Elinor's tone. In fact, they were both smiling and joking a lot more lately, which she really liked. "Promise you won't be angry with me?"

Elinor looked intrigued and put the peeler down and rinsed off her hands. After pouring herself a glass of water, she turned with her back to the sink. "Okay, I'm listening."

"Well, you know how Chris has been coming around here a lot of late?"

"It hadn't escaped my attention. There's been much more music and laughter since he has. What of it?"

Marianne took a deep breath to grow her courage. "I think Chris is coming to propose to me tonight."

Caught off guard, Elinor spit her water back into her glass.

"Well, say something!" Marianne said, laughing.

"I, um, are you happy about it?"

"I don't know. I think so."

"You think so? Bonding is for life, Marianne. Chris is a great man, and he deserves someone who loves him heart and soul. If you do it, do it because you love him, not because you feel you owe him anything. You both deserve much more than that."

Marianne smiled. "Same old Elinor, such a worry wart." She picked up an apple off the table and took a big bite out of it. "I've been thinking a lot about everyone, and about everything that happened over this summer."

Elinor nodded, and taking a seat across from Marianne, she grabbed a banana from the same bowl. "And?"

"I'm not sure how to put this without sounding cheesy."

"So just say it, and if it's cheesy, I can have a good laugh at your expense."

Marianne grinned. "Well, I was thinking about you and how you've always been there for me no matter what, telling me what you thought was right, whether it bothered me or not or whether I was a pill about it."

"Maybe you should have listened, huh?" Elinor teased, as she peeled her banana open and took a bite.

"Ha, ha. Anyway, you've never let me down."

"Because you're my sister and I love you, banana brain." Elinor tapped her banana against the side of Marianne's head.

"I know. And I love you too. And Chris, he was also there for me, all the time. Even when I gave him cause not to be."

"Which was a lot!"

Marianne blushed. "Maybe so, but he never let me down. He's like family."

"Like I said, he's an awesome man. But again, that still sounds more like gratitude than love to me, Marianne. Be careful."

"It's hard to explain my feelings when they're so new to me. All I know is I feel secure when he's around me. When I know he's coming, I can't wait for him to arrive. When he leaves, I miss him before he goes. I don't think there's another man on the planet who could replace him. Is that love, Elinor?"

"Do you think it is?"

"Maybe?" Marianne chewed on her apple and went quiet.

Elinor arranged her banana peel in a starfish pattern on the table in front of her. "What time are you expecting him?"

"I invited him for dinner. Did you peel enough potatoes?"

"Don't I always?" Elinor laughed.

"You may have a point. I guess I'm just questioning myself. A minute ago, I thought I was so deeply in love with...someone else, and now I'm in love with Chris. I just want to be sure." She started pulling the seeds from her apple core and placed them on a napkin.

Elinor leaned forward in her seat and cupped her chin in her palms. "Unfortunately, that's something you're going to have to work out for yourself. Although you know, it is the twenty-first century. There's no law that says you have to bond with anyone at all. Not until you're both ready. And in any case, you could be wrong. He might not ask you. He knows what a twit you are, and I know I'd think twice about asking you."

Marianne laughed. "Cheek. Well, I'm going up to get changed. Whatever happens I'll want to look drop-dead gorgeous for it." She put her hand to her face and caressed it. "Your lotion is amazing. I can't see a crack or anything, even if I look really hard."

Elinor smiled and stood up also. "I'm glad. Now skit, I have stuff to do too."

As Marianne reached the stairs, she looked back to where Elinor was already back at the sink, rinsing off the potatoes. There had been something else she'd really wanted to say, but somehow she hadn't found the right moment to say it.

Although her sister never said anything, Marianne knew Elinor was still all beat up about Edward. She wanted so much to comfort her, as she had been comforted herself, but it was hard when Elinor went to such pains to keep her own emotions in check. Marianne ached for her and felt a little guilty that fate had been so kind as to send her Chris. She opened her lips to try to express this, but the words wouldn't come. She would have to bide her time until the moment was right. Hoping that time would come soon, Marianne put her hand on the banister and ran upstairs to change.

For once, Marianne was as keen to make everything perfect as Elinor was. They were both fussing about in the kitchen when Chris arrived. Marianne glanced at the clock. He was bang on time.

"Full marks for punctuality," Elinor joked.

Marianne opened the door and invited him inside. His aftershave smelled like orange blossom, although that was probably just a trick of her dryad nose. She took his coat and hung it up on a peg, enjoying how warm it felt.

Mary, Elinor, and Margaret said hello when she led him into the kitchen, and he smiled and returned their greetings, all very formal, no one giving anything away. It was all she could do not to burst out laughing. She sat him at the table and took her seat beside him.

"I hope you like potatoes," said Elinor.

"Oh boy, do I," he said.

"I sense this one is strong," Margaret whispered eerily. "Give unto him the test of the potato and see if he survives."

Marianne crossed her ankles and tried not to pee herself.

"Let us bow our heads and give thanks to Gaia for the feast we are about to enjoy," Mary said.

Marianne's appetite had returned with a vengeance, but even she wasn't up to the mountain of newly dug-up potatoes drenched in butter and vegetable quiche Elinor had piled in front of her. She pushed away her plate and stretched. "Are you trying to fatten me up?"

Elinor smiled. "Maybe. There's barely any meat on them bones as it is."

Chris grinned, but wisely kept his mouth shut. He looked out the window. "It's a beautiful evening. I think after all that food, I wouldn't mind a stroll." He looked meaningfully at Marianne.

Marianne ignored Elinor's knowing grin. "What a lovely idea. Does anyone else want to come?"

Elinor, Margaret, and Mary all shook their heads, clearly pretending they didn't know what was going down.

"Well, it looks like it's just me then," Marianne said. Was it her imagination, or did Chris look relieved they'd all declined to come?

"Thank you for a lovely dinner," Chris said, rising from the table.

"You're very welcome," Mary replied.

Marianne held the door open, indicating she was ready, and Chris wandered ahead of her, then waited for her to close the door behind them.

"Which way would you like to go?" Marianne asked.

"Let's head back to my place, there's something new I'd like to show you there. You don't mind a little walk, do you?"

"No, not at all," Marianne said, a little intrigued and more than a little excited.

They strolled together for a while, making small talk. Marianne was struck by how at ease she was with him, and how often they discovered they liked the same things. Suddenly, he didn't seem that much older at all.

When they were almost at his house, Chris stopped in his tracks and put his hand in his pocket. Whatever it was he'd pulled from it was concealed inside his hand, but he looked *mischievous*.

"What is it?" Marianne asked, sensing the moment was on them.

"Do you trust me?" he asked, a playful look on his face.

"Yes," she smiled, "though I have a funny feeling maybe I shouldn't."

"Okay, well then put this on." A long strip of black cloth fell from his hand.

"Is that...a blindfold?"

"Nothing gets past you, does it!"

"And you want me to put it on?"

Before she could say no, he stepped behind her. "Yes. Let me help you. Don't worry. You won't have to wear it for long. But I want what I'm about to show you to be a complete surprise."

Marianne held her hand to her face as he tied the blindfold, making sure it sat right. Chris was careful and tied it securely. He took her hand.

"We'll go slowly, and you'll be on the path for most of the way, and I'll tell you when we get to the end."

She nodded and slowly began to walk forward, even though she knew the path was flat. In her mind's eye, she roughly calculated the distance to his front door, but after a while she began to wonder if they were going inside at all.

"Where are you taking me?" she laughed.

"We're almost there—just a few more steps."

"Now."

They had come to a pause, and Chris removed her blindfold. What she saw in front of her left her utterly speechless.

They were at the back of his house. Once, a long time ago, she'd spotted a kind of neglected little wilderness that could have used a bit of TLC, and she remembered saying something on those lines to Chris at the time.

He'd clearly paid attention. The fallen wood and overgrown shrubs had been cleared away, and in their place, Chris had used his magic to create a beautiful, enchanted orchard. Set inside ornate, silver railings were the most beautiful trees Marianne had ever seen. As they walked inside, she saw silver birches, dogwoods, and all kinds of fruit trees and nut bushes. Set in the center of them all was a great yew. Though the fall was upon them, the orchard was lit by a surreal golden light and all the trees were magically in blossom.

Singing birds tended the garden, and Marianne clapped her hands in delight when she saw the tiny pixies flittering about, tending to the flowers inside. A curious hummingbird came to check her out, and content she was no threat to it, it darted to the blossom, where it continued to collect pollen.

Marianne closed her eyes, opening her heart to the spirits in the garden. They embraced her at once, claiming her as their mistress. She opened her eyes, delighted. Oh Gaia, how much *work* must he have put into this? She couldn't imagine it had been a casual undertaking. And he'd said nothing, nothing at all the entire time, wanting it to be a special surprise just for her. The gods had truly blessed her.

"Oh Chris, this is the most beautiful thing I've ever seen. It's enchanting."

"Thank you," he said. "It was inspired by the woman I love."

Marianne smiled and lowered her eyes, blushing, too full of her love for him to play coy. And it was love, she was sure of it now. Her heart was bursting with happiness, and when at last she had control of her emotions, she raised her head and smiled at him.

"I love you, Marianne. I know you've had a difficult year, and I've no desire to force you into a union you're not ready for. But I will wait for you, for as long as it takes. I've loved you since the first time I saw you, but I was afraid to speak up because I had no right."

At this, Marianne placed a finger on his lips.

"It's okay," she said. "I love you too. You did all this for me?"

He nodded. "It's yours, all of it. I want to make you happy."

"You do," she said. "Happier than I've ever been in my life." Her gaze swept around the enchanted garden, taking it all in. "This is a good beginning. Are you going to be able to keep it up? I have expensive tastes, you know!"

Chris laughed, and gathering her into his arms, he kissed her. Marianne closed her eyes, enjoying his tender caresses and the whispers of the tree spirits as they poured their blessings upon the couple.

Chapter Thirty-Two

LITTLE BOOK OF BACHELORS

ELINOR WAS PROUD OF HER SISTER AND FELT ONE HUNDRED PERCENT sure she had made the right choice. All the talk between Chris and Marianne was of love, not bonding, though she was pretty sure the two would be bonded when the time was right. For them.

They were at Chris's now. He had arranged an impromptu gathering, and Elinor had just filled her cup with some rather wicked-smelling punch. Marianne and Mary were sitting on the back steps to Chris's house, catching up on gossip with Gemini, Cousin John, and Betsy. Margaret was running around with the other children, and everyone was laughing and in great spirits. Chris was just a few feet away doing his Jedi thing with his barbecue tongs. He looked so happy, like a man who had everything he'd ever dreamed of. As for Marianne, she looked like the proverbial cat with the cream. No one looking at her would have guessed what she had been through. It was like none of it had ever happened. Elinor couldn't have been happier for them both.

The air was infused with the aroma of ketchup and honey barbecue sauce. Elinor's tummy gurgled, as along with everyone else she anticipated some really great food. She joined the others on the steps, placing her punch between her feet. All the talk was of Chris's new enchanted garden.

"How long have you had it, you sly fox?" Betsy asked. "All this time and he didn't breathe a word about it, not a single one! I supposed you concealed it with some kind of magic so Marianne would be the first to see it. I know your silly ways. You can't fool me, you know!"

"May I remind you the surprise was supposed to be for Marianne." Chris tossed a pineapple ring in the air, and it landed perfectly on the upper grill, exposing its nicely seared upper side. Everything looked so delicious. "Of course, I used an enchantment. We all practically live on top of each other. How else was I supposed to keep it a secret?"

Betsy grinned, just happy to tease him. "Well, I suppose now we have these two lovebirds sorted out, we ought to find someone for you, Miss Elinor. You can't be outshone by a younger sister for long. I shall rummage through my little book of bachelors and see if we can't find a nice Romeo for you."

Elinor shook her head, afraid Betsy might actually have one. She wouldn't put it past her. "Don't trouble yourself, Betsy. I'm perfectly content just as things are. In any case, I'm not sure my mother would want another young man on the scene. Things are chaotic enough in our house as it is."

Now it was Mary's turn to shake her head. "You do talk such nonsense sometimes, girl. Betsy, if you have someone in mind for my eldest, by all means bring them over for supper. Get her off my hands, for the love of cookies!"

"For that matter, if you have someone in your book for Mom, send them too," Elinor retorted. "She could use a good flirt, just like the rest of us."

They all laughed.

"How long before the driver gets here?" John asked, his hungry eyes fixed on the succulent meats on the grill. "I'm famished."

Chris had had a good supply of everything he needed for his last-minute barbecue, except for burger buns. One call to the local grocer's had fixed that, and the driver was supposedly on his way. Chris looked at his phone. "He just left. I'd say no more than five minutes. Grab some salad. Or have a bunless burger if you can't wait. There's plenty."

While John did just that, Elinor sat back on the steps and let the autumn sun stream down on her upturned face. As the others chatted, her thoughts drifted away. It had been a while since her last text from Edward. It was just as well—he was with another now, and she probably wouldn't hear from him ever again. It was time to accept it and just move on. The worst was over, surely?

She took a swig of her punch and watched as, at last, the awaited driver drove slowly up to the house. As soon as the car stopped, the driver popped open the trunk, got out, and pulled a whole tray of buns from inside it. Chris certainly never did anything by halves.

Elinor recognized the young man at once. Harry was the son of the local grocer, and she would sometimes have a friendly chat with him in his dad's shop. He nodded to everyone as he carried his tray over.

"All right, Harry!" Chris said as the young man dropped his buns on a tray beside the grill. "How are you?"

Chris reached into his pocket and pulled out some bills, which he handed over. When Harry started pulling out some smaller notes, Chris held up his hand. "Keep the change, it's a tip."

"Thanks, Chris! Oh, I've nothing to complain about," Harry said. "Dad's been keeping me busy."

"How is he?" Chris asked. "I haven't seen him about much."

"No, well, he's had his hands full lately, that's for sure. He'll be glad when that Ferrars bonding is over, and things get back to normal again."

It was as if someone had slapped Elinor in the face. She froze and was conscious of her mother and Marianne suddenly staring at her.

"Dad hates it when they spring these last-minute events on him," Harry continued. "Then he has to scramble to get all the right orders in. Not that Dad would turn good business away. It's a lot of work, but it's going to be lovely. We're pulling out all the stops for them. The lady wants it just perfect, and that's what she's going to get."

Suddenly, he had a wistful look in his eyes, and Elinor knew beyond all doubt that he was thinking of Lucy Steele, imagining what it must be like to carry a succubus to your honeymoon bed and pleasure her nonstop for a week.

"Lucy Steele got bonded up here?" Marianne asked. "In Maine? I thought they would do it in New Jersey?"

Harry shrugged. "Last-minute change of heart, I heard. Another Bridezilla probably—there's plenty of them about this season. Oh well.

There's one born every minute. Oh, that reminds me, she had a very particular message for you, Elinor. Now what was it?"

"Oh?" Marianne asked.

"Oh yes, she said to be sure to tell Elinor Dashwood that Lucy Ferrars sends her love and to let her know everything went down like a piece of cake."

He smiled at Elinor.

Summoning all her strength, she said, "Thank you, Harry, that was kind of you to pass it on."

His business concluded, Harry waved goodbye and climbed back into his car. A moment later he was gone, and though Elinor's gaze remained fixed on his taillights, she barely registered what she was looking at.

This was a shock. Her heart was racing, and she felt a little dizzy. She wasn't quite as over Edward as she'd thought. Conscious that everyone was staring at her, she picked up her punch and took a sip, more to hide behind the cup than anything. Her hand trembled a little, so she put the cup down quickly.

Chris, who had been following along with everyone else, turned his attention to the newly arrived buns and opened the first bag.

"Right," he said. "Who's hungry?"

Grateful for the distraction, Elinor took the opportunity to get up and walk inside Chris's house. She needed a moment alone to gather her thoughts. She wasn't by herself for long though, because her mother came in right after her.

"I'm sorry," her mother said. "That was a dreadful way to hear about it. Are you okay?"

Elinor shook her head, hardly able to comprehend what she felt. "I will be. I just need a minute, Mom."

Mary nodded, but before she left her daughter alone, she gave her a little hug. Elinor felt the tears well in her eyes, but conscious that she wasn't safely at home to shed them, she fought to keep them in check. Mary must have sensed her misery, because she pulled her daughter even closer, then kissed her on the cheek. "Come out when you're ready. Take your time. I'll make sure they save you some food. Or maybe they won't, so don't wait too long."

"Thanks, Mom," Elinor said, then turned away, knowing if she looked at her mother now, she wouldn't be able to stop the tears from falling.

Mary must have understood this, because without another word, she slipped away. Elinor wandered over to Chris's fireplace and rested her hands on the mantel. The spirits in the wood were long dead, and the mantel felt empty. As did she. She bowed her head, and controlling her sorrow, finally accepted that her love was lost and that this was how things had to be.

Chapter Thirty-Three

MUD FIGHT

ELINOR AND MARGARET WERE UP TO THEIR NECK IN MUD, WEEDING THE flower beds around the house. It had rained last night, leaving the soil super-soft, perfect for weeding—and mud fights.

"Oh no you don't, you little scallywag!" Elinor cried as she took another mud pie to the chest. "I'll get you for that." She scooped up a handful of wet mud, ready to sling it back.

Margaret shrieked and immediately jumped up and ran to the side of the house, inviting Elinor to chase.

"You can run but you can't hide!" Elinor shouted, jumping up and taking the bait.

Her little sister could have made her escape easy, but enjoying the fun, she teased Elinor by keeping herself only just out of reach.

"I'll tell Mom if you splat me!" Margaret cried. "You're supposed to be looking after me. Not chucking mud balls at me."

"I'll look after you all right!" Elinor took aim, and screaming, Margaret ran off again.

They'd been running around the perimeter of the house, and just as she turned the corner to the front, Elinor tossed her mud ball as hard as she could, expecting Margaret to be about six feet or so ahead of her.

Splat! The mud ball found its target all right, but it wasn't Margaret standing there with a chest full of wet dirt. It was Edward! And Margaret was standing right beside him, frozen to the spot and her mouth wide open. Elinor could relate.

"Holy crap cakes!" Elinor said, feeling the blood drain from her face in shock as his presence knocked her off guard. "What are you doing here?" she managed to say.

"Hello to you too," Edward said, wiping the mucky mess off his once perfectly white shirt. "Don't hold anything back, will you?"

Feeling a little foolish, Elinor rushed forward, intending to help brush off the mud, but then she hesitated, in case he didn't want her to. Also, her hands were muddy; she might make an even worse mess of his crisp, white shirt and silk tie.

"I'm so, so sorry," she said, feeling it. "That was supposed to be for Margaret."

"I'm glad to hear it." Thank Gaia, he was laughing. "I thought maybe it was some new ritual dryad greeting or something."

A million and one thoughts and emotions fought for dominance, but she couldn't focus on anything. Not that Margaret helped. She kept grinning like some perverted Cheshire Cat, as if something saucy was going on between her and Edward—and as if nothing had changed. Didn't the big twit realize, everything had changed? He'd bonded with Lucy. Things had to be different now.

"Um, maybe you should come in and get yourself cleaned up?" Elinor said at last.

"Thank you, yes. That probably would be a good idea." A large clump of slick mud slid down his chest. Elinor groaned.

Wiping her own filthy hands on her jeans, she led the way inside, glancing with horror at the mirror inside the door when she saw how much dirt was caked to her face. *Really, Gaia*, she thought, *you had to bring him round now?* And her hair, omg. And her clothes, yikes. She looked like a vagrant. Why didn't the floor open up and swallow her? She fumbled for something, anything, to say.

"Mom and Marianne went out earlier to get some shopping. They'll be sorry they missed you."

"Yes, that's a pity," Edward said. "Still, another time maybe."

He said it like they had all the time in the world, like he could pop in any afternoon he wanted to and they would all sit down and politely eat some cake and drink tea. It was time someone reminded him that things were different now. He couldn't just swan around here when the feeling took him, just to tease her. Could he really be that cruel? She angrily ripped a few sheets of paper towels from a roll, dampened them under the faucet, and handed them to him. Then she ran Margaret a glass of water and passed it to her.

"So how is *Mrs.* Ferrars?" Elinor hoped her special emphasis would not be overlooked.

Odd, because Edward looked genuinely confused. "Um, I would guess she's fine? Probably as crabby as ever."

Weird. If this was how he talked of his sweetheart, maybe Elinor had made a lucky escape. But then the penny dropped. "No, I didn't mean your mother, I meant Lucy."

A shadow of realization crossed Edward's face, and she could see his thoughts racing.

Whatever he was thinking, Margaret had had enough. Sensing that her mud fight was well and truly over, she set down her empty glass and skipped across to the door. "You're both boring," she said in a huff. "I'm going to find someone fun to play with. Bye, Edward."

Normally Elinor should have upbraided Margaret for her rudeness, but the truth was she was struggling for words as it was. And where on earth was Lucy? Not that she wanted the smug little twerp there, but still.

As soon as the door closed, she turned back to Edward. "I'm sorry, Edward, but what are you doing here? Shouldn't you be with your darling partner?"

"Actually, I was here visiting Chris talking job-related stuff." Edward took a step toward her, but uncertain, he hesitated. "I'm guessing then, er, that you haven't heard the news?"

Elinor shook her head, bewildered. "No, not a whisper. What's happened? Is Lucy all right?"

The faintest smile turned the corner of his lips, and Elinor couldn't help observing just how adorable he looked, with his unruly mop of green-black hair and his tawny goblin eyes, now dancing and playful. Not to mention the mud. Maybe it was the dryad in her, but that little splatter of mud made him look so hot. *Shush now, brain, you can't have these thoughts anymore. He's not free.*

"Well," he began. "I suppose it's all been a bit chaotic, so maybe I shouldn't be surprised my news hasn't reached you."

Elinor could barely restrain herself. "What news?"

"Then you haven't heard." He sighed. "Lucy and I, we're not bonded. She chose to bond with my brother, Robert, instead."

Wait, what? The room began to spin, and Elinor collapsed onto a kitchen table chair. Her breath came in fast, shallow gasps, and she pointed frantically to the drawer where they kept all the paper bags.

Panicked, Edward tore the drawer open, and finding one, handed it to her. Putting it to her mouth, Elinor breathed in and out, desperate to restore her lungs to a natural rhythm. *Lucy and Robert. Wait. Was he serious? This couldn't be a bad joke, could it? Was Edward free? What did all this mean?* Oh Gaia, how she wished Marianne and her mother were with her right now!

While Elinor hyperventilated, Edward dropped to one knee, gazing with concern into her face. As her breathing returned to normal, he took her free hand in his own.

"When my mother cut me off without a penny, I don't think she realized she was doing me a favor. I could never have broken my vow to Lucy, you know that, but because of good old Mother, it turns out I didn't have to. As soon as the money shifted from my name to Robert's, Lucy dumped me and took up with him. Turned out she didn't love me after all, can you imagine?"

Elinor laughed at that and put the bag down. It was wet. Oh shit. Was she crying as well? Was her face now streaky with muddy tears? Stunning!

"There's a lot more I need to tell you, but right now the most important thing is this. My darling, I've loved you since the first day I saw you at Norland Park. I should have claimed you then and saved us both all this heartache, but what can I say, I was an idiot. I came today not just to explain everything about Lucy, but to tell you that I adore you and to beg you to forgive me. I love you, Elinor. I couldn't stand not being with you— I just didn't know how I could go on without your love. My life has been miserable, every day has been a black cloud of gloom and despair. But not now. Now, I want to be with you forever—if you'll have me. If you can forgive my stupidity."

The fool was still talking. Didn't he know he'd already said enough? Her tears were an odd mix of saltiness and mud, but she didn't care. He'd just have to live with it. In a burst of passion that even Marianne would have been proud of, Elinor jumped up and flung herself into his arms, desperate to claim at last the very thing she had wanted for so long.

Months of denial, sense, reservation, and caution were washed away in a delicious heartbeat. Explanations could come later. This was her moment, and she was damned well going to claim it. His tears mixed with her own as they embraced. Apparently, Edward was as soppy as she was, which was pretty cool for a half-goblin in anyone's book.

Chapter Thirty-Four

THE WHITE PINE

GIFTS OF HERBS AND SPICES IN ORNATE CONTAINERS FILLED THE ROOM. Elinor closed her eyes and enjoyed the sensation of having them painted all over her body. Her mother dabbed a final line of saffron on the back of each hand, and Marianne had just finished painting her toes with cinnamon. Elinor imagined she and Edward would have a lot of fun with that. Later.

Barton Cottage was filled with laughing women, and even Fanny managed a chuckle or two when she thought no one was looking.

"I still can't believe that Lucy was working for a demon all that time," Marianne said. "I knew she was a twit, but I had no idea she was such a scheming twit."

"Lift your hands."

Elinor did as her mother instructed and waited while she pulled the bonding robe over her head, careful not to disturb the paint.

"Edward told me she approached him when they were alone and made a sign in the air and spoke words he didn't recognize, and the next thing he knew he was promising her everything. You know druids. Their word is their bond, and as soon as he said he'd bond with her, he was stuffed. She turned off the magic after that, but it was too late by then."

"Couldn't he have resisted her?" Margaret asked. "I know I would have if a nasty succubus was all over me."

Elinor and Marianne exchanged meaningful glances, careful of what they said around Margaret. "Not if she turned her dark enchantments on him," Elinor explained. "Trust me, kiddo, no man on earth can resist that."

"Yeah, just look at our brother, John," Marianne snorted. "He starts burbling off the second one walks into a room."

Fanny shot Marianne a nasty look. But perhaps for the sake of the day, she didn't react beyond that.

Elinor gave Fanny a grateful smile and mouthed, "Sorry."

Fanny let out a little sigh and shrugged, turning away and accepting the apology.

Maybe she isn't all bad after all, Elinor thought. "Um, have you heard from Robert? Or Lucy?"

Fanny rolled her eyes. "Oh heavens, yes, ever since he heard Momsie's talking to her lawyers, trying to change the will again. He's positively pooping his pants."

"I thought it was irrevocable?" Elinor asked.

"It's supposed to be. But now she wants it all settled on me." She smiled, and Elinor could imagine what Fanny was thinking.

"It'll be funny if she does," Marianne said. "Poor Lucy." Her eyes sparkled with merriment.

Mary glanced at a clock on the wall. "It is time."

Elinor's heart was steady as she got to her feet and walked barefoot to the door. She stepped aside as, one by one, everyone but Mary left the cottage. Elinor grasped her mother's hand as she stood by her.

"I wish Dad was here," she whispered.

Mary's eyes were full of tears. "He is, child. I believe he is." Her mother squeezed her hand warmly, then let it go.

Elinor and Mary were the last to leave the house, and Mary closed the door gently behind them all.

It was a short walk to the white pine. Elinor was conscious of the dirt and grass under her feet, and the gentle wind that kissed her loose hair, setting it flying softly behind her. Mostly, her heart was full of the joy she felt, the joy of being supported by the people she loved more than anything in this world, and the joy of knowing the one man she loved with all her heart was waiting just a few feet away, as they prepared to unite their lives forever.

She smiled as she passed Betsy, John, and Gemini and the kids, who watched her in awe as she walked along the rose petal aisle they had strewn for her earlier. And then her brother, John, who despite Fanny's misgivings had paid for a lavish buffet they could all enjoy once the ceremony was over. He was a good egg really, and she loved him and was glad they both could come, even if Fanny was such a pain in the butt. Sometimes. It did not escape Elinor's notice that Fanny must have defied her mother's wishes to be here at her outcast brother's wedding. She hoped the punishment, if any, wouldn't be too severe. Though Barbara Ferrars probably wouldn't want to change her will three times!

Marianne, Chris, and Margaret were waiting for her beside the white pine, which they had already dressed in ribbons and painted in spices. All three were holding hands, and she couldn't resist the chance to kiss each of them, needing to share her happiness before it overwhelmed her.

And there, last but not least, stood Edward. His robes were cut from the same natural fibers as her own, and like hers, his body was adorned with all colors of natural spices. She wondered just how much of his body they had painted and where the sweet spots were. She would find out soon enough.

Elinor would have kissed him, too, had custom not decreed otherwise. Instead, she took her place by his side and waited as Mary walked between them to take her place in front of the pine. Then Elinor and Edward knelt before her, signaling that the ceremony was to begin.

Mary smiled at everyone present, then took a deep breath and began. "Sisters of Gaia, I bring to you these souls, who have declared their love and have promised to be true to one another until death recalls them to your bosom. I, and all here present, seek your blessing on their union. Do you offer your consent?"

All went quiet. For a moment Elinor feared that they might not, that they might reject Edward and his goblin blood, forcing her to choose between the two halves of her soul. It would be an impossible choice to make if they forced her to do it. But they did not.

Above her, the branches began to stir, and she was filled with a sense of calm she had never known before in her life. The white pine had spoken.

Permission had been given. Their bonding was blessed. They had accepted him. Her relief must have shown, because Edward turned to look at her. She nodded slightly, signaling she was okay.

Her attention returned to her mother. Mary nodded, and Elinor shuffled around to face Edward. They locked hands, and recited together:

"My honor is yours, my soul is yours, my life is yours. To you I am given. We are as one. For always."

Then two branches swept down, forking together to form a seat. Once the couple was on it, the two were hoisted up, clinging to each other as well as to the limbs. To Elinor, it felt as if they had indeed become one body, one heart, one soul.

High above the trees, the autumn sun cast a golden light upon their little bower. They had known darkness, but for now, all that was overcome. In this moment, there was only family, friends, love, and joy. Neither knew what the future held for them—they were surrounded only by love. Edward brushed a lock of hair away from Elinor's cheek. And then he kissed her. He was wickedly good at that. Life was awesome.

Angus had stared into his cranberry daiquiri for quite long enough. The image of the dryad and druid embracing above that ridiculous tree was nothing short of sickening. Stupid bet. Next time he'd be sure to gamble on something he had more control over than destroying a girl's happiness, and not with a dying satyr. Betting on capturing female hearts! By Gaia, sometimes he was a chump. Och well, you win some, you lose some.

Angus picked up his cocktail stick and used it to stir the drink. The image faded then disappeared. Without a blink, he picked up the glass and swallowed it down in a single gulp. It didn't taste bad, considering.

A rather hot-looking succubus named Brianna with curves that could only be forged in Hades leaned across the bar and put her hand on the stem of the glass. Her tail wagged playfully behind her and her leathery wings were nice and tight, just as he liked them. He'd liked Lucy's wings too, but she was in his bad books at the moment, his *very* bad books. And Willoughby too. A pair of failures. Maybe this one would know how to stick to the job he had given them.

Brianna motioned over to the end of the bar, where a rather dejected young woman had just sat down, looking like she'd just dropped her trust fund at the tables.

"Another?" Brianna asked, smiling her most winning smile and teasing the rim of the empty glass between her fingers.

"Why not?" Angus said. He smiled, stood up, and sauntered over to the young woman at the end of the bar. Let the games begin. "May I join you?"

**

Thank you for reading! Did you enjoy? Please add your review because nothing helps an author more and encourages readers to take a chance on a book than a review.

And don't miss more in the Soul and Shadows series with book 3, NECROMANCER ABBEY, coming soon!

Until then read more paranormal romance like HEX, LOVE, AND ROCK & ROLL by City Owl Author, Kat Turner. Turn the page for a sneak peek!

You can also sign up for the City Owl Press newsletter to receive notice of all book releases!

SNEAK PEEK OF HEX, LOVE, AND ROCK & ROLL

By Kat Turner

Helen Schrader hated witches. After all, they'd gotten her thrown into foster care. But as her thirtieth birthday approached, she sat across from a supposed witch named Nerissa and worked up the nerve to ask her for a spell. Funny how the past refused to die.

Pentagram knickknacks and a crystal ball collection decorated the old lady's living room, along with vintage furniture and a framed art print of three women mixing brew in a cauldron. A bookshelf full of texts on witchcraft, world religions, and philosophy completed vivid testimony to authenticity.

People all over Minneapolis swore the crone could conjure fast cash. The pagans who took classes at Helen's yoga studio spoke of Nerissa in the reverent tones of worshipers.

Perhaps the universe began orchestrating the current turn of events when one of Helen's students walked in on her crying over unpaid bills and handed her Nerissa's business card. Unless her visions from years ago kicked some grand plan into motion.

Did everything happen for a reason?

Though the hardened cynic in Helen scoffed at bullshit magical thinking, an atrophied, softer side not yet demolished by life's cruelty yearned to believe in synchronicity and magic.

Sweat glued her jeans to the backs of her thighs as she adjusted her weight on the sofa cushion. She could stand to do some Zen breathing to calm her nerves. Besides, she'd run out of options to save her business. Her credit was shot, so no more loans. But Light and Enlightened would not become Dark and Forgotten without a final, radical attempt at salvation. Time to take one last shot at rescuing the only permanent home she'd ever known. Throw a Hail Mary pass. She met Nerissa's keen blue eyes and managed a smile.

The universe has a plan. Everything happens for a reason. You've got this.
You are fucking idiot and a loser who is destined to fail.

"You have an impressive book collection." Helen picked a chip in her nail polish as if repetitive motion would banish negative thoughts. "I'm not sure if you got my email about your fee for today. Does twenty dollars work? I'm so sorry I can't offer more."

A lopsided smirk deepened the wrinkles in Nerissa's cheeks. She petted the arm of the leather recliner she sat in and uncrossed her legs beneath a maxi skirt. A knowing tone smoothed the kinks in her low timbre as she said, "Is that why you made an appointment? To discuss literature? Or did you mention the books as a way of confirming my legitimacy?"

Helen drew in a deep inhale and willed the room's sage scent and mellow lighting to relax her before she blundered another attempt at small talk. "Just curious. I've read some of those books. Not the witchy ones, but the Sartre and Nietzsche. 'That which does not kill me makes me stronger' was my motto for awhile. I have an undergrad degree in philosophy. Sorry. I'm rambling."

Yikes, she was a hot and simmering mess. Intelligent aliens were welcome to zap her with a space laser and implant competence into her brain.

Without a word, Nerissa rose. She walked across the living room to the bookcase and ran her finger across spines. "Don't sell yourself short. You have more than an undergrad degree, you started a doctorate. You're smarter than you think, and I can assure you that failure is not in your destiny. Let's have a peek at my favorite book. It's one of the *witchy* ones."

Helen's heart seemed to jump to her throat, and an icy ribbon threaded up her spine. Nerissa must've figured out the facts about her education through research. The other part? Mere coincidence. A nervous laugh bubbled out with her next words. "Is my aura that strong? You practically read my mind."

Nerissa's gray braid swished back and forth as she turned her head over her shoulder. A twinkle in her eye caught slices of afternoon light streaming in through gaps in the drapes.

"There's no *practically* about it. My ability to access your surface thoughts is a sign of our spirit-born connection. I see magic swirled into those beautiful amber irises of yours, too. You are gifted, but we can't step into our deepest truth until we believe in ourselves."

Helen snorted when her stomach went sour. She'd been called a lot of things over the years, but gifted wasn't one of them. Mind reading amounted to an easier sell. This woman was patronizing her due to some ulterior motive. Everybody had one.

"Oh, please. If I was gifted, I'd have more to show for myself by now. Behold, my impressive roster of accomplishments: a pit of debt, a retired stripping career, and a useless degree. Not exactly ticking off boxes on those 'things every woman should have by thirty' checklists."

The self-flagellation lashed Helen to the bone, and her trusty armor of sarcasm didn't protect her from those whip stings. She covered her face and trained her gaze on an area rug, not looking up until the floorboards creaked.

A massive tome in her hands, Nerissa ambled back to her chair and sat. "There will be bigger birthdays if you're lucky. I still remember the sixties. Woodstock. I was the girl in a famous picture, twirling and twirling. I slept with *all* of those rock stars and enjoyed free love."

Heat spread under Helen's breastbone, tightness squeezing her midsection. Was the 'rock stars' comment a sly knock on Helen for falling for the musician ex who cheated on her with every available groupie? A catty little mind-reading trick of Nerissa's?

Whatever. With her life circling the drain, she could not endure head games. Lisa still refused to speak to her. Bad news for a business partner or best friend, let alone both. She had major problems to solve and not a minute to squander.

"Cool. Sounds like fun. I'd like to talk about your services now. My business goes in to foreclosure next week, and my closest friend blames me. I need money. You can do wealth spells, right?"

A grating guffaw rolled out of Nerissa's throat. She opened her volume and leafed. Pages warped from water damage and crowded with words offered coy peeks at possible solutions.

"Patience isn't among your virtues. Hence your tendency to act before thinking and leave projects unfinished. But your drive is noble, and your will is strong. You dare to chase success by any means necessary, which I admire. Takes gumption to sell the spectacle of one's naked flesh to keep the lights on, and don't beat yourself up about the studio. There's a yoga place on every block these days. Lots of entrepreneurial young women such as yourself are losing their shirts teaching Downward Dog."

Helen clamped her teeth down on the tip of her tongue and swallowed a snarky comeback. Not wise to risk alienating the witch. Better to summon tact and diplomacy.

Nerissa hummed a tune while reading.

Helen tapped her foot. She needed to hit the road before traffic became a zoo, and the final notice of foreclosure stuffed in the bottom of her purse wasn't about to dematerialize.

"Finding any good abundance spells?" The fake-casual lilt in Helen's tone prompted her to roll her eyes at herself. She sucked at tact and diplomacy.

"I want to try an experiment." The gray-haired woman flipped to the front of her book and touched a circle inked on the inside of the cover.

"Alright. Sure." Helen snuck a peek at her watch and squirmed.

"This grimoire was an inheritance from my foremothers. My coven daughter will inherit my sacred text from me to learn the spirit witch's craft and begin the work of the six-fold sisterhood. The spirit element is the most cerebral of the six circles."

God, enough with the pointless anecdotes. Nerissa might have all day to meander, but Helen did not. "Whoever she is will be lucky. Like I said, I'm broke as a joke—"

Another laugh from the old witch made for a jarring interruption. "You may be the *she* in question. Here's a free lesson. Your defeatist tendencies stem from fear of finding your true power, so you self-sabotage in an effort to make yourself less threatening. I understand. We wise women have been taught by the patriarchy to hate our gifts."

Helen ground her molars. Aggravation shot through her in a frying jolt.

Cash, not a feminist lecture, would solve her problems. She grabbed her purse off the couch and jumped to her feet. "This was a mistake. I assumed—"

Nerissa muttered in some throaty, incomprehensible language. The old woman's eyes rolled back in her head. Blank slates of white remained.

Breath vanished from Helen's lungs. The bizarre sight and sounds boggled her imagination until skepticism intervened. Nerissa's eyeball move could be a trick, a result of training ocular muscles.

"A trick? I don't deal in cheap parlor tricks, dear. Now let's see if you are the one."

A pop sounded in Helen's ears. She blinked a few times as a dazed, sleepy sensation disoriented her. Lost to pleasurable mugginess and an odd feeling of time slowing to a crawl, she didn't snap back to lucidity until she noticed the cauldron painting again.

The painting was upside down. No. Correction. *She* was upside down, hanging in midair.

Blood roared in Helen's ears while she scrabbled unsuccessfully to reclaim control of her faculties. A scream tore its way up her throat but somehow died before erupting. Electric with panic, she flailed, spinning in a dizzy circle. A few chaotic seconds later, she recovered some semblance of her bearings and managed to stay still despite waves of queasiness.

The room returned to focus as blurs of color reformed into bookshelves, furniture, and other familiar shapes. *Almost* familiar. Her perception was weird.

Helen gaped when she figured out was was wrong with her surroundings. The furnishings and Nerissa were below her. She was stuck to the damn ceiling. To make matters weirder, another woman now stood in the spot she'd occupied, someone in jeans identical to Helen's.

Shock slammed into her as a realization dawned. She wasn't looking at a third person. She looked down at herself, her own body, while her consciousness floated above. Brunette waves streaked with blonde highlights tumbled over her shoulders. At least she was having a good hair day, because the out-of-body experience blew her mind. Separation from her physical form had been the last thing she'd been expecting during the visit.

A coil of phosphorescent light spiraled upward from the middle of the open book while the witch chanted, "Coven daughter, come to me. Show us truth and clarity."

Discombobulated, Helen squinted against a glare. The beam bent and twisted into a hoop. The space in the middle of the illuminated circle glimmered. Images appeared. A highlight reel of her life played while she gawked.

Nerissa pulled from Helen's memories and projected them at her. *Now* her mind was blown. What else could this be besides hardcore magic?

"I can help you, Helen, but you need to listen. Can you?"

She ought to get in line and embrace the insanity, or she'd soon be begging Dreamgirls to let her hump their germ-infested pole again. Hard pass on the humping. "Yes."

Helen crashed back into her physical form with a boom, knees weak and mind spinning. Reeling from the loss of control, she plopped her butt on the couch and shook herself out of a daze.

"Did your mother and grandmother have the gift?" The witch's eyes returned to normal.

Mother. The sound of the word was profane, like the filthiest curses flung at her.

What should have carried a connotation of loving nurturance dredged up a memory of the time the mother in question shrieked about original sin while she forced Helen to eat the pages of her diary. Recollections of the incident still scraped her raw with phantom pain. She should have learned to stop talking about her visions after that day. Or after the next morning, spent whimpering on the toilet.

"I didn't know my grandmother. My mother had major issues."

"You never had a mother figure who embraced your gift. Tragic." A soft tremble rounded the edges of Nerissa's words. "The visions began at the onset of your menses and lasted for years, didn't they? Trances? Seizures? Mine showed up at menarche and didn't leave until I mastered my craft."

Wow. One other person on the planet could relate to her secret.

"One foster family returned me because my episodes scared their pet rats. Yep. I ranked below rats." She spoke the words in a jesting tone, but the long ago rejection still made Helen's chest ache with old hurt.

"Rats are inherently nervous creatures. Let your pain go and describe the episodes."

"Speaking in tongues, chattering teeth, muscle spasms. Visions of spinning out of my body and flying through the air, seeing women burning at the stake. Wild times. Of course none of my temp families believed me." Helen shrugged, over-affecting nonchalance as the uncomfortable topic poked at her insecurities. Too weird and too spacey. Dissociative. Broken. Bad girl, crazy bitch.

"Flying through the air. Oh, yes. You are spirit born."

For the first time, Helen settled back in her seat, her muscles loosening, curious to know more. "Okay, so I'm spirit born. What should I do to save my studio?"

"You must choose a path to proceed on your actualization."

"Excuse me?"

"To actualize means to coax your abilities to the surface, where you may direct and control them. The power you possess is dormant and churning in your subconscious, so you endured episodes. When witches repress what we do best, we suffer."

Helen put her hands up, palms facing out. She could accept the idea of having some psychic abilities, but being a witch...the notion stretched the limits of plausibility. "Hold up. I don't think I'm a witch."

A shadow passed across Nerissa's eyes. She leaned forward in her chair, close enough for Helen to smell her rosy perfume. "Are you calling me a liar?"

"No. It's difficult to take in, though."

"Why? You came to me for help, and I'm showing you how to get what you want. But if you've changed your mind about needing money, this can end right here." Nerissa closed the book with a definitive snap.

"I'm not quite convinced is all. What's in this for you?"

"When witches practice, our powers enhance each other. Mine will grow in relation to yours. So while I wish to help you because I care about the spiritual health of my coven daughter and want to see the sisterhood come to fruition, I'm also being a teeny bit selfish."

Outlandish, but what if Nerissa was right? God, the possibilities for turning her life around. She hadn't taken a chance coming to the witch's home only to run out when things got strange. No more quitting, no more failure. Time to nut up or shut up.

"Fine. I'm all in. You were saying. Initiation. Spirit element. Smash the patriarchy with our broomsticks. How do I choose a path?"

"Your choices are Right Hand or Left Hand path. The Right Hand path draws from your internal strengths and abilities, in your case latent color magic. Astral projection and remote viewing would also come from marshalling the Right."

"How does color magic work?"

"The expression is unique to the witch. You'd call out to meaningful colors in your life and weave emotional union with them to perform spells."

"Such as visualizing the color green for money."

Nerissa shrugged. "If you're thinking long-term, sure."

The words "long-term" bounced around in a series of bothersome echoes. Long-term might not suffice. "What's up with the Left?"

"Left Hand powers originate from outside. Think transferring energy into objects in order to manipulate them, or splitting your psyche so as to exist in two places at once. The Left is potent and capable of producing immediate results, but also volatile and dark."

A surge of curiosity charged through Helen. She scooted to the edge of her seat. Potent power and speedy results could save L&E before the bank snatched it away and Helen and Lisa trudged out carrying boxes.

Helen had slunk out of many front doors with tears in her eyes. Never again.

She pursed her lips, though, wavering at what volatile and dark might mean. In all likelihood, something bad. Yet depending on inner strengths didn't seem like the right move, not when one of Helen's dumb mistakes all but catapulted the studio into the abyss.

"Have you chosen?" Nerissa drummed her fingers on the book's cover.

Bottom line, she could not afford to wait. "I choose the Left Hand path."

"There will be a cost." Nerissa rose and offered Helen the grimoire.

"What is it?" Helen accepted, her arms straining under the book's weight.

Nerissa walked to a credenza. Jars filled with liquids in a variety of colors cluttered the top. Helen watched with interest as the old lady rummaged in a drawer.

The elder witch returned with a small sack made of black velvet and a jar half full of clear fluid. She handed over the pouch. "Depends on one's constitution. Could be as trivial as a stomachache."

Helen took the bag, taking a moment to stroke the silky material. She loosened a string and peered in. Crystals in a rainbow of colors sparkled one after the other as if they communicated. "But it could be worse."

"Oh, yes."

"What's the worst case scenario?"

"If the universe decides the darkness wasn't yours to take, it might generate a hex as punishment for selecting the wrong magic. Think karma, but magnified tenfold."

Helen's insides dropped. "Hold up. I don't need more trouble. How would I deal with a hex?"

"Read your book. That's the answer to all of your questions. But first, deploy the crystals. They are sentient and absorbent, and the clear ones are the most pliable and receptive to their witch's will. Give both clear stones away to good people before you undertake your study, as cultivating others' energies will refine your powers. Make sure to set a mental intention before gifting this pair of crystals. Done correctly, this means giving each one precise directions. Otherwise, the hex might begin with dark entities latching on to one or both stones. Once demons establish communion, they can possess crystals."

Yawning, Nerissa thrust the jar at Helen. "Drink this and leave. The Reveal spell I did drained my energy. If I don't get my nap in, my weakened state could compromise you."

Though her pulse accelerated, Helen took the container and unscrewed its lid. She chugged, gag reflex lurching as she downed the sour glop. Her eyes watered, and nausea roiled her insides, but she finished the nasty potion. Go big or go home. "So twenty bucks is okay?"

"We'll settle up down the road." The old woman's eyelids fluttered closed as she sagged in her chair. "Study now."

A rush of pride prompted Helen to straighten her spine. She could be a decent student. Armed with a big book of witchiness and the crystals, she placed her empty jar on a coffee table and sauntered to the front door of the bungalow with her head held high.

The plan: give away two crystals, figure out magic, get L&E solvent, and save her dearest friendship. Doable? Helen smiled and hugged the grimoire to her chest. Hell yeah.

"*Sacrificium.*" A calm, male voice spoke inside of Helen's head. An itchy surge of adrenaline shot to her toes. Though she'd never taken Latin, she sure got the gist—sacrifice.

Her hand tensed on the doorknob, and she glanced at Nerissa. "Did you hear that?"

"No!" Nerissa bolted upright. Her mouth dropped, and her eyes stretched wide, but the show of fear in her expression fled as fast as it came.

Helen's mouth dried. Talk about a bad omen double whammy. "Are you okay?"

Rubbing her temples, the elder looked around the room. "I'm fine. Take care."

Helen jetted to her Mini Cooper. As she fumbled for her keys, a plume of milky smoke erupted in the recesses of her consciousness, vanishing a second after it arrived. She tried to disregard the inexplicable intrusion. Probably just her magic settling in.

She drove to the Minnesota State Fair, but by the time she squeezed between two cars in a dusty makeshift lot, she hadn't managed to forget the creepy voice and smoke.

A definitive slam of her door shoved the unsettling events out of her mind, and she strode to the flapping banner marking the entrance to the fairgrounds.

Today belonged in the win column, damn it.

Don't stop now. Keep reading with your copy of HEX, LOVE, AND ROCK & ROLL by City Owl Author, Kat Turner.

And find more from Adrienne Blake at authoradrienneblake.com

Don't miss book three of the *Soul and Shadows* series with NECROMANCER ABBEY coming soon, and find more from Adrienne Blake at authoradrienneblake.com

Until then, discover more paranormal romance with HEX, LOVE, AND ROCK & ROLL by Kat Turner!

With a business skidding toward bankruptcy and bone-dry bank account, Helen Schrader is willing to do the unthinkable. But what will happen when she hires a witch to cast a money spell?

When the spell sets in motion her own latent magic and her inexperience causes her to accidentally hex her celebrity crush, rocker Brian Shepherd, all that good fortune she hoped for flies out of the window.

Now, Helen and Brian struggle to break the curse and tackle their growing feelings for each other. Problem is, the harder they fall for each other, the deadlier the curse becomes.

But as a dark magic cult with an unquenchable thirst for power closes in on them, the couple will have to face more than just their inconvenient desire. With time running out and danger mounting, can they beat the hex before Brian becomes its next victim?

Please sign up for the City Owl Press newsletter for chances to win special subscriber-only contests and giveaways as well as receiving information on upcoming releases and special excerpts.

All reviews are **welcome** and **appreciated**. Please consider leaving one on your favorite social media and book buying sites.

Escape Your World. Get Lost in Ours! City Owl Press at www. cityowlpress.com.

ACKNOWLEDGMENTS

I would like to acknowledge the entire team at City Owl for taking my rough diamond and helping to make it shine. May Gaia walk with you.

ABOUT THE AUTHOR

ADRIENNE BLAKE is a *USA Today* bestselling author of paranormal mystery and urban fantasy. She is also an Amazon Top 100 bestselling author. Her stories blend plot, humor, and darkness, all in one sizzling cauldron. Born in the UK and writing in the US, she and her partner are managed by three ruthless cats.

authoradrienneblake.com

ABOUT THE PUBLISHER

City Owl Press is a cutting edge indie publishing company, bringing the world of romance and speculative fiction to discerning readers.

Escape Your World. Get Lost in Ours!

www.cityowlpress.com

facebook.com/YourCityOwlPress
twitter.com/cityowlpress
instagram.com/cityowlbooks
pinterest.com/cityowlpress

www.ingramcontent.com/pod-product-compliance
Lightning Source LLC
Chambersburg PA
CBHW020830260626

47169CB00003B/920